THE DEATH OF BRIDEZILLA

When Caroline Tucker's wedding-planning business goes bust, she gets sucked into organising her cousin Barbara's nuptials, in Haven, New Mexico. But Barbara turns out to be a Queen Bride — a Frankenbride — Bridezilla even — and driving Caroline round the bend. And when Barbara's car crashes, Caroline is accused of her murder! Luckily, the arrestingly handsome Sheriff, Travis Beaumont, is on the case — not so luckily, he's also Caroline's ex-husband. She's not impressed with this unwanted blast from the past, but she will have to work closely with him if she wants to avoid a future behind bars.

LAURIE BROWN

THE DEATH OF BRIDEZILLA

Complete and Unabridged

ULVERSCROFT
Leicester

First published in Great Britain in 2010 by
Little Black Dress
an imprint of
Headline Publishing Group, London

First Large Print Edition
published 2011
by arrangement with
Headline Publishing Group, London

British Library CIP Data

Brown, Laurie, *1952 –*
 The death of bridezilla.
 1. Weddings- -Planning- -Fiction. 2. Cousins- -Fiction.
 3. Murder- -Investigation- -Fiction. 4. Chick lit.
 5. Large type books.
 I. Title
 813.6–dc22

ISBN 978-1-4448-0821-6

Published by
F. A. Thorpe (Publishing)
Anstey, Leicestershire

Set by Words & Graphics Ltd.
Anstey, Leicestershire
Printed and bound in Great Britain by
T. J. International Ltd., Padstow, Cornwall

This book is printed on acid-free paper

To my husband Brit, my real life hero
and the wind beneath my wings.

Acknowledgements

Many thanks to Claire Baldwin, Leah Woodburn, Sara Porter, and everyone at Little Black Dress for making the production of this book a wonderful experience.

Thanks to awesome agent Lucienne Diver for thinking of my work at the right time and place.

A Special Mention goes to Mary Micheff, my critique partner through many stories. We will find a way to continue working together in spite of everything.

Thank you to my co-workers at Poplar Creek Public Library, especially Darly Doyle, Sue Haisan, Kathy Kirstein, and Pat Hogan, for your understanding and encouragement.

Last but never least, thanks to my fabulous family for believing in me, supporting me in so many ways, and putting up with the craziness that being a writer sometimes causes.

Prologue

Some things a man never forgets: the day he got his driver's license, his first car, first bad hangover, first woman. And if he's a cop, he never forgets his first stinker.

'You all right?' Sheriff Travis Beaumont asked without looking directly at his deputy. If the young man was going to toss his cookies, the least Travis could do was to allow him the same consideration he'd been shown nearly eight years ago.

'Yes,' Bobby Lee Tucker answered, his voice thick. 'It's not the same as . . . ' He swallowed convulsively. 'You know, like at the funeral parlor.'

Travis nodded. There was nothing peaceful or antiseptic about the scene before them. The supply room of the courthouse was little more than a long, narrow closet, approximately twelve feet deep by six feet wide. Two strips of harsh fluorescent lights illuminated the neatly labeled shelves of office paraphernalia that lined the walls from the black-and-white-tiled floor to the ten-foot-high ceiling. The body lay at the far end near the copy machine, her feet next to a tipped-over wastebasket.

Poor Mrs Crocket. A person of her dignified age should have passed away gently at home in her sleep, not collapsed doing the same job of Records Clerk that she'd held for more than forty years. Judging by the smell, she'd been there the whole weekend. Sadder still, no one had reported her missing. She'd been found that morning when a co-worker had entered the area to retrieve some highlighters and paperclips.

'It won't be much longer,' Travis said, tamping down his own impatience and filling out the rest of his report form. The representatives from the Rondale Funeral Home had already arrived and wheeled a gurney into the closet, but they seemed to be taking an inordinate amount of time.

'Hey, Beaumont,' Marlene Rondale called out. 'You might want to look at this before we move the body.'

'Look at what?' He stepped to the doorway. Marlene still wore her jet-black hair in one long braid down her back, just like in high school. Even though she'd been several years ahead of him, her majorette routine using fire batons and her penchant for orchestrating gradiose pranks had made her a local celebrity. Growing up over the funeral home had given Marlene a macabre sense of humor. Either that or it was hereditary. One of her brothers had quit the family business to do stand-up comedy.

'If this is some sort of ghoulish joke . . . '

She stood up and, after digging in her black leather case, tossed him a mask and pair of latex gloves. 'I never joke about murder.'

Travis quickly donned the protective gear. Why would anyone want to kill Mrs Crocket? He squatted beside the body. 'What makes you think it's murder?'

'This.' Marlene bent down and used a pen to move aside the body's high lace collar. 'Not too many folks slit their own throats.'

'Damn.' How had he missed that? Six months in this sleepy small town and he was losing his edge.

'Especially after they're already dead.'

'What?'

'Look around. There's not enough blood. If she wasn't dead when her throat was slit, spatter would be everywhere. And these abrasions? Something was wrapped round her neck. Notice the eyes? Those striates indicate suffocation.'

'Are you bucking for a job on *CSI*?'

Marlene snorted. 'Don't even get me started on unrealistic television.'

'Fine.' He stood up. 'If you'll move your gurney, I'll take some photos and process for trace.' He would have to do it himself because Haven, New Mexico didn't have a staff of evidence techs like the big city departments.

'I'll do an autopsy as soon as possible.' Not only did Marlene work for the family business, she was also the county coroner.

'Do you know — ' He paused when she glared at him. Although the mask covered most of her expression, her gray eyes shot daggers.

'Do I know what I'm doing? Is that what you were going to say?'

He held up his hands. 'Hey, cut me some slack here. I'm still getting my bearings as acting Sheriff. This is the first forensic autopsy we've needed.'

'Okay.' Her shoulders relaxed. 'Sorry. I was at a coroners' conference last week and I got a lot of flak from the good old boy types there.' She wheeled her empty gurney out into the main room and took off her mask.

He followed and sent Bobby Lee to fetch his evidence kit. The deputy left with a grateful nod. Travis turned back to Marlene and resumed their conversation. 'I guess you get the old 'What's a sweet little thang like you doing in a job like this?' ' Travis said with an exaggerated drawl even though he couldn't imagine anyone calling her little, seeing as she was nearly as tall as his six foot three.

She tipped her head to the side and propped one hand on her hip. 'I sincerely hope you're kidding. I bench press two hundred pounds, have a black belt in karate, compete in triathlons, and I can whoop your ass with one hand tied behind my back.'

Although fairly certain he could hold his own, he nonetheless eyed her with new respect. 'Really?'

'Let's just say there's an FBI agent from Albuquerque who used to not believe me. He's real polite to me now whenever our paths cross.'

Anyone who could teach a Fed some manners was all right in his book. 'You don't have any unresolved hostility against sheriffs, do you?'

'Not yet,' she said with a grin.

'Remind me not to get into any arguments with you.'

'Now you sound like my brothers. And they're the reason I started karate classes in the first place.'

For the next few minutes they talked about her family and what her brothers had been up to for the last ten years. The whole time questions churned around the back of his brain. Why would anyone want to kill old Mrs Crocket? And why slit her throat *after* she was dead? Was it a signature MO? Some sort of weird ritual?

In his years on the force in Chicago he'd handled some strange cases but he hadn't expected that sort of crime in his sleepy little hometown. And certainly not in the County Courthouse only one floor above the Sheriff's Department.

Bobby Lee returned with the evidence kit and Travis set to work with grim determination.

1

Dear Desperate,

If you didn't want your rich but uncouth relatives at your ritzy wedding, then why did you invite them? Were you expecting an expensive gift by mail? Shame on you. When you send an invitation you should hope and anticipate the recipient will attend.

Ungraciousness after receiving the RSVP reflects worse on you than your aunt and uncle using the wrong fork at the reception would.

So paste a sweet smile over your gritted teeth and display your good manners by not making a scene. Even people who are considered high society (maybe especially those) know you can pick raspberries; you can pick your friends, but you can't pick your relatives.

Yours truly,

Mrs Bea Correct

$\star$ $\star$ $\star$

Caroline Tucker finished typing the last of the letters and responses. After checking it carefully, she emailed the article to the Features Editor of *Weddings! Weddings!* magazine. At least Kathy Anderson hadn't turned her back on Caroline after the fiasco like everyone else in LA. Probably because the nom de plume kept Caroline's identity a secret. What reader would take advice from the woman who'd ruined the wedding of the daughter of the most powerful man in Hollywood?

As if the groom announcing at the altar that he was gay and intended to run off to Mexico with Caroline's assistant Anthony was her fault. The emotional debacle could have been handled with discretion if the bride hadn't chased Caroline out of the church swinging her bouquet like a cudgel and screeching like a banshee. The tabloids had latched on to the story, big surprise, and for the last three months Caroline's Weddings had booked nothing but cancellations.

Her throat tightened. *I will not cry.* She took a couple of deep breaths and blew each one out, slowly repeating the mantra that had served her so well over the last seven years. *Any negative can be turned into a positive.*

While writing an advice column didn't come close, financially, to owning a premier wedding-planning agency, at least she didn't have to deal with demanding brides face to face. The column had also provided bona fides that had helped her get other writing assignments for a variety of magazines. Not that she had a consuming interest in *Building Winter Dioramas for Model Railroads* or *Traveling California With Kids*, two of her better-paying articles, but she did know how to research a subject and interview experts.

She'd latched on to the new career direction like a frugal bride at a designer wedding dress clearance sale. The ability to work anywhere was a distinct advantage since she'd had to sell her beautiful condo to meet the final expenses of her defunct business.

'Is there anything else you want carried down to your car?' Naomi asked as she re-entered the dining room.

Caroline looked around the apartment, now devoid of personal touches. 'No, I think that's it. The building manager will let the guy in to pick up the furniture on Monday.'

'Memorial Day?'

'I meant Tuesday.' Of course, she'd gotten a fraction of what she'd paid for the pieces she'd lovingly selected, but she had no place to store five rooms of furniture and no means to move it. Practicality won out over sentiment yet again.

'I can manage the last of it,' she said as she packed her laptop into its case.

'Won't you at least stay through the holiday weekend?'

Caroline shook her head. 'Can't. It's a long drive.' And she planned to treat herself to a relaxing day at a spa and two nights at a bed and breakfast in El Paso before facing the entire family on Memorial Day. 'Am I supposed to tip Adonis and Apollo?' she whispered, jerking her head toward the two muscular toy-boys her friend had recruited at the pool as helpers.

Naomi shook her head and waved to the men with a seductive smile. 'I've taken care of it,' she whispered back. 'Thanks, guys,' she called to them. 'I'll see you both later,' she added, her voice full of sensual promise.

Caroline reached for her purse as the two grinning men backed toward the front door. 'I can — '

'Don't be silly. Money would insult them.' Naomi waved again and they returned the gesture. One of them, Adonis, giggled as the door shut behind them.

'Nice young men,' Naomi said with a sigh. 'They were glad to help after I promised them both blow jobs.'

Caroline's jaw dropped.

'Oh, don't look at me like that. I'm not actually going to do it.' Naomi put her hands on her hips. 'I can't believe you're — what? Twenty-seven?'

'Twenty-nine.'

'Always subtract at least two years, you'll need it eventually. As I was saying, I can't believe you've reached your age and know so little about men.'

'What does that have to do with — '

'Everything. Promise a man a blow job and he'll do anything you ask.'

'But don't you have to — '

'Do it?' Naomi shrugged. 'I never have. Unless I wanted to, that is.'

'Won't they expect — '

'That's the point. Men are creatures of fantasy. Those two guys who just left are thinking about my promise and getting so turned on, they'll either jack off or rush to visit their girlfriends. Whichever, that fantasy will be good for them every time they think about it, and will probably just get better and better. So good, they'll never call me on the promise. Now that's what I call a win-win situation.'

'But they could. Then what?'

Naomi laughed. 'If all the men I've promised decided to show up on the same

11

day, I'd have them lined up around the block. Trust me. Men know reality rarely lives up to imagination, and they won't want to lose the fantasy. They won't call.'

'Still . . . '

'It works. You should try it.'

Caroline shook her head. 'There aren't any hunky pool guys in Haven, New Mexico.'

'What a shame. Why are you going again? Never mind, I know why. But it works on non-hunky men as well, if not better. Promise me you'll at least try it.'

'Speaking of going . . . ' Caroline stood up — 'I should be hitting the road.'

'Promise you'll try it?'

Yeah, right. When pigs fly. But once Naomi got an idea in her head she was like a vegetarian's poodle with a juicy bone. Caroline knew she wouldn't get away easily unless she agreed, and she wanted to get across the mountains before dark. 'Okay. If the opportunity arises that I need a man to do something for me and there is no other way I can get him to do it, I promise I'll try your method.'

'Good. Now I know you'll be fine. I can't believe you're actually leaving,' Naomi said, giving Caroline a hug. 'Who's going to do my next wedding?'

Caroline had to smile at Naomi's absolute

faith that there would be another. Of course, she was probably right. Caroline had planned Naomi's last three weddings, and if she ran true to course there would be another within the year since her latest divorce was already three weeks old.

'It won't matter because you'll be beautiful, even if you get married barefoot on the beach.'

'Don't say that even in jest.' Naomi shuddered. 'If a man can't afford a decent ceremony and reception, I'm not interested. Why won't you take the loan I offered? This whole mess will soon be so yesterday's scandal and you'll be back on top in no time. If there's one thing Hollywood always recognizes *eventually*, it's talent.'

Caroline shook her head. 'Put your money in some blue-chip stocks and bonds. You may need it some day.'

Naomi waved off her concern. 'I consider you a good investment.'

'Thank you for that, but the answer is still no. Maybe it's that whole Cosmos-conspiring-to-do-what's-best thing you're always talking about. Right now I need to spend some time with my grandmother. Our last few weekly phone conversations have been . . . well, strange.'

'Is she sick?'

'I — '

'I'm getting a vision.' Naomi put her hand to her forehead and sank dramatically into one of the Sheffield dining chairs. She grabbed Caroline's arm and pulled her into an adjoining seat. 'A terrible vision.'

Caroline yanked herself free. 'I don't believe — '

'Death is stalking your grandmother,' Naomi intoned, an unnatural and ominous timbre in her voice. 'One life only whets an evil appetite. And Death is hungry, so very hungry.' Her eyes rolled up, her eyelids closed, and she slumped on to the table.

'Naomi?' Not knowing what else to do, Caroline rushed to the kitchen, grabbed some paper towels and a bottle of water from the cooler she planned to take in the car with her. After pouring some of the icy water on the towels, she wrapped one round each of Naomi's wrists and placed another on her forehead.

Naomi stirred, then sat up holding the wet paper towel to her forehead. 'If you messed up my hair, I'm going to be pissed. I've got an important lunch date.'

'Are you all right? What happened?'

'Don't worry. I just fainted. It sometimes occurs when I get a really strong vision. I'll be fine in a minute.'

'You scared me half to death.'

14

Naomi flashed her an odd look. 'Apparently, that's not enough to make you change your mind about leaving.'

Caroline sank slowly into the chair. If anything, her friend's prediction, whether true or not, made her more determined to leave, now with a sense of urgency.

'If you go home, I have a feeling you will not return,' Naomi said, tears in her eyes.

'Nonsense. I'll be back in time to attend your next wedding. Cross my heart and — '

'Don't say that. Don't ever say that.'

★   ★   ★

Right back where she'd started. Whoever it was that said you can't ever go home again was wrong. In truth you could never escape. The people you loved most kept dragging you back.

Unfortunately, this wasn't Caroline's usual quick visit and she hated returning a failure. Starting over was a bitch. Keeping your chin up during the process was even harder.

The old Queen Anne-style Victorian that had been her family's home for generations was around the corner on Harvard Street. But just as she had every day after school for all those years, she headed directly to her grandmother's studio. With a resigned sigh, she parked in the driveway leading to the converted carriage house.

She got out of the car and stretched out a few of the kinks two days of driving had put in her shoulders. Spending the previous two nights in a quaint and relaxing bed and breakfast had been a good idea in theory. Unfortunately, the historic stagecoach inn had retained the original mattresses along with the ambiance and charm. Sleep had been elusive even if the treatments at the nearby spa had been heavenly.

She lifted her car key to press the lock button, and shrugged it off instead. Why bother? Haven was a throw-back, a post-modern Mayberry. She wasn't in LA any more.

But there had been changes in the almost six months since her last visit the previous Christmas. The studio had been repainted, noticeable even though the cream walls, green shutters, and lilac gingerbread trim were the same colors she remembered from childhood. The main doors, still the original heavy planks with large iron clasps, had been restored and re-hung straight. The left one probably opened more than a crack now. And the twin eagle weathervanes on the roof's cupolas had been repaired. No longer one-winged or headless, Icarus and Ichabod postured in their new brassy finish like aloof runway models clad in gold lamé.

As she had so many times before, she slipped through the service door quietly so as not to disturb her grandmother if she was working. A few steps inside, Caroline skidded to a halt on the smooth concrete floor. The sense of stepping into a strangely distorted familiar world intensified.

Space and silence. No hiss of the welding torch. No whine of the grinder or saw. No banging as Mimi hammered some scrap of metal into the shape she saw in her mind. And emptiness. The area, large enough to hold half a dozen cars, was swept clean. All the bits and pieces that usually littered the floor were sorted into large neatly labeled bins against the far wall. Auto parts. Bicycles. Appliances. Ranch equipment. Toys. Tools. The shelves above were filled to overflowing with everything from blenders to old telephones.

Not scary, but peculiar. She shivered despite the late-afternoon sun flooding in the large windows that had been installed on the back wall when Mimi had made the garage into her studio.

'I thought you might come here first.'

Caroline started at the interruption of her thoughts. Then she sprinted across the room to the back door to give her grandmother a hug. The familiar scent of Chanel No. 5 made her absence melt away. Even though Mimi had the same short, thick cap of white hair, and wore one of her usual denim work shirts and a profusion of silver and turquoise jewelry, the dear woman seemed smaller, frailer than Caroline's memory. Had her grandmother been ill?

'I'm glad you're home,' Mimi said.

'Me, too.' Not a total lie. She just wished it had been under different circumstances. Moving back felt a little too much like running home with her tail tucked between her legs even if she did have a plan for her future. She looked around. 'Where is everyone?'

'Up at the house. Waiting for you.'

'No.' Caroline waved her arm to encompass the studio. 'I meant where are all your people? Your statues?'

'Oh, them. I sold all but the one.'

Caroline's knees wobbled and she gripped Mimi's arm in order to steady herself. For more than thirty years her grandmother had refused to sell any of her wonderful articulated statues, not since she'd learned a buyer used one for a hat rack. If she was selling her darlings, something was terribly wrong. 'Why?'

Mimi shrugged. 'It was time for them to move on, find new homes. Time for me to clear some space.' She grinned. 'And I got a really good offer.'

Caroline could only shake her head, feeling like her childhood friends had been sold. Roy Cowboy made of branding irons, bridle bits and spurs; Emma Socialite with her glass coffee-pot head. George Miner made of picks, shovels and a wheelbarrow body, a salute to the town's Wild West beginnings when the nearby silver mines had made fortunes overnight. Jaunita Dancer, Chief Two Horses, Suzie Homemaker. Caroline could not go on remembering or she'd start bawling.

'Why didn't you tell me before you did such a thing? I can't believe you sold all your people and didn't even mention it.'

'They aren't people. They're statues, artwork, meant to be sold and shared. And as for getting your permission to sell my work — '

'That's not what I meant and you know it. You're attacking as a form of defense and I'm not falling for that trap. Stick to the subject. Why didn't you tell me?'

'You can't expect an hour or so on the phone once a week to take the place of being here. Things happen. Big stuff, little stuff.

When you condense a week's full of days into an hour, not everything can be included. You get the *Reader's Digest* version.'

'That makes me wonder what else I've missed?'

'Come on,' Mimi said, putting an arm round her shoulders. 'Let's go up to the house. We've had a bit of work done to the old place.'

As they exited, Caroline blinked in disbelief. Instead of the familiar rocky path, a multi-tiered deck spiraled up to the house.

Before she could recover enough to ask about the changes, the screen door slammed against the wall, opening the floodgates to a sea of Tucker relatives. Aunts, uncles, cousins. Second and third cousins she hadn't seen in years and could barely remember. Fatter, thinner, taller, older. Uncle Henry had lost his hair. Her sister Mary Lynn had gone blonde, and the baby that Caroline remembered in an infant seat was running around on chubby legs. Her other sister Dee Ann had switched to maternity clothes and was attached at the hip to her husband Stephen. Aunt Ellen had lost fifty pounds and Aunt Wynetta had found them. The entire clan had shown up for the annual Memorial Day barbeque.

Her brothers Bobby Ray and Bobby Lee

opened the large gate in the fence and unloaded her car, passing out the smaller items to an assortment of young children branded with catsup, mustard, and chocolate pudding on their little faces and T-shirts. The munchkin pack train wound up the deck steps past her cousin Barbara, the last relative to exit the house.

Whereas everyone else was dressed ultra casual, blue-jeans-shorts-fishing-trip casual, Barbara wore a pink plaid sundress with matching earrings, and darling pink and white spectator pumps Caroline would have given her eye teeth for. Not that she would let her cousin know that. Ever.

'Hello, Franny,' Barbara said as she approached and gave her the obligatory cheek-to-cheek air kiss. As usual her make-up was flawless and not a hair was out of place.

'I go by Caroline.'

'I told Dirk you'd come back to town for my wedding,' she continued as if she hadn't heard the comment. 'Even if it's only to point out what you would have done differently.'

'Actually I only — '

'You of all people should know the importance of sending back your response card.'

Impossible since she'd pitched the invitation into the garbage.

'Mother,' Barbara called over her shoulder, 'we didn't get a response card from Franny, did we?'

Aunt Rose, struggling to wash the face of an unwilling toddler, replied without looking up. 'For Pete's sake, Barbara Jean, I can't remember every little . . . stand still, Jeremy.'

Barbara rolled her eyes but Caroline was glad to see Aunt Rose standing up for herself. As a single mother she had focused all her emotions and attention on her daughter. After Barbara moved out, Aunt Rose buried herself in her work. Then two years ago she'd gone on a two-week self-empowerment/learn to dance cruise and had returned five pounds thinner, ten years younger, and no longer her daughter's doormat. Obviously Barbara still hadn't adjusted to the change. She narrowed her eyes and pursed her lips into a tight white pucker.

'I haven't seen Dirk yet,' Mimi interjected before Barbara could say something to her mother. 'I'm sure Caroline is looking forward to meeting him.'

Like she anticipated dental surgery. She forced a toothy smile.

'He sends his regrets,' Barbara said with a sigh. 'He remembered at the last minute that he'd committed to play in some big charity golf tournament in Florida this weekend.' She turned to Caroline. 'My fiancé is one of the Miami Vandergelts, you know. They're big in philanthropy.'

'Really?' Well, at least Dirk had been good for Barbara's vocabulary. That was assuming she didn't think philanthropy had anything to do with extramarital affairs or stamp collecting. 'I'm surprised you didn't go with him.'

'Pa-leeze. There's nothing more boring than standing around watching grown men in tacky clothing chase a little white ball — even if it is for charity. And besides, I have so much to do for the wedding.' She turned and glared at her mother's back. 'How am I supposed to have a perfect wedding with help like her?'

'I'm sure it will all work out,' Mimi said.

She linked arms with Caroline and steered her away before she could come up with an appropriate remark about perfect weddings needing perfect brides. They followed everyone else back toward the house.

'We've put you in your old room,' Mimi said as they mounted the wide plank steps of the deck. 'Bobby Ray and Bobby Lee are sharing just like when they were children.'

'That should be interesting.' The ex-con and the deputy bunking together. Bobby Ray had returned home last February for a year's probation after serving a stretch at the county work farm for breaking and entering, just four months after Bobby Lee, the youngest of the five Tucker children, had joined the Haven police force.

Some people might think it strange that she had two brothers named Bobby. Robert Raymond had been named after his two grandfathers, and then when her mother gave birth to another boy three months after the death of her husband, she'd insisted on naming him Robert Lee, Junior. Made perfect sense. If you were a Tucker.

'Oh, they're doing fine,' Mimi said.

Caroline bit her tongue. She held the screen door open and followed her grandmother into the house. The previous surprises should have provided a warning but Caroline was unprepared for the magnitude of the changes.

Not only had the kitchen been redone in a manner fit for a gourmet cook, but an octagonal breakfast nook with floor-to-ceiling windows had also been added where the laundry room used to be.

'Wow! What's going on here?' Her family couldn't afford this. She grabbed her grandmother's shoulder and turned her around to face her. 'How . . . ' — apprehension shot a chilly cramp between her shoulder blades

— 'did Bobby Ray rob a bank?'

'Don't be ridiculous. He's reformed. He's got an Internet ministry now, Brother Ray's Salvation dot com, and he spends most of his time on his computer.'

'Then how . . . ' Caroline waved her hands all around her in a frantic search for words — 'How this?'

'Before we talk, you need a cup of tea.'

'No, I — '

'Then I need one.'

With the push of a button, a gleaming new appliance filled a teapot shaped like an English cottage with steaming water. Mimi added loose black tea, covered the pot with a made-to-match cozy, and set two cups and saucers on a tray with the creamer and sugar bowl. All the dishes coordinated — another change. Gone were the odds and ends of decades. There were enough colorful Fiesta dishes in the glass-fronted cabinets to serve a church supper. She carried the tray to the new breakfast nook and Caroline followed and took a seat, sure she couldn't get even a sip of tea past her closed throat.

'I told you I sold most of my pieces. That nice young man from Sotheby's kept coming around, and he finally convinced me that I could get a good price at auction.' She shook her head. 'I'm still amazed. Imagine, my statues in the Guggenheim, the Louvre, and in the Queen of England's private collection.'

'That's wonderful,' Caroline said, suitably impressed. But the reason behind the unprecedented move worried her so much she couldn't concentrate on any other aspect. 'Why did you decide to sell them?'

'I'm — '

'Lou Beaumont is on her way over,' Mary Lynn called, sticking her head far enough into the doorway to flash a knowing smirk at her sister. 'And Travis is with her,' she added in a singsong tattletale voice.

Caroline stood up, bumping the table so hard the dishes rattled. Even though no one except her grandmother knew the whole truth, her entire family, hell the entire town, knew she'd had a crush on Travis since she was twelve years old. Her siblings had always teased her unmercifully. 'Why are they coming over?'

'Because I invited them. Lou wants to welcome you home, dear,' Mimi answered with a frown. 'What's wrong with that?'

'You invited him, too? Why?'

'Travis? Of course I invited him. How could I ask Lou and not ask him when he's staying with her?'

Travis was living next door again? 'You never told me that either,' she said, her

26

whisper a harsh accusation. Caroline hadn't expected that complication. Why wasn't he in his own apartment? Like on the other side of town. Or maybe a neighboring state.

'Didn't I? Surely, I must have mentioned it.'

'No, you didn't. And I can't believe you invited him when you know . . . everything.'

'He's probably just seeing that Lou gets here safely,' Mimi continued, apparently unruffled by Caroline's agitation. 'Lou doesn't get around like she used to. I expect he's too busy to stay long. He's the sheriff now, you know.'

Caroline knew that all right. She'd heard more than she wanted to about Travis. During her years at college and ever since, it seemed as if not a single phone conversation with her mother or grandmother had passed without some mention of his exploits. Motorcycle racing. Military service. Chicago Police Department. And then he'd come back to take over as temporary Sheriff when his grandmother had a stroke and was forced to take a leave of absence from her job. Oh, yeah, Mimi had kept her updated on every little detail, except that he'd moved in next door.

Travis's grandmother, Louise Beaumont had been the first woman to be elected to the office of Sheriff and she'd held the job for thirty-two years. The entire town must have forgotten Travis's bad boy hell-bent for leather youth in order to go along with her choice of replacement. But then everyone adored Lou and respected her opinion.

Caroline peered out the window. Travis and his grandmother had crossed through the gate between the properties and were walking toward the deck, clearly headed for the kitchen door.

Travis Beaumont was one of only a few men on the planet who could pull off that bad-to-the-bone swagger while wearing a tin star and escorting his grandmother. Her insides quivered as if a guitar riff resonated deep within her.

He looked good, dammit, and that just wasn't fair. Ex-husbands should be balding and have beer guts. His dark hair was quite a bit shorter than she remembered, and he'd bulked up a bit in the chest and shoulders like he'd been working out. A lot. She chased that image from her mind. She already had enough trouble with memories of her ex-husband. Although far from perfect, Travis had become the de facto yardstick against which all other men had measured short. And like it or not, he still cranked her tractor. So not fair.

The only saving grace was that her family didn't know about her quickie teenage marriage and even quicker divorce. Well, her grandmother knew, but she'd been sworn to secrecy. Unfortunately, that left everyone else thinking the high school sweethearts would resolve whatever it was that had caused their break-up and that they would get back together eventually. Which was never going to happen. The pain went too deep for Caroline to ever forget, or forgive.

Her sister Mary Lynn peeked over her shoulder before adding, 'I'll stall him for a few minutes if you want to pull a brush through your hair and put on some lipstick.'

'Why would I want to do that?' Caroline asked, pleased when her voice remained calm even if her hand did automatically move to smooth her hair. She clasped her hands tightly and raised her chin. 'I couldn't care less if Travis Beaumont sees me without make-up or any other way. His opinion is of no concern to me.'

'Right,' Mary Lynn said. 'Don't worry, you look fine. Maybe a little pale, but it works with your auburn hair.' She ducked back outside.

However, Caroline didn't want to confront Travis, not now. Not until she could get her careening emotions under control. She turned to her grandmother. 'I'm going upstairs to lie down for awhile.'

'But you just got here.'

'I drove through the night and I'm exhausted.' A lie. For some reason she felt more energized than she had in months. 'I'm sure I'll be fine after a short nap. A couple of hours.' Or however long it took Travis to leave.

'But Lou — '

Caroline glanced out the window. Her sister had waylaid Travis but his grandmother headed for the door like a train on a one-way track, her wheeled walker clearing the way like the cowcatcher on an old-fashioned steam engine. Once she got inside, Caroline's chance of escaping was nil. 'Please tell Lou I'll give her a call later. I'll be here for more than a day this time and we'll have a chance for a nice chat soon.' Some time when Travis wasn't around.

Mimi gave her a calculating look before nodding. 'I'll make your excuses.'

'Thank you.' Caroline turned away with a sigh of relief.

'Franny?' Mimi called.

'Yes?' She paused in the doorway to the hall.

'Sorry, I meant Caroline.'

'That's okay.' She turned. Her feet itched to run and she shifted her weight from one foot to the other. 'Did you want something?'

'Your mother called earlier. She expects a mare to foal sometime today or tomorrow and can't come to town until she knows everything is all right.'

'I talked to her about an hour ago. I told her I'd come out to the ranch in a few days and save her the trip. It's been a while since I've been out there.' Her usual quick trips didn't allow for the long drive into the foothills, and most holidays the family gathered at her grandmother's house.

'Don't you think it's about time you told your mother about your marriage and — ' Mimi asked.

'Shh!' Caroline glanced around the room to make sure no one had overheard. 'No,' she whispered. 'I — I can't.'

She couldn't face that look of disappointment her mother did so well. Jean Tucker believed you faced your problems and fears head on, and that had stood her in good stead while running the ranch and raising five children alone. Mimi had taken the kids during the school term to save them the long bus trip back and forth. Even though she'd spent more time in her studio than in the house, Mimi had always made time to talk to Caroline about whatever was on the little girl's mind. When she'd been in trouble, she'd turned to her grandmother for help.

'You might be surprised,' Mimi said. 'Your mother is a very understanding person. You two are more alike than you realize.'

Caroline shook her head. She didn't have the steel nerves of her mother or even the quiet strength of her grandmother. Neither one of them would be acting like a flushed jack-rabbit. When the going got tough, Caroline Tucker got going. Literally. Adios, sayonara, bye-bye.

Lou burst through the door.

Only this time Caroline hadn't moved fast enough.

★　★　★

Travis escaped from Mary Lynn's babbling the moment her attention was distracted by her child. He rushed to follow his grandmother, yet hesitated with his hand on the doorknob. He'd expected to have a few awkward moments seeing Caroline for the first time after so many years, but if anyone had suggested his gut would clench he would have called him a liar.

Then again, if anyone had said he'd wind up back in Haven babysitting a cantankerous old woman he wouldn't have believed that either. Not that he didn't love his grandmother, but his plans had never included serving as Haven's Sheriff. But he was the sort of man who did his duty, regardless, and that obligation had somehow brought him to this moment.

Maybe fate was finally giving him a chance to get some honest answers from Caroline. At the very least she owed him that much. Even if the truth were unpleasant, it would be better than not knowing why she'd left him. He gave the doorknob a resolute twist and stepped into the neighbor's kitchen.

'... upstairs to take a nap. The long drive gave me a headache,' Caroline said, edging towards the doorway.

'I understand,' Lou commiserated as she reached for a coffee cup.

At an almost imperceptible signal from Mimi, Lou sat the cup back down and pushed it away.

'Do you have any decaf?' she asked.

'Evening, Miz Mimi,' Travis said, removing his well-worn cowboy hat and wiping his boots on the braided mat by the door.

'Oh, there you are, dear,' Lou said, turning to him with a smile.

Travis wasn't fooled by either her sweet tone or innocent air. If he hadn't come in, she wouldn't have switched to the doctor-recommended decaf. He'd never met another woman as determined to drive him up the wall.

Well, maybe one. But lately even Caroline could take lessons from Lou. Every few weeks he had to find a new place to hide his keys in order to prevent her from taking the cruiser and driving down main street with the lights flashing and siren wailing.

And he'd had to take Lou's gun away from her and lock it up in the cabinet down at the jail. When she'd seemed genuinely distressed, saying she felt naked without it, he'd returned her belt and her holster with a neon orange water pistol inside. Contending with complaints from soaked jaywalkers, litterbugs, and those unfortunate enough to get caught spitting on the sidewalk was better than the alternative possibilities.

'Come on in, Travis,' Mimi said. 'Sit a spell. You can have a nice visit with Caroline. You two haven't been around home at the same time in years.'

Even though he'd been aware of her presence, he'd avoided looking directly at her. He turned and let his gaze trail slowly from her head to high-heeled sandals, her bare toes painted bright pink. Just as slowly, if not more so, he let his gaze return to her face and the defensive coolness of her expression. 'Well, well, well. Look what the cat dragged in,' he drawled as he sauntered into the room.

'Drop your spurs, cowboy,' Lou said,

poking her grandson in the back.

The quaint warning to mind his manners reminded him that he had an avidly attentive audience for this meeting, not an ideal situation. 'Pardon me. It's just such a shock to see our little tomboy Franny, all growed up and city-fied,' he said over his shoulder to his grandmother. 'And looking good enough to trot around the dance floor,' Travis added to Caroline with his best boyish grin. For good measure he shuffled the toe of one boot on the floor.

'Does that aw-shucks-ma'am shtick still work? I can't imagine any self-respecting woman going for . . . oh, I'm sorry. I'd forgotten the type of women you usually hang out with.'

'Caroline!' Mimi exclaimed, censuring her granddaughter's rudeness.

'It always worked on you,' he whispered for Caroline's ears alone, and was gratified when she blushed and stiffened her spine.

He turned to face the other women. 'Lately, I've been spending all my time with my best girl.' He kissed his grandmother on the top of her head and she brushed him away with pretend aggravation.

'I could do with a little less attention,' Lou said.

'Can I fix you a plate?' Mimi offered.

'No, thank you, ma'am,' he said.

'Do stay for supper,' Caroline said in that mocking oh-so-sweet, butter-wouldn't-melt-in-her-mouth tone that he knew all too well hid rattlesnake venom. 'I, however, must excuse myself,' she continued. 'I had a slight headache before, but it's intensified beyond endurance.'

With that she spun on her heel and practically marched from the room, taking the spark of the evening with her.

'Something to drink?' Mimi offered. 'A beer? The boys are in the library watching a ball game.'

'Thank you again, but unfortunately I can't stay. I'm going back on duty so Harlan can take his daughter to some Girl Scout thing. If someone could walk Lou back to the house later . . . ?'

'We'll see she gets home safe and sound,' Mimi replied.

'I don't need a keeper,' Lou grumbled under her breath.

'Then try behaving yourself,' Travis said, giving his grandmother's shoulder a gentle pat. 'I should be back around ten o'clock.'

'In time to tuck me in?'

Travis ignored the sarcasm in her voice. She wasn't nearly as tough as she pretended to be, and had even admitted in private that she appreciated his looking after her. The public banter helped her save face because she could pretend she only conceded to her limitations because he insisted. 'Good girls get their beauty sleep,' he replied with a wink.

'Hah!'

He took his leave and headed along the path between the houses, worn smooth by at least three generations of back and forth. As he reached the gate, the nape of his neck tingled. He paused and turned, automatically zeroing in on Caroline's second-floor bedroom window. The lace curtain twitched.

It might have been a breeze.

Imagination supplied the image of her standing next to the window. Tousled red-gold curls, laughter in her brown eyes, summer freckles across her nose. Her lips in that delicious pout that begged a kiss. As usual his mind's eye failed to supply her with any clothes.

His pulse kicked into high gear. The warrior's reaction to an upcoming battle. He wouldn't admit any other cause for the adrenaline rush.

Oh, yeah. There would be another confrontation and he would finally get some answers. He took off his hat and made a low sweeping bow in her direction, a salute to a worthy opponent. And a challenge. When he glanced upward again, her window shade was drawn.

With a deep chuckle, he continued on his way with a jaunty step.

★ ★ ★

'How long did you say it would take for this plan to work?' Lou asked, taking back her cup and gulping a big swig of coffee. 'Oh, that's good.'

'You shouldn't be drinking that. You'll be up all night.'

'Don't you start in on me, Mimi Tucker. I get enough of that at home.'

'Travis is only trying to help you follow your doctor's — '

'I know that and I play along because it makes it easier for him to cope, but that dang decaf tastes like horse piss.' She took another swallow, visibly savoring the flavor. Inhaling the aroma. 'Good coffee is a quality of life issue.' Setting her cup down, she continued, 'So what do you think? A couple of days?'

After a lifetime of friendship, Mimi wasn't thrown by the quick return to the previous subject. 'Patience, my friend, patience.'

'I'm not getting any younger. Travis is the only grandson I have and I'd like to see him happily settled before I die.' She paused and her hand flew to her mouth. 'Oh, I'm sorry. You know I didn't mean anything by that.'

Mimi patted her friend's hand. 'It's okay, Lou. We're all going to take the big dirt nap sooner or later.' Mimi hated lying to her friend, but deception was necessary. Lou was as honest as the day was long and incapable of keeping a secret. Mimi was counting on that fact. The sooner Caroline believed the lie of Mimi's imminent demise, the sooner the plan could be put in motion. And it wasn't a total fabrication. After all, wasn't everyone on the path to death from the day they were born?

'How can you be so calm? I'd hate knowing when I'm going to die. I always figured I'd take a bullet and it would be quick. Yep, I'd rather have it quick.'

Mimi sighed. 'We aren't usually given a choice. Don't worry. Everything is going to be fine.'

'What if Caroline decides to leave town in the middle of the night?'

'She won't.'

'She's done it before.'

'I've got that covered.'

'And what if they don't reconcile?'

'Don't be so negative.'

'It's a possibility,' Lou insisted. 'What then?'

'I have a plan B. And plan C. That one can't fail.'

'Then why don't we use plan C first?'

'Too drastic. We should let nature take her course.'

'Nature has been sitting on her damn thumbs for ten years. I say, let's bring out the big guns, go for the surefire cure.'

'Shhh! She's coming back downstairs. Remember, not a word about . . . you know what.'

'I'm as silent as the grave,' Lou whispered. 'Oops, sorry.'

Caroline breezed back into the kitchen. 'I took some headache medicine and feel better already.'

In order to allow Lou a few minutes alone with Caroline, Mimi excused herself. The new downstairs powder room was in the hall just off the kitchen, enabling Mimi to monitor the conversation. If everything went as she expected, Lou would say just enough to lead Caroline's thoughts along the intended path. The bathroom mirror reflected Mimi's grin. A year's worth of scheming and plotting was finally coming together.

Caroline was a true Tucker even if she denied it, and that meant stubborn. Bull-headed to a fault. Mimi was willing to do whatever was necessary to give her granddaughter another chance at happiness, even if it meant stretching the truth a tad. Or a lot.

Mimi put her ear to the door, ready to interrupt if necessary. If Lou said too much, it could ruin everything.

2

Dear Frustrated,

Interfering relatives are like toothaches, ignoring them only makes matters worse. Sit down with your fiancé and discuss your concerns in non-confrontational terms. Decide together what you want at your wedding, and present a united front.

That said, pick your battles. If there are some things that aren't all that important to you, but are imperative to your mother-in-law-to-be, consider compromise an investment in your future peace and happiness.

Yours truly,

Mrs Bea Correct

Caroline jumped out of bed, shoved her feet into her favorite slippers, the ones shaped like puppies with big floppy ears. Sparing only enough time to splash water on her face and brush her teeth, she raced down the stairs determined to have a heart-to-heart talk with her early-rising grandmother.

The stairs were now carpeted in a maroon pile. She found odd comfort when the third-to-last riser squeaked as it always had. At least some things never changed. Like good old Thurston. The large solid brass eagle perched on the newel post had been named after her great-great-great-grandfather whose portrait in the library sported a similar baldness and fierce expression. She reached up and gave Thurston's head a rub for good luck as generations of Tuckers had done daily, polishing it shiny smooth and slightly flat.

'Good morning,' she called out as she entered the kitchen. Only her younger brother was present, seated in the breakfast alcove. She couldn't help thinking he looked like a teen dressed up as a cop for a school play or Halloween party.

'Morning,' Bobby Lee mumbled in response to her greeting. He shoveled food into his mouth as if the scrambled eggs would escape the plate if he didn't eat fast enough. 'Nice jammies.'

She pulled her Lakers jersey further down even though it nearly reached her knees, noticing the colors clashed with the hot-pink and peach paisley leggings she'd grabbed out of her suitcase late last night.

'Is that what city men find sexy?' he asked

with a teasing grin.

'None of your business.'

'What did you name them?' he asked, nodding to her slippers.

'What makes you think — '

'Because you always name everything. Cute, in an mental-hospital sort of way.'

She raised her chin, refusing to tell him she'd named the floppy-eared slippers Charles and Camilla. 'Where's Mimi?'

He gulped down some orange juice. 'Already in her studio.' He stood and removed the napkin from under his chin that had pro-tected his tan uniform. 'I'd stay and insult you some more but I overslept. I need to get gas and stop at the cleaners before work and Travis likes us on time for our shifts.'

Caroline frowned. She didn't want to think about her baby brother working for that man. No telling what bad habits Bobby Lee might pick up.

'Don't worry,' he responded, carrying his dishes to the sink and running them under the faucet. 'He won't fire me for being late. At least, I hope not. I like being a deputy.'

Caroline grabbed a kitchen towel and handed it to her brother as she elbowed him away from the sink. 'Here. I'll finish that. Though don't ask me why I'm doing you any favors.'

'Thanks,' he said.

After drying his hands, he grabbed his gun belt from the back of a nearby chair and strapped it on while she rinsed the dishes and stacked them in the dishwasher.

'Sheriff Beaumont didn't actually give you bullets for that thing, did he?'

'One or two,' Bobby Lee said, slapping the holstered pistol. 'Just in case.'

'In case what? Has crime suddenly gone rampant here in Sleepytown, USA?'

'We're not as isolated as you might think,' he said, his tone unexpectedly serious. 'Day before yesterday, we had . . . ' Then, as if thinking better of that topic of conversation, he switched gears with a grin. 'We have criminals in Haven. Two weeks ago Henderson's bull got loose and terrorized downtown, but I don't have time to tell the whole tale. Suffice it to say, I was the hero of the day. Those steaks may have been a bit tough to chew, but I enjoyed every bite.'

He paused for a moment, standing on the other side of the open dishwasher with his hat in his hand.

'I thought you had places to go before work and were running late,' she said. 'Isn't that why I'm doing your dishes?'

'I didn't get a chance to say it last night but it's good to have you home,' he said, ducking

44

his head, apparently still unaware that his ears turned pink when he was embarrassed.

The glimpse of the sweet boy beneath the brash young man put a lump in her throat. 'Go to work,' she ordered, sensing that any show of sentimentality would humiliate him further. 'And be careful.'

Bobby Lee plunked his hat on his head at a cocky angle.

'I always am,' he said and strutted out the door, whistling 'I'm Too Sexy'.

She shook her head and smiled as she wiped down the counter and finished setting the kitchen to rights. And just in case she'd been wrong about the twenty-first century bypassing Haven, she whispered a prayer for her brother's safety, for the safety of the entire police force. Even Travis.

Shaking off the direction of her thoughts, she poured a cup of coffee and carried it out to the new deck. She sucked her lungs full of the cool morning air. You couldn't get oxygen like that in LA. Although within walking distance of downtown Haven, the house could have been in the country if judged by the sweet scents. The air smelled . . . green.

The grape arbor to the left of the back door had been salvaged and the trellis enhanced, the vines growing up and over a new pergola. The plants gave privacy to the patio and would shade it in the heat of the day. The tiny sour grapes were perfect for the jellies the women of the family had always made, and the leaves were the secret ingredient in her grandmother's blue ribbon dill pickles.

With only one other house sharing the block, the Tucker yard was large. Beyond the herb garden near the kitchen and a small patch of lawn, the rest of the area was a higgledy-piggledy arrangement of small garden plots tumbling down the slight slope. Dahlias and daisies. Tomatoes and cucumbers. Seemingly everything from asters to zucchinis. Flagstone and gravel paths crisscrossed and looped around, perfect for wandering on a soft summer night.

She closed her eyes. If she concentrated she could pick out the heady scent of the damask roses in the area just beyond the stand of birch trees. The cuttings had been brought westward in a covered wagon, a symbol of the life left behind at a time when a woman couldn't expect to ever see her old home again. The heritage rose bushes had a place of honor in a private little garden with a stone fountain and iron bench. Perhaps she would take a book out there later.

The sound of a door closing punctured her reverie. She peeked through the grapevine. Travis! He paused on the porch and covered a wide yawn. Dare she hope he hadn't slept any better than she had? Then he stretched and breathed deeply. Oh yeah, he'd definitely developed a few new muscles. And they definitely looked good on him. As did the uniform. Snug in all the right places.

The very sight was a turn-on. Or it would be, if she were the type to get excited by a thrill-seeking, danger-loving, adrenaline junkie, which she wasn't. No way. She'd learned that lesson the hard way. Give her a nice, normal guy whose idea of a great weekend was grilling burgers and renting a movie. Not the kind of man who took off for Colorado on a moment's notice because some fool friend of his thought it was a really cranking idea to enter a motorcycle race. She wanted normal. Still she didn't look away. Even if she wasn't interested, she appreciated eye candy just as much as any other woman.

Travis took the back stairs two at a time and started across the yard. Caroline ducked inside the house and peeked out the kitchen window. He vaulted over the gate and sauntered up the path, gobbling up the space between them with his long-legged stride, obviously headed in her direction. Why would he come over this time of the morning?

She didn't wait to find out. She scurried across the kitchen and down the hall, slip-sliding on the newly refinished wood floors and juggling her cup to keep from leaving a trail of coffee drops. Rounding the corner, she grabbed Thurston's wing to steady herself and skidded to a stop.

Footsteps upstairs could only belong to her other brother. Bobby Ray was as bad as their mother about facing your problems head on, only in a different way. A knock sounded on the back door. Travis! If Caroline didn't get out of there, her brother would have the three of them sitting at the kitchen table holding hands and praying for their sins faster than he could say the Lord's Prayer. She had nothing against praying, mind you, but she was dead set against holding hands with Travis.

Caroline took a deep breath. Don't panic. Think.

'Hello?' Travis called from the kitchen. 'Anyone home?'

'Be right down,' Bobby Ray answered. 'Make yourself at home.'

She spun round and headed out the front door. If she could make it to her grandmother's studio, she'd be safe. She flipped the remainder of her coffee into the hydrangea bush as she dismounted the front steps. Then she ran down the sidewalk, Charles and Camilla's big droopy ears flip-flopping and waving as if controlled by demented cheerleaders.

She almost made it to the corner before being called to a halt.

'Franny, dear. I thought that was you.'

She turned and forced a smile, facing Gloria Stanley, an elderly woman who lived down the street and was the town's biggest gossip. Considering gossip was one of Haven's favorite pastimes, that was saying a lot.

'Good morning, Mrs Stanley, Mr Stanley.' Of course Gloria stood on the sidewalk alone, Mr Stanley having passed away some thirty or so years ago, before Caroline was even born. But since Gloria had always spoken as if Mr Stanley were at her side, everyone else did the same. 'Lovely morning, isn't it?'

'Yes. We were just out for our morning constitutional, when I saw you racing down the front steps. I said to Mr Stanley, 'That's Franny, isn't it?' 'Of course,' he agreed. You've always been a favorite of his, you know.'

'Thank you,' Caroline said, sidling toward the corner where the fence would shield any view from the house, at least any view from downstairs.

'And then I said to Mr Stanley, 'I wonder what could be wrong? Surely something is causing her to behave so erratically?' 'Of course,' he agreed. What's the matter, dear? Maybe we can help.'

'Oh, nothing's wrong. I was just on my way to Mimi's studio.'

'In such a hurry? Is she all right?'

'Oh, she's fine. Everything's fine. Really, fine. I was just . . . ' Unable to think of anything, she spread her hands. And noticed she still held the cup. 'I was bringing her this.'

'An empty coffee mug?'

'Yes, because . . . it's for a new piece she's working on. And I'm in a hurry so . . . so that she doesn't forget her brilliant idea.'

'Oh, you don't have to tell us about the creative muse. Mr Stanley is a painter. Aren't you, dear?'

Gloria Stanley nodded at the answer only she could hear, but Caroline found herself nodding too.

'I'd better go now,' she said. She took a step backward. 'Have a nice — '

'Before you run off, dear. Mr Stanley and I were having a bit of a disagreement regarding the reason you've returned to Haven after all these years.'

Caroline recognized the opening dig-for-information gambit. Gathering gossip was like a chess game. A little move here. A little slide over there, sacrifice a couple of pawns, and then before your opponent expected it, bam, checkmate. And in this game, Gloria Stanley was a Grand Master. Caroline was way out of her league.

Because years of training would not allow her to be rude to the older woman, Caroline's best strategy was to volunteer a chunk of unimportant information and then run like hell. 'It's no secret that I've been writing some magazine articles.'

'Oh yes. Mr Stanley and I quite enjoyed that article you wrote on the Indian Pueblo. And also the one on the use of martial arts in video games. Quite informative.'

Caroline had to blink away the image of Mrs Stanley reading a gamer magazine. 'Um, thank you. Well, an opportunity presented itself, and I decided to pursue a writing career full-time. I might even try a novel.'

'I see,' Mrs Stanley said, nodding. 'I see.'

And Caroline wondered if she'd said too much or not enough. 'I really must get going. Have a nice — '

'We were actually hoping you'd decided to come back and open your own business here. You know people in Haven and the surrounding towns get married just like anywhere else. We no longer have a wedding planner in the area and a girl with your skills could earn a tidy living.'

'Oh. That's . . . I'll think about that. Thank you for that suggestion.' Give a little, take a little. 'Now, I should — '

'One more thing, dear. What is your grandmother working on, I mean with the coffee cup and all?'

The question caught Caroline by surprise. 'I don't think I can say . . . '

Mrs Gloria Stanley crossed her arms and leaned back on her heels, a smug little *aha, I caught you lying* smile on her face.

'Actually,' Caroline said, glancing around the yard for inspiration, scrambling for something to say, anything. 'It's . . . It's a tree, a . . . coffee tree. Very surrealistic and avant-garde. Sort of a philosophical . . . nihilistic comment on the current coffee-drinking mania. I'm sure Mr Stanley, as a fellow artist, quite understands the need to make a statement about the cyclical recurrence of cultural phenomena.'

'Mr Stanley and I were discussing that very matter just the other day. Of course, he agrees. Well, we won't keep you from your errand. Give Mimi our regards.' Gloria Stanley turned and started back up the street.

'Have a nice day,' Caroline called, but not too loudly. Then she ducked inside the studio.

And found her grandmother near the door, slumped over and leaning against the wall.

Caroline rushed to her side. 'Omigod! Mimi, what's wrong?'

Mimi took a deep breath and straightened up. 'A nihilistic coffee tree? I nearly busted a gut trying not to laugh out loud. Gloria Stanley might be old but she has the ears of a teenager, one who doesn't listen to rock and roll. I didn't want her to catch me listening.'

'You were eavesdropping? You heard everything?'

'Every pretentious, polysyllabic, bullshit word of it.'

'And it never occurred to you to come out and rescue me?'

'Why? You were doing fine.' Mimi put her arm around her granddaughter's shoulders. 'You're a lot stronger than you think you are. You can hold your own with anyone, once you make up your mind to do it.'

'I handled a crazy woman and a dead man. Big deal. It's not like she's Mother.'

'Hey, never underestimate the Stanleys. Those two have put me on the spot more than once. Why do you think I stayed in here? Prudence is the better part of valor.'

'I can't believe you did that to me.'

'What about what you did to me?' Mimi held out her hand. 'You might as well give me that cup and let me see what I can do with it. By this time tomorrow everyone in town will know I'm supposed to be making a coffee tree. A surrealistic, avant-garde tree.'

'But you don't have to do it. All artists have ideas that seem good at first but just don't pan out.'

'I might as well try. I haven't had a decent idea in months. Not since . . . '

Mimi shook her head, turned and walked toward the corner where her office area was defined by a dilapidated desk, drafting table, and a couple of overstuffed chairs covered in old quilts worn soft and a bit ragged. She sat in one of the easy chairs and picked up a tablet of paper and a pencil.

Caroline followed and sat in the other chair. 'You mean you haven't worked on anything since you sold your pieces?'

Mimi shrugged. 'Guess I got used to having them around, like old friends. I saw them every day, told them my problems, bragged to them about my grandchildren.'

'Did you sell them because — '

'Let's go up to the house and have a cup of tea,' Mimi said as she jumped up. 'Then — '

'No! I mean, we might as well stay here. Don't you still have that hot plate? I could heat some water and — '

'What are you hiding from?' Mimi sank back into her seat, eyeing Caroline with curiosity.

'Isn't that the pot calling the kettle black? Why are you avoiding talking to me? What are *you* hiding?'

'I asked you first,' Mimi said with a petulant lower lip.

'Fine, I tell you then you tell me. Deal?'

'Agreed. You first.'

Caroline took a deep breath. 'I'm prudently avoiding Travis. What's up with him coming over so early and letting himself in like he owned the place?'

'Oh, that. He only has decaf over at their house because Lou isn't supposed to have regular. So I told him any morning he wants coffee, he could come on over and help himself as long as he puts his dirty cup in the dishwasher.'

'Great! You could have warned me.'

'Guess it slipped my mind. Age, you know. Memory is the first thing to go.'

'Your memory is as good as mine.'

'See, it's already happening to you. Lack of sex does it, too.'

'Mimi!' Caroline could hardly believe her ears. 'It does not. And what makes you think I don't have sex, even if it were your business, which it's not.'

'You never talk about a boyfriend.'

'Just because I don't discuss my love life with my grandmother doesn't mean I don't have one.' Caroline had dated. Some. Okay, occasionally. There'd been that whole yardstick thing. Travis was a hard act to follow, no pun intended. 'End of my turn. Now you talk.'

'Why are you hiding from Travis? You can't avoid him for ever.'

'Because I'm smart enough to recognize a lost cause. We're polar opposites. We have incompatible goals. We want different things out of life.'

'Opposites attract for good reason. They complete each other.'

'Believe me, it would never work. And yes I can avoid him for ever if I'm not sabotaged by an interfering grandmother.'

Mimi snorted.

'Your turn,' Caroline said. 'What did Lou mean last night when she said it'll all be over in four to six months? She refused to explain.'

Mimi slumped over and heaved a big sigh. 'The doctor said . . . ' She sniffed and pulled a handkerchief from her sleeve to wipe her nose. 'I asked Lou not to tell anyone. I don't want people looking at me with pity in their eyes. I couldn't stand it.'

Caroline leaned forward and squeezed her grandmother's hand. 'Do you want to tell me about it?'

'I can't talk about it just yet. Maybe later. I

just want to live every day of the rest of my life with the people I love near me, doing the things I love to do for as long as I'm able. I want to concentrate on living not dying.'

Caroline swallowed the lump in her throat. Naomi's vision had been right. Death was stalking her grandmother. Was it her heart? Cancer? By marshalling all her self-control, Caroline managed to hold back her tears, to not break down into a blubbering child seeking comfort rather than giving it. Mimi needed her to be strong. Caroline would respect her grandmother's wishes and not pry. But she also decided to pump her other relatives for specifics at the first opportunity.

'I haven't told any of the others yet.'

Nix that last idea.

'So you can't treat me any different,' Mimi added. 'Even though I get tired more easily than before, I refuse to be treated like an invalid. I want to go on as if nothing has changed.'

'If you're — '

'As if nothing has changed. Please.'

'Okay, I can do that.' Mimi had trusted her with a huge responsibility and Caroline would not let her down. 'But I want your promise that you won't waste any of your precious energy on matchmaking between Travis and me.'

'But — '

'I want your word of honor, and no crossing your fingers or any other body parts.'

'If I do that, and mind you I haven't agreed to do it, but if I do, then you'll have to do a favor for me.'

Mimi scooted forward in her seat, way too eager for Caroline's comfort. Almost as if her grandmother had engineered the whole conversation. Even though that couldn't possibly have happened, Caroline hesitated before asking, 'What favor?'

'Well, your Aunt Rose is at her wit's end with those stepchildren. Four spoiled rotten little monsters, that's what they are. And that new husband of hers isn't any help, what with practices and games and whatever else he does with his time.'

Caroline suppressed a smile. Mimi never referred to Rose's husband by name. He was always That New Husband even though it had been over a year since Rose Tucker Jennings, respected widow and vice principal of Haven High School, married Chuck Siznewski, the freshly divorced gym teacher and athletic coach who was fifteen years her junior. A scandal of Olympic proportions.

Bigger than back during the Depression when Mayor Dooley's boy Howard used his father's 1923 Model T Ford to run moonshine. Bigger than the discovery in the sixties that for years Diane Cummings had used canned filling laced with rum in her blue ribbon cherry pie. Bigger than when she and Travis had been caught skinny-dipping up by the family cabin in the woods. Those poor fishermen had had a shock that morning, as had Caroline. As if losing her virginity the previous night had not been memorable enough.

'School's out next week and Rose could really use your help.'

'I thought she and Chuck only had the kids every other weekend.'

'Their mother had emergency gall bladder surgery two weeks ago and she needs another month before she's able to take the children back. Maybe the rest of the summer.'

That seemed a bit excessive to Caroline but then if she were in the same position she might stretch out her recovery, too. 'So what do you want me to do? Babysit the kids to give Aunt Rose a break? For a day,' she added in hopeful self-defense. 'She could go to a spa in El Paso, get a facial and a massage.'

'Actually, I had something in mind that's more in line with your experience.'

'I've babysat before.'

'But you've never been a prison guard. No, you're uniquely qualified to . . . '

Caroline had a sinking sensation.

'. . . help your cousin Barbara with her wedding.' Shit! Damn! No way! 'I'd rather not.'

'Poor Rose is pulling her hair out. And you're the perfect choice to help.'

'You should hire a professional wedding planner.'

'You *are* a — '

'I'm not in the business any more. Besides that, you need someone with local contacts. There must be dozens of agencies in El Paso and it's less than an hour away.'

'We tried. The first wedding planner we hired collapsed in tears. The second one threw a wedding dress out the window. And the most recent one suddenly decided to become a forest ranger and was last seen headed for the wilds of Montana.'

'Montana is nice.'

'Don't even think about it.'

'The wedding is three weeks away. Surely everything major is done. Anyone could follow up on the guest list and do the last-minute things like giving a final head-count to the caterer.'

'See, you know what you're talking about. It would be easy for you.'

'No. I don't want that responsibility.' Meaning she didn't want to deal with

Barbara. 'Someone else — '

'There is no one else. Word seems to have spread. I've been through the phone directory and not one agency has returned my calls.' Mimi reached over and took Caroline's hands in hers. 'I'm not asking you to do this for Barbara or even for Rose. Do this for me. For my peace of mind.'

'Why is Barbara's wedding so important to you?'

'When I got married my family had fallen on hard times and couldn't afford a fancy wedding. Years later I promised myself I would do whatever I could to help my daughters, and granddaughters if I was so blessed, to have the weddings of their dreams. Dee Ann wanted hers at Christmas with a sleigh and fur hand muffs instead of flowers.'

Caroline had named hers Fluffy. Naturally.

'Mary Lynn wanted a hot air balloon.'

And Caroline had learned she wasn't fond of heights.

'You wanted — '

'Never mind me,' Caroline said. 'We're talking about Barbara the Beast.'

'Now, dear. I know the two of you haven't always gotten along.'

That was an understatement. From the day Caroline was born, Barbara, the one-year-old darling of the family's collective eye, had seen her new cousin as competition, deserving of nothing better than being crushed beneath her dainty patent leather Mary Janes. Barbara had been nasty yet sneaky, making Caroline's life miserable in such a way that Sweet Barbara had never been held accountable for her acts. Except once.

Okay, blackmail wasn't a pretty word, and Caroline wasn't proud of her actions, but it had meant her last two years of high school had been free of Barbara-inflicted mortification. Not free of embarrassment, not by a long shot. But Caroline had managed that all by herself. At least Barbara had finally left her alone. Conventional wisdom told her to let sleeping dogs lie.

'And I know Barbara can be . . . ' Mimi hesitated as if unwilling to say something unflattering about her granddaughter.

Caroline had no such aversion to the truth. 'Self-centered, demanding, a royal pain in the — '

'She's still a Tucker.'

'Or the product of an alien abduction,' Caroline muttered.

'Barbara deserves her dream wedding as much as my other granddaughters.'

The matter of dealing with Barbara aside, Caroline had just spent the last three months saying goodbye to her business and her former career. Getting involved in another wedding would only dredge up all that grief. 'I'm sorry. I can't.'

Mimi closed her eyes and hung her head. 'If you do this for me, I promise on my word of honor not to come up with any new schemes to get you and Travis together.'

Her grandmother wasn't playing fair. One of the worst things Caroline could imagine in exchange for something she definitely wanted — needed — if she was going to live in Haven for any length of time. She couldn't dismiss a sense of unease, a feeling she was getting the short half of the candy bar.

'For as long as I live,' Mimi added in a pitiful whisper.

Caroline stifled a groan. How could she refuse? This was practically her grandmother's dying wish.

'All right, I'll do it. But when I'm arrested for killing her, you're paying the lawyer to get me off on an insanity plea.'

A horrified look crossed Mimi's face. She jumped up, spun round twice, crossed herself and spat through her fingers.

'What in heaven's name are you doing?' Caroline asked, leaning way back in her seat and staring transfixed. Her head swiveled back and forth as her grandmother circled her chair. Mimi waved her arms in a sweeping-away motion as she faced each of the four cardinal directions and blew out long puffs of air, a modern dance version of the weather channel.

'I'm warding off the curse. Never, ever say things like that. You're tempting fate to make it come true.'

'That's silly. It's just a figure of speech. I wouldn't kill anyone, not even Barbara.'

'Go up to the house and bring me all the salt you can find, that bottle of whiskey hidden over the refrigerator, and your Great-aunt Annie's picture from the front parlor.'

'Voodoo Annie?' Caroline slid up and over the arm of the chair, never more desirous of fleeing a scene than at that moment.

'Yes. And don't call her that. She doesn't like it and it's not voodoo.'

'Pardon me if this seems like a stupid question, but why do you want Voo — ah, Great-aunt Annie's picture?'

Mimi gave her granddaughter an exasperated look then she sighed. 'I've always said there's no such thing as a stupid question. Annie's spirit is attached to her picture and I'm going to need her help from the other side if we're going to ameliorate the damage done. Now go.'

'Why do you want the other stuff?'

'I asked you to fetch those things because I thought you'd be faster than me and time is important. I could've been there and back by now.'

Caroline put her hands on her hips. 'Do you want my help? Well, then, what is the salt for?'

'Salt by a door keeps evil spirits away. We'll put some by each of our doors and then go over to Barbara's house and then Rose's for good measure.'

'And the whiskey? What is that for?'

Mimi rolled her eyes. 'I stand corrected. That's a stupid question. Whiskey is for drinking. By the time we're done, I'm going to need a double. Now, hurry up before it's too late.'

Caroline ran up the hill on her bizarre errand muttering to herself, 'Too late for what?'

3

Dear Anxious,

Yes, choosing the bridesmaids' gowns is the bride's prerogative but for heaven's sake don't make lifelong enemies by insisting your dearest friends spend a small fortune on something atrocious. Look for fashions and fabrics that will flatter everyone in the wedding party. If your bridesmaids vary greatly in size, consider different styles in a unifying color. Or if color choice is a problem, consider a single style in several coordinating hues. Be considerate and everyone will look their best on your special day.

Yours truly,

Mrs Bea Correct

★ ★ ★

Two short days later, Caroline sat at one of the tables near the window of Maybelle's Diner, sipping iced tea and wishing it were a

Bloody Mary. Wishing she were anywhere but here. Wishing she was having lunch with anyone other than —

'Hello, Franny.'

— Barbara.

Caroline set down her glass and laced her fingers together. 'Let's get one thing straight from the start,' she said in her most professional I'm-the-wedding-planner-in-charge voice. 'I agreed to help you as a favor to Mimi, but if you persist in calling me Franny, the deal is off.'

Barbara looked down her nose, and for a few seconds Caroline thought her cousin would leave the restaurant in an indignant huff. A bubble of hope surfaced.

'Fine. *Caroline.*'

Pop! The bubble burst and was gone as quickly as it had appeared.

Barbara pulled out the other chair, inspecting it with a disdainful eye before sitting. 'As long as *you* understand this is *my* wedding and I'll accept nothing less than perfection.'

In that one sentence Caroline recognized the syndrome she'd frequently observed in the rarified atmosphere of bridal salons. Queen Bride. Franken-bride. Bridezilla. However, Barbara morphing into Bridezilla wasn't exactly an extreme makeover.

After clearing a space, and wiping the already-clean table with a paper napkin, Barbara reached into her tote, which matched her white strappy sandals, envelope purse, and the braided trim on her pale pink sheath dress with bolero jacket. She placed a white leather-bound volume on the table.

'Mother sent you this,' she said. 'Along with her gratitude for your assistance,' she added with obvious reluctance.

Caroline stared at the book, *Our Wedding, Barbara Jean Jennings and Dirk Aaron Vandergelt,* and the wedding date in gold script letters on the cover. Judging by the bulging contents and haphazard way bits and pieces of paper attempted to escape, Caroline was going to need the entire three weeks before the ceremony to get the mess sorted out.

'Everything's in there. At least everything Mother could find on short notice. She is *so* disorganized lately.'

'Well, she does have her hands full with four young kids.'

'This is my wedding we're talking about.' Barbara shook her head. 'Need I say it?' She flung her hands out palm up as if in an appeal to logic. '*Priorities.*'

Caroline moved the book to the side, carefully so as not to dislodge anything. 'After

68

lunch I'll take this home where I can spread everything out and look through it.'

'You want to eat here?'

'Absolutely.' Caroline looked around the diner, a fixture downtown for as long as she could remember. Not much of the original fifties malt shop remained. Maybelle's granddaughter Susan had redecorated in a trendy ranch-house style with Tex-Mex and Native Indian accents. She'd added low-carb and vegetarian selections to the menu along with the heartburn chili, green enchiladas, and shredded beef tamales that were favorites. Her brother Lewis, a classically trained chef, had returned to the family business and had started a catering business. 'I eat here whenever I can. Susan makes a great taco salad.'

'The service is so slow,' Barbara complained, not bothering to lower her voice.

'Not for my friends,' Susan said, stepping up to the table. She gave Caroline a wink and a smile before turning a bland face to Barbara. 'What'll it be?'

'I suppose I'll have the taco salad if the lettuce is fresh. No boiled eggs or cheese. No beef. Can I substitute chicken? No? Well, then just leave off the meat. No guacamole, no sour cream and no tortilla shell. Water to drink. Bottled water.'

'One plain salad,' Susan said and turned to Caroline.

'I'll have the taco salad with everything you can find to put on it. But rather than guacamole, can I have gobs of your fabulous homemade blue cheese dressing?'

'On taco salad? That's disgusting,' Barbara said.

'Don't knock it till you've tried it. I could eat Susan's blue cheese dressing on just about anything short of ice cream.'

'And I won't be shocked when she orders that.' Susan picked up the menus with a grin. 'Speaking of shocked, did you hear about old Mrs Crocket?' she asked Caroline.

'No, I — '

'The poor woman was found murdered.'

'You're kidding.'

'No. Right in the courthouse. They say it happened Saturday afternoon. Can you imagine?' Susan's voice dropped to a whisper. 'I heard — '

'Excuse me,' Barbara interrupted. 'We do not gossip.'

'News isn't gossip,' Caroline said, dismissing Barbara with a wave. 'What — '

'Not only is that an inappropriate topic for table talk, but we have other matters to discuss,' Barbara hissed back, her immaculately groomed eyebrows arched high. She turned to Susan. 'Don't forget my water. Bottled water. Please,' she added with a condescending smile, effectively putting a stopper in Susan's characteristic effervescence.

Susan bowed in mock acquiescence, promising under her breath to call Caroline later. As Susan left the table Caroline bit her bottom lip to keep from telling her cousin that in some restaurants such behavior would earn her spit — in her food.

'Why did you do that?' she asked instead. 'Murder is big news. You'd think someone would have mentioned it since it happened the day before I got here.'

'Two days. And Bobby Lee asked that it not be discussed in his presence. Some stupid thing about professional ethics and him being afraid he'd reveal privileged information. As if he had any.' Barbara paused to inspect the fork she'd rubbed with another napkin. 'I personally can't see why everyone is so upset.'

'A woman was murdered!'

'A crotchety old witch. Last time I was at the court-house she made me wait forty-five minutes for some stupid motorized copies.'

'Do you mean notarized copies?'

'Whatever. As if I didn't have better things to do with my time. If Dirk hadn't insisted we needed the papers for the pre-nup, I would have walked — '

'He's making you sign a pre-nup?'

'That is what rich people do.'

'Did you have a lawyer look at it?'

'A waste of money. I don't own anything except my clothes and my car. Even my little house is mortgaged to the hilt.'

'Still, it's a good idea — '

'Are you a wedding planner or a lawyer?'

'I've had some experience with pre-nuptial agreements.'

'And I'm not stupid. I read every word of it before I signed. If the marriage ends in divorce I get a hundred thousand dollars a year. Really it's for my protection so his family can't protest any settlement.'

If she'd already signed there wasn't much point in arguing. However, they weren't married yet. 'If you — '

'Forget it.' Barbara leaned forward and pointed the fork at Caroline. 'This marriage is my ticket out of this dumpy town and into the good life. I'm going to make this wedding happen, come hell or high water, and if it takes signing a pre-nup, it's done.'

Caroline blinked at the fierceness of her cousin's tone. 'Why did you stay here if you hated it so much? You could have left at any time.'

'For what? Some menial nine-to-five job and a dreary one-room apartment in the city?

No thanks. At least here I still have . . . '
Barbara pursed her lips together as if to stop
the flow of words. She took a deep breath and
laid the utensil on the table with exaggerated
care. 'Let's just say Dirk and I are going to
have the life I've always dreamed of. Now
then. Where is that waitress with our food? We
have an appointment in El Paso at two-thirty
and I don't want to be late.'

'What appointment? Mimi didn't say
anything.'

'The fitting for your bridesmaid dress.'

'Oh, no, no, no. I'm not — '

'Yes, yes, yes. You are. Fortunately, you're
the same size as Dee Ann.'

'Not only no, but hell no.'

'You're probably tight on money — '

'I'm not.'

'But you don't have to worry about the
cost.' Barbara picked up the spoon and
frowned at it. 'The dress is already paid for.'

'Money is not the issue.' A lie, but Caroline
would never let her cousin know that. 'I never
said I'd be a bridesmaid.'

'You agreed to help make my wedding
perfect and the perfect wedding has four
bridesmaids.' Barbara held up four fingers
then bent one for each attendant as she
named them. 'My college roommate Sue
Ellen, Judy my best friend all through school,

cousin Mary Lynn, and you. You're taking your sister Dee Ann's place.'

'But Dee Ann loves being a bridesmaid. Her feelings will be hurt if she isn't — '

'She's pregnant. Not only will that ruin the lines of the dress I've chosen, the scent of roses makes her puke. And I must have roses.' Barbara stared off into space and sighed. 'Everywhere pink roses. Perfectly lovely.' She tipped her head to the side, her smooth blond pageboy swinging to her shoulder, and laid her cheek against her hands folded together. An angelic vision.

Caroline gagged. She shuffled her feet to fight the itch that urged her to run, hide. Escape! But she'd given her word to her dying grandmother. Through gritted teeth she said, 'Please tell me the bridesmaid dresses aren't hideous.'

★   ★   ★

Caroline stood on the pedestal and stared into the three-way mirror with something akin to morbid fascination. Although by definition a bridesmaid dress was expected to be dreadful, her reflection went beyond her worst nightmare. The Pepto-Bismol color alone was enough to make her nauseous. But, oh no, the fun didn't stop there.

74

Wide organdy ruffles around the scoop neckline itched and made her look like she was wearing football pads. The huge skirt could double as a car cover for a VW. The taffeta lining rustled with every step as if saying, *Fashion impaired coming through.* Even the freaking shoes were pink, and unattractive plain pumps with clunky one-inch heels at that.

But wait, there's more. No outfit from the Barbie Goes To Tara Playset would be complete without a floppy garden hat including long satin ribbons to tie into a big-ass bow under the left ear.

'Lovely,' Barbara said, clapping her hands while the bridal shop employees beamed their approval.

Caroline rolled her eyes.

'Now we have ze walking lessons, no?' Madame, *just Madame no other name was needed*, the owner of the shop, said.

Caroline pointed out that she'd been walking since the age of ten months but apparently that wasn't sufficient practice.

'*Vite! Vite!* Around ze room.'

So Caroline *vited* around the perimeter of the salon, the hoops under the circus-tent-sized skirt causing it to sway from side to side with every step like a drunken pink elephant on parade.

'*Non, non, cheri.* You look like ze, how you say, ze pendulum on ze grand clock.'

'The skirt isn't supposed to move when you walk,' Barbara pointed out with way too much enjoyment. 'Lead with your hips and keep your knees slightly bent so you glide elegantly.'

Caroline glided around the room in a sort of crouching belly dancer movement.

'*Maintenant,* ze alterations.' Madame snapped her fingers, and three assistants rushed forward proffering a pincushion, tailor's chalk, and a tape measure like they were frankincense, gold, and myrrh.

'Actually, I think the dress fits pretty well as is.'

Madame gave her a pitying look. 'We take in ze bust. You are not, how you say, well-endowed,' she added maliciously.

Barbara burst into a fit of poorly muffled giggles.

And it was just one pinprick too many. Quitting wasn't an option, but Barbara didn't know that. Caroline turned and *glided* over to where her cousin sat in a throne-like chair.

'If I choose to ignore the rudeness of a stranger rather than make a scene, that's my business,' she whispered. Leaning closer, she pushed her face to within inches of Barbara's. 'But if you tick me off, you know what will happen,' Caroline said in her most threatening voice. She sliced a finger across her throat. 'I'll be out of here faster than you can say Mendelssohn's *Wedding March.*'

She returned to the dressing room, pausing only long enough to tell Madame, 'Thank you, but no alterations will be needed.' Taking her time, she changed into her usual jeans and vintage T-shirt, using the extra minutes for calming deep breathing. Three weeks until the wedding. Only three weeks. Less time than it took a broken bone to heal. Less time than recovery from an appendectomy. She'd endured a toothache for three weeks during one June with seventeen weddings, for Pete's sake. She could do this. For her grandmother's peace of mind. Three long, miserable weeks.

When Caroline returned to the salon, Barbara was on the pedestal in her wedding finery, a frothy concoction of satin and lace, the Hollywood version of *Scarlett Gets Married.* Barbara was obviously not a happy bride, and she harangued the staff with the minute details of her dissatisfaction. The hem was a full quarter inch lower on the left. The train pooched where it should pouf. The sleeves were supposed to end a half-inch below her wrist not a disastrous half-inch above it, and the waist simply hung on her. The alterations would have to be redone yet again.

As the assistants scurried and Madame groveled, Caroline announced to no one in particular that she would wait at the book-store across the street, as if anyone cared. Maybe she could find some details of the murder in the newspapers. At least she could get a few moments of peace and a mocha cappuccino before the long drive home.

Three weeks.

★   ★   ★

Travis supervised the collection of fingerprint evidence, schooling the impatience from his voice. His men were doing a decent job even if one was slower than the other. He could have done it a bit faster himself but deputies Bobby Lee Tucker and Harlan Keyes needed the practice. Watching them laboriously dust and lift was about as exciting as inspecting drying paint.

'What the hell is going on? My God! Look at my office.'

Walter DeShane burst through the yellow CAUTION tape that Bobby Lee had strung because they were out of CRIME SCENE DO NOT CROSS, if they'd ever had any to begin with. Walter hardly looked like the county's leading attorney dressed in his fishing clothes. Which was surprising in itself. Even as far back as high school Walter had been preppy, wearing socks that matched his sweater and polishing his shoes daily. The two men had not been boyhood friends but now had a polite working relationship.

'Afternoon, Walter,' Travis said, blocking the path into the inner office. 'Seems you had a break-in.'

'So my secretary said.'

'I suspect she called you before she called us.'

Walter, just like the good lawyer he was, neither confirmed nor denied. 'I came back right away.'

'The guys will be through in a few minutes. Then I'd like to know what, if anything, is missing.'

'Look at that mess. There goes my vacation and I haven't caught a single fish.' Walter took off his canvas hat with the fishing lures attached and threw it across the room.

File drawers had been emptied onto the floor and papers were scattered from wall to wall. The desk and chairs had been upended and all the pictures and diplomas were off the walls, revealing an apparently undisturbed wall safe. Everything was covered with a fine film of graphite dusting powder, including both deputies.

'It'll take weeks to clean that up,' Walter whined. 'Why would anybody do this? I don't keep any valuables here. Petty cash in Earline's desk but that's less than fifty bucks.'

'I'll need a detail of that, but off the top of my head, I'd say this looks as if someone was pissed at you.' Travis also was careful with his wording. Appearances were often deceiving. 'Got any unhappy clients?'

Walter looked at him. 'I'm a lawyer and the county prosecutor. Unhappy clients go with the territory.'

'You know I'll need a list of your cases.'

'Yes, yes. I'll have Earline get it to you as soon as possible.'

'If she could include last known addresses, that would be helpful. I expect we'll find this guy is local.'

Walter cocked his head to the side. 'Why do you say that?'

'Somebody knew you would be out of town, that your office would be closed. If Earline hadn't come back to get that scarf she'd forgotten, the break-in wouldn't have been discovered until your return.'

'I always take the month of June off to go fishing. I've been doing it for years.'

'That would be at Judge McKay's place?'

'I was at my uncle's fishing camp,' Walter said, bristling. 'It's a family tradition.'

'Nice place.' The twelve-room log mansion wasn't exactly what Travis would call a campsite.

'If you need to verify my whereabouts, that can be arranged.'

'I'm sure that won't be necessary,' Travis said. But it was interesting to note that from Walter's tone he still had a major chip on his shoulder. There must be others besides Travis who thought the prosecutor's meteoric rise had as much to do with connections as it did with Walter's talent.

'All anyone would have to do is phone the office,' Earline said, stepping between the two men. She'd run Walter Senior's law office before he'd retired early in favor of his son and she acted more like Walter Junior's mother than his office manager. 'I changed the message and gave all that information. Not that he was fishing, of course, but that the office would be closed until the first of July.'

Her protective instincts made Travis smile. He backed off a few steps and nodded toward the other room where the deputies were still hard at work. 'What sort of files do you keep in there? Don't you have an office at the courthouse?'

'I do, and most of my case files are there,' Walter answered. 'But I still have a small private practice of a few long-time clients.'

'Any of them unhappy? Violent?'

'If any of them were dissatisfied, which no one has mentioned, I'd think they'd just get another lawyer. I can't see any of them doing something like this.'

'What's in the safe?'

'Nothing exotic like jewels or bank notes. Mostly papers I'm keeping for clients, a couple of wills, a few property settlements. One divorce case,' he added with a go-ahead-and-ask-me-I-dare-you smile.

Travis chose to ignore the lawyer's riposte because he knew damn well who that client was.

'And before you ask, yes, I have a master list of the contents,' Walter added. 'But obviously whoever did this didn't get into the safe.'

'That's an assumption at this point. When the guys have finished with the outside, I'd like you to open it. There might be something missing.'

'How much longer?' Walter asked. 'I haven't even been home to change my clothes yet.'

'Really?' Travis asked, unable to suppress a grin. 'I hadn't noticed.'

'Okay, Beaumont. You've gotten in your digs, and asked your questions. Now give me a break. I've never been the victim of a crime before and I'm justifiably upset.'

'Is that possible? I've heard you're a heartless machine.'

'Don't believe a word of it,' Earline said as she returned to her desk and started sorting through papers. 'He may be tough on the outside but inside he's a marshmallow.'

Travis smiled and relayed the earlier question to the guys inside the office.

'Not too much longer,' Bobby Lee answered. 'Man, there are a lot of prints in here. Totally cool.'

Travis could only shake his head and curse the janitor for not wiping the surfaces better. The likelihood that they would find usable prints was inversely proportional to the number of prints found. Most of them were probably going to be unclear or turn out to belong to Walter or Earline.

Two hours later, Travis didn't have much else in the way of evidence. The break-in had taken place between five-thirty Friday evening and about ten o'clock Wednesday morning when Earline discovered the mess. Ed, the janitor, had been in the building over the weekend on his regular schedule, but he'd bypassed that particular office knowing he had several weeks to clean it. He hadn't heard anything unusual.

According to Walter nothing had been disturbed in the safe. The petty cash box had contained only seven dollars and thirty-two cents because Earline had just bought postage stamps the week before. The stamps were still in the box. Based on appearances, the robber had gotten pissed at the small amount of cash and had trashed the office in retaliation.

However, several things struck Travis as odd. For one, not a single drawer or cabinet had been left untouched. Such a methodical execution did not fit someone who was enraged and irrational. And nothing had been smashed. Overturned, upended, dumped, yes, but no broken glass, or splintered wood. Nothing had been crushed, trampled, ripped, or thrown against the wall. It almost seemed as if the deed had been done purposefully, sort of premeditated chaos, which sounded crazy. Still, he couldn't shake the notion.

If the intruder had been searching for a specific item and had trashed the room to cover his or her tracks, did that mean he or she had found that particular something? Or not?

Travis jotted down a few notes and then helped bag and tag the evidence for transport to the State Crime Lab for processing. If he were lucky the results would be back in weeks instead of months depending on the lab's current workload. In the meantime there was plain old-fashioned grunt work to do, asking everyone who had been in the vicinity over the weekend if they'd witnessed anything out of the ordinary.

Since the surrounding neighborhood included several popular restaurants, the movie theater, and a couple of bars, that could mean questioning just about everyone in town. A major effort for a simple break-in, but instinct told Travis there was more to this than met the eye.

Four hours later, he still didn't have the slightest idea what it could be. Not yet anyway. But two non-typical crimes within such a short period of time made the hair on the back of his neck stand up. Not a good sign.

4

Caroline stared in dismay at the neat piles of papers covering the large dining-room table. Simulated organization couldn't disguise the underlying chaos. And where was Barbara, who was supposed to be helping get the mess she'd created under control? Late. Conveniently MIA. As usual when there was work to be done.

'If you keep frowning like that your face is going to freeze that way,' Bobby Lee said. He leaned against the doorframe and took a bite from the drumstick in his hand.

Caroline stuck her tongue out at her younger brother.

'So mature.'

'Don't talk with your mouth full.' Her stomach growled. Since he was still wearing his uniform she assumed he had come home for lunch. 'Did you bring enough to share? I'm starving.'

'This is Mimi's famous Honey-mustard Fried Chicken.' He took another bite with an ostentatious flourish. 'Mmmmm. Just as good cold.'

She hadn't seen any chicken in the

refrigerator earlier. 'Where did — '

'Obviously you missed the big green cooler in the corner.'

'The one with the note on it that said, *Do Not Open. This means you, too, Bobby Lee.*'

'Yep. That's the one. Nobody makes chicken like Mimi. Add to that her potato salad, slaw, a veggie plate, cheese tray, brownies, and sugar cookies. There's even a full half of a Lemon Coconut Snowball Cake. My favorite.'

'Everyone's favorite,' Caroline said with a *Duh!* shake of her head.

'Mimi must be going on a picnic with four or five friends.'

'And you reached that conclusion how?'

'Elementary, my dear Watson. Since there's nothing wrong with the refrigerator, and plenty of room for food, Mimi chose to put the food in the cooler for portability. The amount of food suggests five or six adults — '

'Or two people with your appetite.'

Bobby Lee rubbed his flat stomach with his free hand. 'Gotta keep the lean machine's fuel tank full. Hey, maybe you can horn in on her picnic? That is, if you can tear yourself away from whatever it is you're doing.' He pointed at the table with the chicken leg. 'Isn't that the same stuff you were working on when I left the house this morning?'

'Barbara's wedding plans.' She slumped forward and rested her forehead on the table. 'Just shoot me now and put me out of my misery.'

'Helloooo. Where is everyone?'

Caroline recognized her cousin's voice and groaned as she sat up. 'Better yet, give me your gun and I'll shoot the source.' But her brother was gone. 'Chicken,' she called after him.

'There you are,' Barbara said as she swept into the dining room. 'Why aren't you dressed?'

Caroline glanced guiltily down at her cut-off jeans and Mickey Mouse T-shirt before catching herself. Why did she still allow Barbara to do that to her? 'Where have you been?' she demanded, sounding more defensive than she wanted. She stood up and cleared her throat. 'You were supposed to be here at nine o'clock to help sort through this paperwork.'

'Do you *need* help? Aren't you a professional organizer?'

'Wedding planner.'

'Whatever. I assumed you could handle it.' Barbara walked around the table, eyeing but not touching. 'All sorted by major category; cake, caterer, flowers, RSVPs. Alphabetical and date order. Impressive.'

'Hardly. I learned my ABCs and numbers before first grade.'

'I'm trying to pay you a compliment.'

'And not doing it well.'

'You've done more in one morning than Mother managed to do in the last two months.'

Caroline narrowed her eyes and crossed her arms. 'You're never nice without an ulterior motive. What do you want now? I've already promised I'd help with your wedding, and I agreed to be a bridesmaid and to wear that stupid costume — '

'That dress is not — '

'Whatever you want, the answer is no.'

Barbara gave her an arch look. 'Actually, this falls within your promise to Mimi to do everything you can to make my wedding perfect.'

'You're playing the grandmother card?'

'If I have to.'

Caroline bit her bottom lip to keep from saying what she really wanted to say.

Apparently satisfied with the silence, Barbara said, 'I want you to write some wedding vows for me.'

'You're joking.'

'I never joke about having the perfect wedding. And you're the writer in the family.'

'But your wedding vows?'

89

'Dirk has this crazy idea we should each say our own words, but I have no intention of baring my soul in public.'

'And *I'm marrying you for your money and social position* doesn't sound all that romantic.'

'Just write up something suitable. Doesn't have to be long. Stay away from words like obey and for ever. Make it sound thoughtful and intelligent and . . . okay, romantic. But not overly sentimental.'

Actually it wouldn't be the first vows Caroline had written. More brides and grooms needed help with those important words than anyone might think. Although a little coaching and a few suggestions usually sufficed to get their thoughts flowing, there had been times when she'd heard her exact words recited at the altar. 'I'll help you write your own. What first attracted you to Dirk?'

Barbara gave her a blank stare.

'O-kay.' Caroline cleared her throat. 'Think about why you love him. Anything? No. Let's see. How do you see your future together?'

'Can't you do this without my help?'

She made it sound like a challenge. Caroline had never been able to resist a dare, especially from Barbara. 'Don't you want to have *any* input?'

Barbara heaved an exasperated sigh.

'Whatever you come up with will be perfectly adequate.'

Adequate? 'Fine. I'll whip out a few lines later this afternoon.' Caroline counted to ten to regain control of her temper. 'Right now we have to deal with this mess.' She waved her arm to encompass the diningroom table.

Barbara opened her purse, took out her checkbook, and tossed the pink leather wallet with hearts and flowers and BJJ stitched on the cover on top of a pile of papers. 'You'll need to write checks to . . . ' she waved her hand over the stacks of paper — 'those people. They all want deposits.'

'You haven't given them deposits?' Caroline could feel her voice rising in pitch. None of these contracts were binding without a deposit. 'Your wedding is only three weeks away.'

'Two weeks, three days and four hours. Believe me, I know. I signed a dozen checks for you to use.'

'You should — '

'Hello,' Bobby Ray called as he entered the front door. He crossed the hall and came into the dining room loosening his tie.

Caroline hadn't seen her older brother dressed up in a suit in years. 'You look nice. What's the occasion?'

'Monthly reporting to the court and my

probation officer.' Bobby Ray motioned with his head to the man behind him and Travis stepped into the room.

What was Travis doing here?

Another man entered.

'Darling,' Barbara said to the stranger, crossing the room to kiss his cheek.

So this was Dirk Vandergelt of the Miami Vandergelts. The groom. Blond-haired and blue-eyed, he was extremely handsome in a slick, overstyled sort of way, like he belonged on the cover of *GQ*. Like the after picture in a plastic surgeon's office. Like the wannabe stars that populated LA hoping to be discovered. Not Caroline's taste. When he was introduced to her, rather than shake her hand, he took hers in his soft fingers, bent at the waist, and drew the back of her hand to his moist lips.

'Isn't he the gallant one,' Barbara said with a pleased sigh.

'I'm glad to finally meet you.' Dirk looked up at Caroline from under his lashes and his hungry eyes said way more than his innocuous greeting did.

She jerked her hand away from his. Somehow their movements knocked Barbara's checkbook off the table. Caroline bent over and snatched it off the floor using the disruption to camouflage her steps backward away from Dirk. She surreptitiously wiped her hand on her sleeve as she crossed her arms and glanced over at Travis. He seemed to be avoiding looking at her.

'I should be going,' he said to her brother. 'I'm still on duty.'

'I appreciate the ride,' Bobby Ray said. 'Hang on a minute and I'll get you that CD we were talking about.'

Travis shrugged his shoulders. 'I can't leave until Dirk moves his car. He's parked behind me.'

Bobby Ray nodded and left the room. Caroline heard him clomping up the stairs.

'We should be going,' Dirk said to Barbara.

'Yes, of course. Mimi said she'd put our picnic lunch in a cooler in the kitchen. Why don't you take it out to the car? I'll just finish up with Caroline.'

'That picnic is for you?' Caroline asked her cousin as Dirk left to follow instructions. 'I can't believe you asked Mimi to get up at the crack of dawn to bake and cook for you . . . ' she stopped herself from saying *in her condition*. Barbara didn't know their grandmother was dying, and Travis was still there, even if he was leaning against the wall as if he were a disinterested bystander. 'At her age,' she finished lamely.

'Mimi loves to cook and she gets up at

93

dawn every day. And for your information, I didn't ask her. She volunteered when I told her we were going up to the lake today.'

'You hate the lake.'

Barbara looked over her shoulder before continuing. 'Dirk thinks communing with nature will help us come up with ideas for our wedding vows.'

'You hate nature.'

'No, I don't.'

'You spent every summer of our childhood complaining about the log cabin, the bugs, and the dirt. Wild animals like deer and rabbits caused you to run screaming in terror. You refused to swim in the lake because it didn't have a blue cement bottom.'

'Because the water wasn't filtered,' Barbara corrected her. 'Fish poop in that water, you know.' She glanced over her shoulder again. 'Just because I don't enjoy rustic pursuits doesn't mean I hate nature. I'll enjoy spending time with Dirk regardless of where we are.'

In that moment Caroline realized her cousin was not as confident of the groom's feelings as she pretended to be. Her attitude toward Barbara softened a bit. Did she know he already had a wandering eye?

A horn's impatient beep captured Barbara's attention. She headed for the front door. 'Got to run. You know how to handle everything.'

Suddenly Caroline realized she was alone in the dining room with Travis. 'Wait! Come back,' she called after her cousin as she raced around the table and down the hall. Her plea had no effect.

Barbara had the audacity to smile and wave like royalty as they drove away. Any soft feeling she might have had toward Barbara dissipated.

'One of these days,' Caroline muttered under her breath, shaking her head as they drove away. She slumped back against the doorjamb.

'Don't take it so hard.'

Caroline jumped at the sound of Travis's deep voice. She whipped around to face him. 'Don't sneak up on me like that.'

'Not my fault the floor doesn't squeak anymore.'

'I'm sure you have important sheriff-type things to do so don't let me keep you.' She managed just the right tone of haughty dismissal in her voice.

He smiled. And she stiffened her knees to keep from stepping closer to him.

'I'm waiting for Bobby Ray,' he said with a glint of amusement in his eye.

The not-so-subtle reminder that he hadn't come to see her hurt her feelings more than

95

she wanted to admit. Hurt her pride, she amended to herself. Her feelings were well under control, thank you very much. She raised her chin a notch. 'Then you'll excuse me.' She started to walk past him with her head held high, but he sidestepped and blocked her path.

'Running away again?' he asked.

'I have business appointments and must get ready. And I do not run away.' *Liar, liar, pants on fire.*

He smiled wide enough to flash a dimple. 'You can't avoid me for ever.'

Watch me.

Suddenly serious, he added, 'You owe me an explanation.'

He didn't have to say for what. She knew he meant an explanation of why she'd given up on their marriage. 'Why rehash the past?' She forced herself to smile. 'I moved on. You moved on.' *And how.* Mimi had kept her updated on each new girlfriend, the exotic dancer, fashion model, ER nurse. He'd dated Miss Illinois for a few months before moving back to Haven. 'Let's just let sleeping dogs lie.' She headed for the stairs knowing he wouldn't follow her up to her bedroom.

'Caro?' Travis put his hand on her arm.

He was the only person to ever call her that. She paused with one foot on the second

96

step. She didn't turn around because she needed a few seconds to squash down her reaction. Instead, she looked meaningfully at his hand. He dropped his hold and she mounted two more steps before facing him with a bland expression. 'Nothing is gained by dredging up old hurts. I prefer to look to the future.'

'I deserve to know the truth,' he said in a low, slightly hoarse voice.

Maybe he did, but the truth would hurt him worse than believing she'd just stopped loving him and had left him for college and a career. Saying the words would open a wound on her soul that she'd buried deep inside. A pain she couldn't share. 'You already know everything there is to know,' she lied with a straight face. 'We just didn't work out. It's been over for a long time. That's not too complicated or difficult to understand. Even for you.'

Travis smiled. 'You had me going there for a minute, but as soon as you insulted me I knew for sure you're hiding something. You might as well tell me. I'll find out everything eventually. Was it another man?'

Before she had time to think of a clever response, Bobby Ray bounded down the stairs.

'Here you go, Travis. I burned you a copy so if you like his work you can forward it on to that friend of yours in Nashville.'

He'd also taken the time to change out of his suit and into jeans. She gave her brother a glare as she passed him on her way up.

'I suspected you had an ulterior motive,' Travis replied with a chuckle. 'Thanks.'

When Caroline looked back from the safety of the first floor, Travis was looking up at her with that cocky grin that always made her weak in the knees. She made it to her bedroom before rubbing her arm, still warm from his touch.

★   ★   ★

'Excuse me, Sheriff?'

'What's up?' Travis motioned Phyllis O'Conner into his office. An unlikely-looking choice for a police officer, small and delicate, her graying hair in an elegant French twist, she sat on the edge of a chair in front of his desk and smoothed her immaculately pressed uniform shirt.

'Luann Whitson called.'

The name didn't ring any bells so Travis simply nodded for Phyllis to continue.

'She's the manager of the U-Pack-It, the rental storage warehouses out on the highway. In response to a customer complaint she used her master key to open the door of Unit

Nineteen. The smell was so bad she refused to go in. I think we should check it out.'

'Some animal crawled in there and died,' Harlan called from the squad room. 'I say we call county and let the animal control guys clean it up.'

Phyllis pressed her lips into a thin line.

Although he'd only been Sheriff a short time, he'd learned to trust her insight. Phyllis was connected to almost everyone in town, either by blood, marriage, or by one of the many organizations she belonged to: church circle, knitting group, Little Theatre, the Garden Club, Friends of the Library, Band Boosters, and who knew what else.

Travis picked up his hat and keys from his desk. 'Bring along an evidence kit. We'll call Marlene from the road. Harlan, you have dispatch.'

The deputy put down his sub sandwich and swallowed. 'But Phyllis usually . . . '

A lowered brow and hard stare from Travis stopped Harlan's whining. 'Are you refusing to perform your assigned duty?'

Harlan hesitated a long moment before he jumped up and stood to attention, sucking in his ample gut. 'No, sir. I have dispatch. Sir.'

Travis gave him a curt nod and turned on his heel.

Minutes later Phyllis buckled her seat belt.

'Too bad. You almost had reason to fire him for insubordination. That boy's past due for a set down.'

Travis started the engine and kept his face impassive even though she'd verbalized his thoughts. 'Don't worry. I can handle him.'

'Not Harlan I'm worried about. It's his daddy, the high and mighty Mayor, sticking his long nose into police business that scares the begeesus out of me.'

Didn't make him all warm and fuzzy either. 'So do you want to fill me in?'

'I'm afraid we're going to find the body of Annabelle Dawson.'

'Call me slow,' he said, 'but you'll have to explain that leap of logic.'

'Unit Nineteen is rented by Dr Dieter for old files.'

'Doc Crane's partner?'

'Except Old Doc Crane has been retired for at least five years. Dr Dieter is the only doctor in town now and his assistant Annabelle has a new boyfriend. She blushes and giggles like a schoolgirl anytime someone mentions love or marriage. But no one has seen her out on a date or with anyone, so I figured she was keeping it secret because he was married or something.'

'So you think they were meeting at the warehouse? I'm not much of a romantic but even I could come up with something better than that.'

'Last season the Little Theatre put on the musical version of *The Princess and the Pea*.'

Travis blinked in confusion. She'd lost him again.

'Dr Dieter lets us store props in the unused portion of his space, including a large rather ornate four-poster bed used in the last production. And Annabelle had access to the keys.'

'Okay, so a little hanky-panky between the royal sheets. That doesn't — '

'She hasn't shown up for work for two days.'

'People — '

'She missed rehearsal last night. Being the fairy godmother in *Cinderella* is her first big role. Annabelle would have waded through a pit of rattlesnakes to make it to rehearsal.'

'Do you know who she's dating?'

'Not a clue.'

Travis parked the squad car in front of the office and let the manager Luann Whitson escort them to Unit Nineteen. Marlene had beat them there and had pulled her service van right up to the garage-type door. Her assistant was pulling out her gurney as she slapped the magnetic *Coroner* sign on the side of the vehicle.

'Aren't you jumping the gun?' Travis asked as they approached.

Marlene grabbed a handful of latex gloves from her black medical bag on the gurney and threw a pair to Travis. 'I'm familiar with the characteristic odor of human decomposition.'

Now that he stood nearer the door, he too recognized the smell. If the body proved to be poor Annabelle Dawson, she must have been murdered two or three days ago. He nodded to Phyllis and she stepped forward with her police evidence kit. 'We might as well start checking for traces at the door,' he said even though there wasn't much chance they'd get any usable prints.

What the hell was happening to his town?

5

Dear Concerned,

A contract for wedding services usually includes a deposit. And yes, if you cancel the wedding, your deposits are usually forfeited. Although you think this unreasonable since the event is not taking place, the vendor will have purchased supplies, food, flowers, and whatever, according to your plans. The date has also been reserved for you and not booked to another bride. Therefore any cancellation results in cost and loss of income.

But sometimes weddings are cancelled and yes that can be devastating both emotionally and financially. If you are so very worried about making deposits far in advance, you can take a chance on booking the services you want at the last minute although I warn you it's rarely successful. You might have to settle for your second, third, or even sixteenth choice.

Perhaps you might reconsider setting the date when you have such strong doubts about the wedding actually happening. A *longer engagement could be your best answer.*

Yours truly,

Mrs Bea Correct

★ ★ ★

Caroline finished typing the column inspired by Barbara's procrastination, emailed it to the editor, and closed her laptop.

'More coffee?' Susan asked, pouring more into Caroline's cup before she had a chance to answer.

'Thanks. I didn't mean to be a bother by taking up a booth for so long.'

'No problem. We're not that busy between lunch and the after-school crowd.' Susan slid into the booth across from Caroline and produced her own cup. 'You'll want to be out of here before three-thirty. It's wall-to-wall kids for at least two hours.'

Caroline put her laptop in her cream-colored leather attaché. The butter-soft case had the Caroline's Weddings logo tastefully engraved near the handle, a gift from her employees on the company's fifth anniversary just last year. 'Actually, I should be going. I still have to meet with the florist.'

'You're using Bennett's? I mean, Barbara is using Bennett's?'

'Of course. If there's one good thing I can say about her wedding plans, she contracted local services. Well, except for the dresses.'

'Can't you just see Barbara wearing one of Miss Eugenia's Classic Creations?'

'Styles from the forties and fifties have to be better than the pink atrocity — '

'It can't be that bad.'

'You'll see. Just promise me you won't burst out laughing when I'm gliding down the aisle.'

Susan shook her head as she stood. 'We're not invited to the ceremony. The hired help, you know.'

'I'm going to kill that woman. Right after I make sure you and your brother get an invitation.'

'Don't bother. Really. Lewis will be too busy with the catering and I've already volunteered to help him. Moving back home after losing his restaurant in the divorce hasn't been easy for him. Mom and Dad try to be understanding, but they're just so set in their ways. Mom frets when he's in her kitchen and Dad won't share the remote. Lewis has been depressed and moody. I pushed him to accept the catering job because I think working will be good for him.'

'He's lucky to have you for a sister. And Barbara is lucky to have him. Not many brides can score a chef of his reputation to handle her reception. I'm still surprised he agreed.'

'At first he absolutely raved about how much Barbara reminded him of his ex, how he'd rather cook for Satan. He calmed down and then suddenly changed his mind.' Susan leaned closer and lowered her voice. 'I think cooking for her is some weird self-imposed penance he needs to survive in order to regain his self-respect and be free to start over.'

Caroline didn't know what to say to that. 'Well, as I told him, I'm grateful he kept the date open.'

Three teenagers came into the restaurant and raced noisily to seats at the end of the counter. One pimple-laden boy slapped the granite repeatedly.

'That's my signal to go back to work,' Susan said with a rueful smile as she stood. 'You might want to escape before it's wall-to-wall braces and raging hormones in here.'

'I don't know how you put up with it.' Caroline stared at the boy but she also remembered Barbara's rudeness.

'I've been working that counter ever since I

was tall enough to see the customers.' Susan shrugged. 'Just part of the job. Drama in the kitchen is what drives me nuts.'

Caroline stood and gave her friend a hug. 'Well, I'm off to see about flowers.'

'Tell Paul I say hi. And don't let his wife know you and he dated back in high school. She's the jealous type.'

'We didn't *date*. We went to the movies together a couple of times. Besides, Paul took out nearly every girl in school, including you.'

'Yeah, but I'm not available and looking for a man.'

'Hey! I am *not* looking for — '

Susan patted her friend's shoulder. 'I know. But you are single, and in the mind of a crazy jealous woman that's enough. Watch your back. I mean it.'

'I'll remember your advice.' Caroline waved and exited, her progress slow, like swimming against the tide as the after-school crowd entered.

Caroline burst out the door and on to the sidewalk like a diver coming up for air, and pulled up short to keep from running over Gloria Stanley. 'Oops. Sorry. Are you all right?'

'I'm fine. Mr Stanley always has my arm.'

'Are you sure? I mean, are you sure you're all right?' The older woman looked a bit pale, but then again she always did.

'Not to worry, my dear.' Mrs Stanley straightened the stack of four plastic boxes she carried. 'I see by your attire that you've decided to set up business after all.'

Caroline smoothed the skirt of her cream-colored linen suit, the one with just enough polyester and lycra to keep it from wrinkling horribly or stretching shapeless if she had to crawl on the floor to fix a bride's hem. 'Not really. Just my cousin Barbara's wedding. I'm on my way to see Paul Bennett about the flowers.' That was her bid to escape and she started to turn away until Mrs Stanley spoke.

'One moment, please.'

Caroline faced her.

The older woman tilted her head to the side listening to something only she could hear. 'Yes, of course.' She straightened and then shoved one of the lidded plastic containers at Caroline.

She had no choice but to take it.

'How fortuitous that we should run into you, even if it was quite literally so. You can give that to Travis for us.'

'No. I'm sorry but . . . ' Caroline shook her head and tried to return the box, but Gloria took a step back.

'It's Red Velvet Cookie Bars. His favorite.'

'I can't . . . '

'We simply could not leave them at his office while he wasn't there. Not with that Keyes boy there. Yes,' she nodded over her shoulder. 'You're right. Harlan is his name. We're quite sure he would gobble them all up. Greedy, just like his father. Mr Stanley thinks it's in their genes.' Mrs Stanley tapped the top of the container with one finger and switched the subject, a tactic that often caught others off guard. 'We have a whole list of errands to run and of course, you'll see Travis . . . '

'No, I won't. I mean we're not . . . seeing each other . . . or anything like that . . . anymore.' Caroline pressed her lips together to stop babbling. Again she tried to return the container.

Mrs Stanley took another step back. 'You do live next door to him.'

True. Apparently Caroline could either give the cookies to Travis or she could chase an old woman walking backwards down the sidewalk while trying to give them back. She blew out a breath and agreed to deliver the container. 'I'll drop them off at his house this afternoon,' she said, hoping she sounded more gracious than she felt. If she hurried he might not be home yet.

'Make sure you give them to him personally so he can hide them from Lou.

She has such a sweet tooth, and the poor dear is on that restricted diet. No sense putting temptation at her fingertips.'

'Of course.' Now she'd promised to deliver the cookies to him personally. So much for her plan to avoid the man. Maybe she could get Mimi or Dee Ann to do it?

'Well, we won't keep you from your business any longer. Oh, yes, Mr Stanley says to tell you to be circumspect in your dealings with Paul. His wife is the jealous type.'

'So I've heard.'

After saying goodbye, Caroline continued along the sidewalk. In The Pink, the Bennetts' family-owned business, was located in the southeast corner of the Town Square, the last shop on East Avenue in the row of buildings that faced the central park in front of the courthouse. She crossed West Avenue, cut across the grassy lawn, and took the path past the gazebo where the band gave concerts on Friday nights in the summer and carolers sang at Christmas.

She considered tossing the container of cookies into the bushes. Unfortunately, if she were asked about it later she wouldn't be able to lie convincingly enough to fool Gloria Stanley.

A wicked idea broke into her thoughts. She'd promised to deliver the cookies to

Travis but she hadn't guaranteed their condition. With a grin, she tipped the sealed box on its side and tucked it under her arm. When she entered the flower shop she was in a much better frame of mind.

'Franny!' Paul Bennett scurried out from behind the counter to meet her with a hug.

He'd put on a few pounds, like maybe forty, and had lost most of his hair, but his lively brown eyes were still warm and friendly. He still reminded her of an eager-to-please puppy and she returned his smile with genuine pleasure. 'I go by Caroline now.'

'I know that but you'll always be Franny to me. Okay, okay, don't give me that look. I'll try to remember. I heard you're opening your business here.'

'What? No, I — '

'Mrs Stanley was in early this morning to pick up her weekly bouquet from Mr Stanley and she let the proverbial cat out of the bag.'

Caroline shook her head. 'I haven't — '

'The storefront next door is available and perfect for you. There's even an apartment over the store where you can live or you can rent it out.'

'I haven't decided yet if I'm going to stay in town, much less start a business. I'm just working on Barbara's wedding as a personal favor. She talked to you about her flowers?'

'Ah, yes, well — '

'Pauly? Are you with a customer?' a woman's voice called from upstairs. 'I thought we were closing early so we wouldn't be late. Didn't you put the closed sign on the door?'

'I'm doing it right now, my love. There's time for me to finish talking about the Jennings/Vandergelt wedding.'

Caroline heard footsteps pounding down the stairs.

'We are doing nothing for her. Not after what she said about us. I'll tear her bleached hair out by its black roots. I'll scratch — ' The woman came to a sudden halt. She pointed at Caroline but looked at Paul. 'Who is that? Why did you say Barbara Jennings was here?'

'Nina, love, let me introduce you to Fran — er — Caroline Tucker who's just moved back into town. She's the new wedding planner for Barbara Jennings.'

Caroline pasted a pleased-to-meet-you smile on her face.

'Are you another one of Paul's ex-girlfriends?' Nina demanded.

Why would Paul's wife be jealous of anyone? Elegantly dressed in a simple sapphire-blue sheath dress and single strand of pearls, her four-inch heels made Nina stand a few inches taller than her husband. She had a slim, willowy figure and thick shoulder-length golden curls. Once she calmed down, her delicate features were quite beautiful. Was Paul that much of a catch? His wife apparently thought so.

'I wouldn't say girlfriend,' Caroline answered for him. 'Friend who happened to be a girl would be more accurate.' She had enough sense not to look in his direction, but held eye contact with the wife. 'I've known Paul since before kindergarten and there's never been anything between us beyond friendship.'

At least not on Caroline's part. She totally skipped over the fact that Paul had professed his undying love and asked her to marry him, once in third grade and again in seventh. Of course she'd declined, gently the first time so as not to hurt his feelings. The second time she'd been firm, telling him her heart had already been given to someone else. He'd sent her so many flowers that someone had asked her grandmother who had died.

'Caroline always had a crush on Travis Beaumont,' Paul said helpfully. 'Everyone knew that.'

'Our new Sheriff?' Nina asked, giving Caroline a measuring stare. 'He's quite handsome. Did you go weak in the knees when he kissed you?'

'Who? Paul? He never — '

'No. Travis.'

113

'That was a long time ago.' Even though she remembered the magic of that first kiss as if it had happened moments ago, Caroline shook her head and managed a creditable chuckle. 'I'm not a silly schoolgirl any longer.'

'By the flush in your cheeks and the sparkle in your eyes, I'd say you still have feelings for him.'

'Nothing more than a few pleasant memories.' And some that she wished she could forget.

Nina relaxed and invited her to sit at a small glass-topped garden table with four wrought-iron chairs.

'I understand you have someplace to go, so I'll get right to business.' Caroline dumped her stuff on the spare chair and pulled out the contract she'd found in Barbara's wedding book. 'Despite your . . . ah . . . differences with the bride, this is a good opportunity for you to showcase your — '

'We understand that,' Nina said. She traded significant looks with her husband and then nodded to him as if in encouragement.

'I won't lie and say that sales aren't down, or that we don't need the business, but even so, we must respect — '

'Before you decline,' Caroline said. 'Is there any way we can salvage this contract? I really don't want to work with someone from El

114

Paso whom I don't know. And don't trust.'

'We appreciate your position,' Paul said.

'But Barbara Jennings is unreasonable,' Nina said, unable to keep quiet any longer. 'She demanded a guarantee of Diana, Princess of Wales roses without paying a premium price. That particular hybrid of tea rose is limited, but if it wasn't available in the quantity she ordered then she said we would just have to overnight them in from wherever without her having to pay any extra for shipping.' Nina's voice rose higher and higher in pitch as she worked herself into a dither. 'We suggested substitutions of comparable blooms that might be more readily available, like the same hybrid renamed Elegant Lady. But she freaked out. Only Diana, Princess of Wales roses would do for her.'

Paul put his arm around his wife's shoulders. 'It's not worth getting upset over. Remember you're still recovering.' He turned to Caroline. 'Her sort of business, we don't need.'

'Would Barbara even know if you substituted Elegant Lady blooms?' Caroline asked.

Nina snorted. 'She wouldn't know if we gave her Summer of Love or Pink Promise roses. But we couldn't, not the way she worded the contract. I wouldn't put it past her to sue us out of house, home, and shop just for spite. How dare we ruin her perfect wedding!'

'Then let's change the contract,' Caroline said.

'Are you sure?' Paul asked. 'Barbara — '

'Authorized me to be her wedding planner and that's exactly what I'm doing. I'll deal with my cousin. I've handled her crap for years, and I have an ace up my sleeve if it becomes necessary. Don't worry. Nothing is going to happen. We're the only ones who'll know she's not getting Diana, Princess of Wales roses, and I won't tell if you won't.'

A long look of silent communication passed between Paul and Nina before they agreed.

Caroline should have felt triumphant as she completed the business transaction and gave them the deposit check, but she couldn't get that last unspoken message out of her mind. That's what a married couple should have and that's exactly what she'd been missing. With excuses about letting them get on with their previous plans, she grabbed her purse and attaché case, and hurried toward the door.

'Wait! You forgot something,' Nina called after her.

Caroline turned. 'Oh. The cookies for Travis.' She took the container from Nina.

Paul raised an eyebrow and his wife gave him a smug nod.

'I'm just delivering them as a favor for Mrs Stanley,' Caroline explained and for some reason that made both of the florists grin. 'Really, it's no big deal. I mean he does live next door to my grandmother. We can meet and speak as two normal adults. After all this time, we're virtually strangers.' She'd said it because it had sounded reasonable in her head. Then she realized it was probably truer than she cared to admit.

'Good one,' Paul said, obviously not believing her.

She turned and left, the door shutting off his laughter.

Caroline was thoughtful on her short trip home, unexpectedly drained. She'd changed so much in the past ten years, why should she think Travis hadn't? What did she really know about him? Was it still his dream to open a motorcycle shop? Probably not. What was his favorite movie? Last book he read? What music did he listen to? She didn't know any of the thousands of bits of minutiae that made up a person. Shirt size? Even that had changed based on her observation. What would he order on a pizza? His favorite cookie used to be chocolate-covered marsh-mallow pinwheels, but apparently weren't now. Everything she once knew about him had probably changed. How bizarre to think of Travis as a stranger.

Her reaction to him was just a physical response and nothing more. Probably fueled by her recent abstinence and maybe a few memories. Understanding the cause of her reaction was the key to self-control.

She entered by the back door, put the container on the counter, gave Mimi a kiss on her cheek, and promised to fill her in on the day after she changed clothes.

Back in the kitchen, Caroline tied a cook's apron over her favorite blouse, a Pucci-esque off-the-shoulder top done in shades of blue and purple that she wore with navy crops. She slipped easily into the rhythm of helping Mimi prepare tamales, drying off the cornhusks that had been soaking in the sink while the older woman finished shredding the spiced beef. Mimi quickly mixed up the corn masa.

'A double batch?' Caroline asked. 'Are we making extra for the freezer?'

'I invited Dee Ann, Stephen, and the girls over.'

Keeping pace with her grandmother, Caroline spread masa on a cornhusk with the back of a large spoon, added spicy beef, then folded it into a neat package and laid it on a

118

tray of the stacked bamboo steamer. Caroline's tamales varied a bit in size and shape whereas Mimi's were even and standard.

'You always tend to make them bigger and bigger as you go,' Mimi said. 'You're in too much of a hurry to get done. Don't you enjoy cooking?'

Caroline scraped off some of the beef from the cornhusk in her hand. 'Sure. I don't get much chance, living alone as I do . . . did. When I lived alone.'

'Enjoy the task at hand. Cooking is as much about taking pleasure in the doing as it is about the end product.'

'Nice try at changing the subject. Who else is coming to dinner? Come on, it's obvious. Fifty tamales, a huge salad in the fridge, the makings of a large pan of enchiladas ready to go, and a pot of beans on the stove. Bobby Lee has a big appetite but even he — '

'Your Aunt Rose, That New Husband, and his children. Poor Rose can use a break. Also Barbara and Dirk. And Bobby Ray has a friend visiting who was just released from the county work farm. I believe he said the man's name is Stubbs.' Mimi set the loaded baskets on the steamer base and set a timer for two hours. She mumbled something under her breath.

'What? I didn't hear you.'

119

Mimi turned to face her granddaughter. 'I also invited my best friend Lou, and her grandson Travis.' She put her hands on her hips and stuck out her chin. 'Do you have a problem with that?'

'No, not at all.' Caroline managed a surprised expression. 'Why would you think that?'

'Because just the other day you — '

'Oh that,' she said with a dismissing wave of her hand. 'That was before I realized just how much we've both changed. I've moved on. He's moved on. As mature adults we can certainly be in the same room, even carry on a conversation.'

'I see.'

'Speaking of Barbara and Dirk — '

'Now who's changing the subject?'

Caroline related the events of her day not diluting the vendor's problems with Barbara. 'There was nothing in the book about music so I still have that to figure out. I haven't spoken to the photographer or the people at the country club, but so far she seems to have pissed off everyone with her unreasonable demands.'

'You're in luck. I made the arrangements at the Country Club since Dirk won't be confirmed as a member for another month,' Mimi said. 'They don't usually encourage outside catering, but Lewis's reputation insured their complete cooperation. All you need to do is stop by to approve the final table set-up.'

'Which I can't do until I get a final head count. Guess that's my next project after I figure out what Barbara had planned for music.'

'Done. I had the club book the band that played at the Spring Social. Dirk has already supplied them with a play list. And I'm sure he said he has a friend who is a professional photographer and he will do the pictures because he can be trusted not to release copies to the Miami press. You can check with Dirk, but I think he said his friend is traveling with the groomsmen and will arrive the day before the wedding.'

'How long has Barbara known Dirk? He seems a bit . . . I don't know . . . slick is the word that comes to mind.'

'Why would you say that?'

'Just a feeling. For instance, when he kissed my hand — '

'He's such an old-fashioned gallant. I think they only knew each other a few weeks before he asked Rose's blessing on the engagement. Said it was love at first sight.'

'Have they done any pre-wedding counseling? Talked to a minister?'

'Bobby Ray is going to officiate at the ceremony. He really is an ordained minister.'

'In what? The Church of Reformed Sinners?'

'Now that was uncalled for. I never thought of you as mean spirited before.'

'I'm sorry. I don't know what's the matter with me lately. I'm glad Bobby Ray has finally got his life on track. I'm actually proud of him.'

'Be sure to tell him that.' Mimi patted her granddaughter's shoulder. 'You're under a lot of pressure right now.'

'It's just that I think Barbara should postpone the wedding and get to know Dirk better before rushing into what could be a terrible mistake.'

'Why would you say that?' Dee Ann asked as she led her family into the kitchen. After hugs and kisses Stephen took their rambunctious daughters out the back door to play in the yard. 'Dirk is handsome, nice, rich, and he obviously adores Barbara. Ohmigod. Are you jealous?'

'What!'

'Well, once Barbara is married, you'll be the only old maid left in the family.'

'I prefer the term independent woman,' Caroline said.

'Call it whatever you want, it has to hurt

that she's getting married before you.'

'She's older.'

'But she's a bitch and she still got a guy to marry her,' Dee Ann said with a smug smile.

'You forgot to say *before you.*'

'Now, girls,' Mimi said, taking Dee Ann's arm and pulling her toward the sink. 'Wash up and you can help me roll enchiladas. Have you picked any names for the baby yet?'

Caroline concentrated on sliding the tortillas into the skillet of hot grease and a few seconds later lifting the softened rounds out and on to a platter without tearing them.

'We had just about decided on Emma for a girl but that's what Stephen's cousin named her new daughter last week.' Dee Ann moved the slightly cooled tortilla to her work surface, added a strip of spiced beef, a large spoonful of sauce, and a generous sprinkling of grated Colby cheese. She rolled it up tight and placed it in a long baking pan. 'I like the name Grace, but Stephen isn't crazy about it.'

'What if the baby is a boy?' Mimi asked. She rolled enchiladas using chicken, Monterey Jack cheese, and placed them in a second pan.

Dee Ann shook her head. 'We found out yesterday she's a girl. Stephen isn't at all disappointed like I thought he would be. What do you think of Victoria?'

'Pretty. Have you thought of Sarah? You

had a Great-aunt Sarah.'

Caroline zoned out of the name game. She liked cooking. Especially for people she cared about. Maybe she should think about totally changing her life and going to culinary school. She could open her own catering business where she wouldn't do weddings. Maybe . . .

'Ah ha! What have we here?'

She turned, blinking back to reality. She hadn't noticed her younger brother's entrance and now Bobby Lee held the container of cookies. She made a grab for it but he raised it above her reach. 'Those are a gift for Travis,' she said.

'Guess we know who you're sweet on.'

'They're from Mrs Stanley, you doofus. Not me.'

Bobby Lee held her at bay with one hand on her forehead while he inhaled a deep breath along the sealed edge of the container. 'Chocolate something.' Sniff. Sniff. 'Red Velvet? My favorite.'

'Everything edible is your favorite.' Her swinging fists could not reach his torso. Her kicking feet did not reach his legs. 'Give that back.'

'If I deliver it, maybe he'll share.'

Caroline stopped struggling forward. If Bobby Lee completed the errand, she was off the hook without confronting Travis. Why hadn't she thought of that? 'Great idea.' The popping of hot oil demanded her attention and she turned back to the stove to rescue the frying tortilla before it became a tostado. 'Why don't you take it next door before dinner?'

'Except she knows I don't share,' a deep voice said.

She steeled herself to not turn toward the speaker but she couldn't stop the warm honey in her veins that hearing Travis speak had always caused. 'I guess I've forgotten more than I remember. It has been a long time.'

'No way, boss. You're the most generous man I know.'

'Can the ass-kissing,' Caroline said to her brother even though it was more likely a case of idol worship. She turned to face Travis. 'Giving is not the same as sharing. Even selfish, self-centered people can give gifts.' She crossed her arms. 'Let's say Travis had a candy bar and offered me half. That would be a gift. Now if he promised to give me half of every candy bar he bought in next year that would be sharing. True sharing requires a commitment to continue.'

Travis raised an eyebrow. 'Sharing takes two. The receiver would be committing to being around to accept all those halves of candy bars.'

'Whoa.' Bobby Lee shook his head as he put down the container and backed away with his hands in the air. 'That sounds too much like you guys are talking about personal problems. I'm outta here.' He opened the back door and had one foot outside before he paused and turned back long enough to say, 'Don't forget to call me when dinner is ready.'

'Burning,' Travis said with a nod in Caroline's direction.

What was that supposed to mean? A reference to her temper? She thought she'd kept her cool quite well, all things considered. Then she realized she'd left her pan unattended and spun around. 'Yikes.' The tortilla was puffed up, dark brown, and crispy. 'Why didn't you say something?' she asked her sister out of the side of her mouth.

'And miss the show?' Dee Ann whispered back.

Is that what others thought when they saw her and Travis together? Bound to be an argument sooner or later. Just wait for the fireworks. Okay, in the past they had provided some spectacular public displays. But that was years ago. She wasn't the same immature girl.

Caroline composed her face while she put another tortilla in the hot oil and then turned around. 'Please make yourself at home,' she said to Travis in her best gracious hostess voice. She gestured to a chair at the table in the glass breakfast alcove. 'Can I get you some coffee or iced tea? A beer?'

A look of confusion crossed Travis's eyes, so swift it might have been her imagination.

'No, thank you. I just stopped by to let you know Lou is resting and won't be over for dinner.'

Mimi wiped her hands and approached Travis. 'Is she all right? Not another — '

'No, no. She just overtaxed herself today.'

'By going to the beauty parlor?'

Travis ducked his head. 'Um . . . '

Mimi gave him an expectant stare and Caroline almost felt sorry for him. While growing up, she'd spilled her guts under that intent look more than once.

'Instead of keeping her appointment, Lou spent the morning chasing jay-walkers and litterbugs, and shooting them with the squirt gun I gave her to replace her pistol. She soaked two truckers who spat tobacco juice into the flower bed by the gazebo.'

'I guess that's better than shooting them,' Mimi said.

'She exhausted herself. I should never have

127

given her that gun. I should have foreseen — '

Caroline spoke up for his grandmother. 'Lou is a grown woman who makes her own decisions.'

'Are you saying that if someone I love is making a bad choice I shouldn't stop her?'

'Just because you think you know what's best doesn't entitle you to make decisions for someone else. She has the right to choose what she wants for herself. You can't take that away.' Caroline surprised herself with her uncharacteristic vehemence. Was she talking about Lou or herself? She pressed her lips together to keep from saying more.

'I'm not trying to take anything away from Lou,' Travis seemed astonished by her accusation. 'I just want her to realize she has limitations now that she didn't have before. Once she learns to take care of herself, I can go back to my real job, my real life.'

'I thought you'd decided to stay in Haven,' Mimi said.

'I promised Lou I'd fill out her term as Sheriff. If she's not capable of going back to work by election time, she'll be forced to retire. Either way I expect to leave town after Thanksgiving.'

'You're the only family she has left.' Mimi laid her hand on his arm. 'She needs you.'

'I'll be around much more often than in

128

the past,' he said, sounding sincere. His cell phone rang. He looked at the number before apologizing and saying, 'I've got to take this.' He put the phone to his ear and stepped away. 'This had better be important.'

6

'Sorry to bother you, sir, but you said to call if we got something new on the murders.'

'Hang on,' Travis said and then, grateful for a reason to escape, he quickly gave his excuses to Mimi, Dee Ann, and Caroline, before ducking outside. As he drove off, he resumed his conversation. 'Okay, Harlan, I'm on my way to the station. Don't tell me the lab sent their report special delivery.'

'Ah, nothing yet.'

Realizing that Harlan was enjoying the moment of knowing more than his boss, Travis curbed his impatience and used an elementary interrogation technique. He said nothing. As expected, Harlan quickly broke the awkward silence.

'Dispatch took a call regarding one Monique Gordon who did not report for work today. When she didn't answer repeated phone calls, her employer became concerned. Phyllis went to the address on record, the trailer park at the edge of town. When there wasn't any response, she had a look around. The sliding glass door in the rear of the premises was wide open and she observed the bloody body of a young woman on the floor of the kitchen.'

From the deputy's first sentence, Travis had dreaded that last one. Damn.

'Definitely dead. Looks like the Mescalero Killer has struck again.'

Travis walked into the office. 'What the hell are you talking about?'

Harlan sat up suddenly, his feet clunking from the desk to the floor. 'Wow, you got here fast.'

'That's what sirens and lights are for. Radio Bobby Lee and have him get to that address as soon as possible. And call the funeral home and have them send a wagon.'

Harlan stood up, cleared his throat, and stuck his thumbs in his belt. 'I thought up that catchy name for the killer,' he said in a boastful tone. 'The Haven Killer doesn't have any appeal — '

'Where's your brain? Don't you think the Mescalero Apache Indians will be offended by the use of their name? Especially since neither murder happened on the reservation.'

'Well, yeah, but — '

'Are you trying to incite an uprising of justifiably indignant Indians?'

'Well, no, but — '

'Secondly, we don't know for sure this is another murder by the same killer. Not yet.'

131

While he talked he grabbed an evidence kit from the supply closet. Catchy name? Just what they didn't need. Keeping the investigation under control would be hard enough without reporters dogging his team's every step.

Travis gave the deputy a hard stare. 'If you talk to anyone from the press, you're fired. I decide what information to release. If you even say the word Mescalero to a reporter, you're fired.'

Harlan sat heavily in his chair, and swallowed deep. Then he stuck out his chin. 'You can't hold me responsible for — '

'Call your cousin over at the *Haven Daily Journal* and retract everything you've already leaked.'

Harlan's mouth opened and closed like a fish landed in the bottom of the boat. Travis crossed the room with long strides and leaned over the other man's desk to retrieve the address of the earlier call. 'Do it before I get back.'

He left with a sinking feeling in his gut. In a conscious effort to clear his mind of preconceived ideas of the crime that might influence his investigation, he tried to think of something else as he drove to the trailer park. Caroline came to mind as she always did on the rare occasions when he didn't discipline his thoughts. Her recent change in attitude to impersonal politeness was more exasperating than outright antipathy, mostly because he didn't know the cause.

No need to ask for directions to lot number thirty-two. From the moment he turned into the entrance of Shady Oaks Trailer Park, the crowd of curious bystanders pinpointed his destination. The deputies had strung yellow tape around the perimeter and Bobby Lee stood guard while Phyllis handled crowd control. Both met him at the back door to the trailer.

'Talk to me.'

'I arrived onsite at approximately five-fifteen,' Phyllis said, consulting her notes. 'Five minutes or so later I saw a body with a pool of reddish-brown liquid beneath her head. I checked for a pulse. An ambulance wasn't necessary. When I went back to the car for my kit, I noticed curious neighbors had already started coming out of their homes — '

'Like buzzards to carrion,' Bobby Lee said as he joined the others. 'I taped off as much as I could without going on to the next lot. These spaces aren't very big.'

Travis looked around the postage-stamp patio. He'd already noted the tiny metal table with a half-eaten salad, empty bag from the Burger Basket, and a glass of tea with the ice melted. Next to the adjacent folding chair a pair of sensible shoes had been set neatly aside. To his mind the victim had known her attacker and had taken him inside the house in spite of the lack of air conditioning to prevent anyone passing by from seeing them together.

'I'll take the inside,' Travis said, pulling on a pair of latex gloves. 'Bobby Lee, you take the outside. Get this patio area first. Hopefully, we haven't contaminated it too much. You know the drill.'

'Photograph, log, bag and tag.'

Travis put covers over his boots to avoid tracking in more trace and said to Phyllis, 'See what you can find out from the neighbors. Someone from Rondale's should be here soon. Have him wait. Let's get this done.'

'Okay, boss,' both deputies said.

Travis turned to the doorway and started his processing there.

Twenty minutes later he was startled to hear Marlene's voice directly behind him.

'This place is a mess. Doesn't look like the same perp.'

'Perp? You've been watching too many cop shows.'

He'd thought the same thing. The other two bodies had been neat compared to this one, but he'd found the signature ligature

134

marks on her neck and the after-death knife wound. Both details he'd withheld from previous press releases. 'Didn't anyone tell you to wait outside until I'm done?'

'Nope.' As if unconcerned by his not so subtle reprimand, she squatted next to the body. 'Don't worry. I know how to behave at a crime scene.' She gave the body a cursory examination. 'Well, she put up a fight.'

'Tell me something I didn't know, like time of death.'

'I really need to get her on my table to accurately measure lividity, rigor mortis, algor mortis — '

'Just give me your best shot.'

'Science is not a guessing game.'

'How about a hypothetical time parameter based on empirical knowledge to be validated later?'

Marlene raised one eyebrow. 'I always did admire a man with a big . . . vocabulary.' She stood up and put her hands on her hips. 'If you put it that way, two to five hours.'

'I could guess that close based on the wilted lettuce in her half-eaten meal.'

She shrugged. 'Whatever works for you. If you're done taking pictures, I'll move her and get to work proving that hypothesis.'

'Not yet. I haven't processed the body for trace.'

Marlene nodded. 'Working the inward spiral. I prefer that technique myself. Need help? I can handle trace on the body before I start the autopsy. And to answer your next question, yes, I know what I'm doing. It won't be my first time collecting evidence off a corpse.'

'If you need a rape kit or — '

'I have everything, including all the appropriate forms. Comes with the coroner job.'

'The chain of evidence should — '

'Stop worrying.'

'When we identify this guy, I don't want any glitch to put him back on the street.'

She saluted.

Phyllis stuck her head in the door. 'I got somebody here you'll want to talk to.'

'Go,' Marlene urged.

'I am besieged by bossy women.' He preferred strong women who weren't afraid to voice an opinion because a meeting of equals was always more interesting, but no way did he want that fact known.

'Just trying to do my job,' Marlene said.

Travis threw her a mock salute with just the right amount of spoof to it. The accompanying heel-click, not so much. He ripped off the protective booties and stomped to the door.

136

'What's up?' he asked Phyllis as he joined her on the patio.

'Neighbor says Monique Gordon was a quiet, shy girl. Lived here about six months. Everyone liked her. She worked two jobs to save money, breakfast shift at the truck stop and evenings at a dress shop downtown doing alterations and such.'

'Which boss called it in?'

Phyllis flipped back through her notebook. 'Eugenia Patterson of Eugenia's Classic Creations. Said Monique had never been late before. Was worried she'd had an accident. Apparently she rode her bike everywhere and was training for some kind of bicycle marathon, neighbor wasn't too specific on that.'

'Did you find the bike?'

'Yes. Over there. Against the wall. Processed it, but don't expect much. It's had more than a few miles on it.'

'Boyfriend?'

'Monique wasn't a party girl. Church every Sunday. Rarely had friends over, and as far as the neighbor knows, there wasn't a love interest.'

'Anything else?'

'Neighbor's name is Jaunita Alverez. She's waiting for you next door.'

'Good job.'

But not a lot to go on. Travis walked the

short distance to the next trailer. His questions would elicit some of the same information for verification, but he also hoped for the names of her friends and descriptions of any cars seen parked in the girl's driveway.

★ ★ ★

Travis sat at his desk and sipped his third cup of coffee as he reviewed the files for the umpteenth time. He was no closer to solving the three murders than he'd been when the last one had happened two weeks ago. The lab reports had started to trickle in, a new one just about every day. Basically, they might be of help convicting or eliminating suspects, if he ever found one. So far he hadn't been able to establish a single connection; an elderly clerk killed at work, a chubby middle-aged thespian killed at play, and an athletic young seamstress killed at home. Different social circles. Different interests. No activities or friends in common.

And yet he couldn't convince himself the victims had been chosen at random. The murder scenes had the feel of advance planning, not crimes of opportunity.

'Lou called and asked me not to let you work past ten.'

He looked up.

'Don't glare at me,' Phyllis said, holding up her hands in defense. 'I'm only the messenger. She also wanted me to remind you to pick up your tux at — '

'I wish I could forget. Standing up at this wedding is the absolute last thing I want to be doing today.'

'The word *no* usually works for me.'

'Have you ever tried to say no when both Lou and Mimi gang up on you? Well, count your blessings.'

'Maybe the groomsmen will show up at the last minute. Where were they coming from?'

'Frankfurt. The whole freaking polo team is delayed by weather.'

'But the groom is here?'

'I heard he got in yesterday. Guess I should be thankful he decided to leave soon after their match or Mimi and Lou would be eyeing me for that job.'

'No rehearsal?'

'Today at noon. Then a luncheon. I hope that doesn't mean frou-frou food. I hate those tiny sandwiches.'

'Maybe they'll have those teeny-weeny pigs in a blanket. I love those.'

'I feel like a fool eating fifteen or twenty in order to equal a decent burger and fries.'

'So you'll be off for the rest of the day?'

Travis shook his head. 'Everyone else may want to hang around the Country Club and then dress there, but I'm planning on coming back here for the afternoon. The ceremony isn't until six.'

'Not necessary.'

'Gee, thanks. Always good to hear you're not necessary.'

'You know what I mean,' she said. 'We can manage without you for a day, and you're only a phone call away.'

'I know, but I'm lousy at golf.'

'You should practice.'

'And I really suck at tennis.'

'It wouldn't hurt you to take some time off now and then.'

'Now you sound like Lou. Maybe later. Did we hear back from the FBI on whether or not they have any record of a similar MO?'

'Not yet. Maybe Harlan is right and the killer was a transient who has moved on and we'll never know — '

'Don't say it. Don't even think it. Not only do I never want to hear you say Harlan is right, I don't want you to jinx the investigation.'

Phyllis turned to leave the office then paused and spun around. 'Word of advice. Stay away from the mayor at the reception this evening. I hear he's gunning for you.'

'I always try to stay away from the Mayor.'

'If all else fails, ask his wife to dance. Irene adores you. Thinks you're sexy.' Phyllis grinned. 'The other day at Garden Club she said you could put your boots under her bed any — '

'Whoa. I do not want that image in my head.' And to make sure it didn't stick, Travis replaced it with one of his favorite memories. Of course that brought Caroline to mind. He hadn't had another chance to confront her alone, which was probably her intention. Whenever they'd seen each other in the past two weeks, she'd been coldly polite. What game was she playing with him now?

The wedding would give him the chance he needed. If he asked her to dance in front of Lou and Mimi, they wouldn't let her say no. Then he could lead Caroline off the dance floor, out the wide French doors, on to the veranda, and to an alcove where they would be totally private. For the first time that day he smiled. Before midnight that very night, he would have his answers.

★ ★ ★

Caroline plastered her professional everything-will-be-fine smile on her face. 'You really should discuss your problem with someone who knows you well. Your best man?'

'He's not even in the country yet,' Dirk said.

'Your therapist? A minister? Doctor?'

'Not available.' He stepped closer. 'You're so kind and knowledgeable about this stuff. I just need someone to talk to.' Dirk paused while a waiter rushed by headed for the Rose Room with a cart full of dishes. 'Couldn't we go somewhere private so we can talk?'

She had more important issues than the groom's pre-wedding jitters. Barbara had changed the menu at the last minute because some TV reality star had served crab cakes with wasabi lemon mayonnaise appetizers and she didn't want it said she was a copycat. Now it had to be prawns with caviar. Lewis was fit to be tied. As was just about everyone else. Her job was to keep everyone from exploding for just a few more hours and then she would be done. Meanwhile, she had to get rid of Dirk.

Caroline used the pretense of adjusting a flower arrangement not only to step away from him but also to put a table between them. 'I'm not the one you should talk to.' Especially not when the guy gave her the creeps. 'You should be honest with Barbara. Tell her what you're feeling and the two of you can work it out.'

'She's not answering her phone.'

Caroline consulted her watch and then her bulging organizer. 'She should be finishing up at the beauty salon. Maybe her nails were still wet.'

'I drove by on my way here but her car wasn't there,' Dirk supplied.

Caroline dialed her cousin's cell number. *Come on. Pick up, pick up, pick up.* No luck. She flipped her phone shut and it beeped before she could tuck it back into her pocket. Caroline quickly viewed the message from Dixie May, owner of Cut 'n' Curl:

Whr is she??? Ive bn wSting snce 7.

What? She shld hve bn thr hrs ago, Caroline texted back.

U think?

Dixie May was obviously not a happy camper. But she would have to wait in line.

Back 2 U asap, Caroline replied.

She turned to Dirk. 'Did Barbara say anything this morning about revising her schedule?' Like she'd already done several times, although she'd always been adamant about getting her hair and nails done early.

'I didn't see her this morning,' he said.

Caroline blinked, then she remembered Dirk had stayed at the Arbor Inn. Barbara's idea. The whole not-seeing-the-bride-before-the-ceremony. Closing the barn door after the

143

horse was gone, as Mimi would say, but Caroline pressed her lips together to keep from speaking.

'In fact, she was acting very strange yesterday. We'd planned a romantic dinner at La Maison in El Paso and she made me cancel the reservation. Practically kicked me out of her house at a little after six. Said she had too much to do.'

What could she have meant? Everything was either done or on the list for today. Caroline shook her head. Something was very wrong. Barbara would never pass up a chance to dine at the most exclusive restaurant in the Southwest, not even for her own funeral. A cold shiver crawled up Caroline's back.

Dirk took her hand. She flinched. Damn. She'd been so deep in thought she missed him sneaking up on her. Stepping back, she pulled her hand away and it took more than a hint of motion to free herself. 'You really should be talking to Barbara. Maybe she overslept and her phone is off.' That would explain everything.

'I went to her house first because I forgot my black silk socks to wear with my tux. Her car wasn't in the drive, so I came here thinking she might have contacted you.'

'No. I didn't expect her here until ten-thirty-ish.'

144

'You're such a wonderful listener. Can't we have a cup of coffee together, or tea, or anything. I really need to talk. I . . . I confess I'm getting cold feet.'

'That's normal,' Caroline said, still distracted by trying to figure out where her cousin could be.

'I think Barbara went out to meet another man last night,' Dirk blurted out.

'What?' He had her full attention. 'Why would you think that?'

'A man always knows.'

Caroline crossed her arms and tilted her head forward. 'How? Male intuition?'

'She said she needed some 'alone' time.'

Why did people make those little quote marks with their fingers?

'She said she had to say a final goodbye to her old life. Doesn't take a genius to figure out that meant a former lover.'

'Not necessarily.' Damn. He was probably right. 'Women get attached to places and things and she'll be moving far away. Saying goodbye to her childhood home makes sense to me.' That sounded good even if she didn't believe a word of it, at least as far as Barbara was concerned.

Dirk shook his head. He wasn't buying it either.

'We already had plans to return in a few

months and build a house by the lake. A cool mountain retreat for summer. Skiing in the winter. Barbara was looking forward to that.'

Sure she was. Miss Nature-lover in person. Caroline wasn't going to be the one to burst that bubble. 'Sounds nice.'

'You don't think Barbara met with a former lover and decided to go away with him, do you?'

Not likely since the one man Barbara had been seeing since high school was still very much married and never going to get a divorce. Caroline shook her head.

'You don't think she changed her mind about the wedding?'

A zillion times. About everything from the invitations to the favors. But never about the groom. Barbara had been very determined to marry Dirk. 'I doubt it. Why don't you play a round of golf before it gets hot outside? That will settle your nerves.' And keep him occupied far away from her.

'I'm not dressed for it. And I'm worried.'

'That's normal. Worry about your friends and family getting here on time. Worry about your hair.'

Dirk's hand flew to his head.

'Worry about anything other than Barbara. I know she wants to marry you and I'll find her. Everything will be fine.'

'I'll go with you.'

'No.' God no. 'It will be better if I find her so I can talk to her alone.'

'But you said I should talk to her — '

'And you'll have a chance to do just that. Later.'

'If we look for Barbara together we can get to know each other better. You know, bond.'

That was one of the last things she wanted. Caroline grabbed a passing waiter by the arm nearly causing him to drop a tray of glasses. 'Would you please show Mr Vandergelt to the pro shop?'

Without waiting for an answer, she ducked around him and ran for the kitchen and a back door leading to where her car was parked. She had no doubt she would find her cousin. Caroline was the one person who knew all of Barbara's secrets.

7

By the time Caroline pulled out of the parking lot she'd checked with Mimi, her sisters Dee Ann and Mary Lynn, and Aunt Rose. She'd even called the Maid of Honor Sue Ellen who was driving in from San Antonio. Nobody had heard from Barbara that morning.

Traveling south on the highway, she noticed a man waving to her from the open garage door of a body shop/gas station. She waved back at her third cousin Tommy G, owner of the shop. No one in the family trusted anyone else to service their cars.

Caroline smacked her forehead. Of course, car trouble. Or a flat tire. That had to be it. She dialed his number even as she made a U-turn.

'You wreck 'em, we stick 'em back together.'

'Hey, Tommy G. Did Barbara Jennings call you this morning about a problem with her car?'

'Well, butter my butt and call me a biscuit if it ain't Franny Tucker. Ma said you was back in town and living at Mimi's again.

148

Imagine that. After all these years. How the heck are you?' Tommy G spoke real slow, choosing his words like a picky eater at a potluck supper.

'I'm doing good. Listen, I hate to cut this short, but I'm in a God-awful hurry. Did Barbara call you this morning?' Caroline pulled into the gas station, and walked inside the tiny office/candy counter/parts store as she talked.

'Nope. Ain't seen her since the last three-thousand-mile check-up on her car.' He scratched the back of his head, causing his baseball cap to rise and fall. 'Late April, if I recollect.'

She snapped her phone shut and greeted him in person.

'I can look up the exact date iffen you want,' he said. 'Got me a computer now and everything.'

'Not necessary. If Barbara does call you, would you let me know? You've got my cell number now.'

'Well, sure. What's going on? You seem a bit frazzled.'

'More than a little. Barbara has, for whatever reason, changed her morning schedule without bothering to let me know. Coordinating a wedding day is difficult enough *with* the bride's cooperation.'

'Yup.' Tommy G nodded as if he had shared a similar experience. 'Ma said you was working for Barbara and we all wondered why.'

She didn't want to give him any gossip to take home, no more than she had already, what with Barbara's weird behavior. Caroline sidled toward the door. 'Tell your ma I'll stop by next week. I want to hear all the family's news. And don't forget to call me if you hear from Barbara.'

'Sure thing.' He smiled. 'Sweet engine, that one.' His eyes got a glassy faraway stare, almost like the expression any other man might have while recalling the memory of a beautiful woman.

Tommy G had been breathing gas fumes for a mite too long.

'Purrs like a kitten. In fact, I said that very thing just this morning when she drove by the shop. Talking to myself, but I tend to do that being here alone so much.'

'Wait a minute. You saw Barbara drive by?'

'I waved, but I guess she didn't see me.'

'What time was that?'

'Let's see. I was sweeping the pump area so maybe seven-thirty, seven forty-five. She's lucky there weren't no cop out by the minimart like there usually is 'cause she was heading north like a bat outta H-E-double

150

hockey sticks. Musta been doing at least eighty.'

'North? Are you sure?'

'I been knowing the difference between north and south since I was knee high to a grasshopper.' He sounded a bit peeved with her question.

What was Barbara doing heading out of town at that time of the morning when she was supposed to be at the Cut 'n' Curl at eight o'clock? 'Sorry. Are you sure it was her?'

'Ain't too many folks in Haven that drive a pink Mercedes SL550. And she was wearing her wedding veil.'

After making sure Tommy G didn't have any more information, Caroline thanked him. 'See you at the wedding,' she called as she drove away.

She sat at a red light, her thoughts a confused muddle. Something just didn't add up. A honk from the car behind her brought her back to the present. At the next intersection she turned around and headed back toward the Country Club.

The town of Haven, New Mexico straddled the main highway with businesses strung out to the north and south of downtown like a double strand of beads getting smaller and smaller and then there was only road. And desert.

After the minimart and the last souvenir

stand there was nothing on the road for a good five miles except the entrance to the Country Club, and then nothing but desert for ninety miles. Halfway to the entrance, she spotted the historical marker for Sentinel Mesa and the scenic viewing site called Indian Point. Caroline had always been fascinated by the legends connected to the location and the stone spires that were supposed to be petrified Indian scouts. As her fifth-grade science project, she'd made a salt dough topographic model of the mesa and nearby foothills of the Sacramento Mountains. The mesa was one of the highest points in the Tularosa Basin, a Connecticut-sized graben, and had been used by Indians and settlers alike to post sentries.

The Point had always been the after-dark make-out spot for the high school crowd, probably still was. No one went there during the day except occasionally lost tourists searching for either the Three Rivers Petroglyph Site or the World's Largest Pistachio Nut.

As a teen, Caroline had enjoyed hiking or biking the trail to the top, a great setting for getting perspective, a good thinking spot. And, as she'd found out one day when she'd skipped school, being able to see the road and anyone coming to or from the mesa made it an excellent meeting place for someone having a clandestine affair with a married man. She'd promised to keep Barbara's secret, for a price. A devil's bargain that Caroline regretted in the long run.

She made a sharp right turn and drove up the switch-back road to the top of the mesa. The scenic overlook was little more than a wide spot in the road with parking spaces for half a dozen cars. Totally deserted. As she turned her car around, she tried to call Mimi to see if Barbara had contacted anyone yet.

Just her luck. The stone sentinels probably blocked the signal from the lousy single tower in Haven. Caroline sighed, put the car in park and paced the gravel parking lot. So frustrating. If it weren't for her grandmother's illness, she'd be tempted to head west and not stop until she hit the beach. She might not have much of a life left in LA but the mess she was in now wasn't much better.

She finally got a dial tone by standing near the edge of the cliff. As she brought up Mimi's number on her phone, a bit of shiny metal glinting in the sun caught her attention. When she squinted she could see something pink that was nearly obscured by scrub pine and tumbleweeds. Pink, just the color of Barbara's custom-painted car. A tiny whisper of smoke signaled disaster. Caroline hesitated only a nanosecond before dialing 911 instead and starting down the almost non-existent path.

Travis thought he'd timed his arrival at the Country Club perfectly. Not the last to arrive, but not so early that he'd have to mingle and chitchat. He should have walked in the door just as the group was being called to start the rehearsal. Instead, the members of the wedding party stood around the lobby in subdued groups. Not the festive atmosphere he'd expected. Mimi detached herself from a cluster of women including Rose and two strangers, one of whom must be the business school friend of Barbara's and maid of honor whom he would be escorting down the aisle.

'Have you heard from Caroline?' Mimi asked, her brow furrowed.

Travis shook his head. 'Why would — ?'

'She went to look for Barbara and now they're both missing.'

Dirk arrived at Mimi's side and took her hand in both of his. 'I'm sure they're both fine and will be here soon. Then we'll all have a good laugh over whatever it is that's keeping them.'

Travis looked at his watch. In two minutes Caroline would be late to an event she'd planned. Not at all like her. His gut did a twisting somersault like the dive he'd attempted into the swimming hole when he was fifteen and trying to impress her. Same result, too. A painful belly-flop landing.

Bobby Lee snagged his attention by waving him off to the side.

'I don't want to worry Mimi,' he said in a low voice. 'I just talked to Tommy G and Caroline stopped by the garage about an hour ago. When last he saw her, she was headed north, and he guessed she was headed here. Wouldn't we have seen an accident on the side of the road?'

Before the deputy even finished speaking, instinct spurred Travis into action. He spun on his heel and headed toward his car.

★ ★ ★

Caroline finished reporting the emergency to the 911 operator and then tucked her phone in the pocket of her chinos as she scrambled down the narrow hiker's trail. The path was little more than a goat track and so steep in some places she had to hang on to a mesquite bush or rock outcrop to stay on her feet. She called out to her cousin several times but when there was no answer she decided to save her breath.

Rather than think about what she might find, she tried to concentrate on her foot placement so she wouldn't fall on the steep, rocky path. Really, if she'd known the morning would be spent tromping through the mesquite and cacti, she wouldn't have worn her Via Spiga sandals that were little more than a leather sole held on her foot by silver chains.

By the time she reached the bottom of the escarpment, thick smoke swirled around her and seared her lungs. Through watery eyes she located the car. Ohmigod. Barbara was still inside, slumped against the window.

'Barbara!' Caroline tried to open the door. Locked. She pounded on the glass. 'Barbara! Come on. Wake up!' There was no response.

The engine was still running and the smoke was getting thicker. *What to do? Think!* Patting the car as if to comfort her cousin, she tried to get her brain out of panic mode and into action gear. *Think! What would Travis do in a situation like this? He'd break the glass!* She whipped off her sandal and smacked the heel against the window several times. She leaned over the windshield and pounded on it with her fist and the shoe.

That didn't work. *Don't give up. Never give up.* Falling to her knees, she ditched the shoe and searched for a large rock or a heavy stick, something solid enough to break the window. Frantic and nearly blinded by her watering eyes, she felt her way crawling farther and farther away from the car without finding anything of use.

An explosion knocked her flat. Searing heat rolled up her back and sucked all the air from her lungs. As she blacked out, the faraway sound of sirens faded, as if they were headed in the wrong direction.

★　★　★

Travis disconnected after taking Phyllis's call about a reported explosion just off Indian Point. Without slowing down to anywhere near the speed limit, he made a tire-squealing left on to the access road, and led the procession of emergency vehicles, fire engine, ambulance, and the Fire Chief's red pick-up truck, to the top of the mesa.

Noting Caroline's abandoned vehicle, Travis beat the firemen and paramedics down the trail. 'Damn fool woman doesn't have a lick of sense,' he muttered to himself. Why didn't she wait for the professionals to handle the dangerous situation? He took a deep breath and shoved his worries aside. If he were going to maintain his professional focus, he would have to treat this like any other emergency situation and not let his emotions affect his actions.

When he arrived at the bottom of the precipice, Barbara's car was engulfed in flames. He noted the blaze but passed it by, his unerring Caro-radar locating Caroline about ten feet to the left of the vehicle. He knelt beside her and gently turned her over, his breath and very heartbeat stopping until he felt the pulse in her neck. He scooped her up and carried her out of further danger.

Although his first reaction was to hold her until she woke, he knew she needed medical help. And he was a cop with a job to do. He carried her to the paramedics, and laid her on the stretcher, kissing her on the forehead. Then he returned to the burning car where the firemen were battling the blaze. Because they'd known there would be no water supply, the firemen had brought canisters of foam that they backpacked down the trail.

Travis followed the paramedics as they maneuvered up the trail with Caroline strapped to the stretcher. Still in full cop mode, he automatically scanned the area for possible clues as to what happened. Skid marks were visible in the gravel, stopping short of the cliff edge. Stranger still, one of the concrete tire bumpers had been moved, creating just enough room for a vehicle's wheels to fit between two of the safety features. The bumper had been moved quite recently because the dirt under the former position was still darker than the surrounding area, meaning it was still damp.

He narrowed his eyes. The terrible accident might not have been an accident.

Even though it wasn't likely he'd get useful tracks from the gravel, Travis steered the emergency personnel around the area. He borrowed a walkie-talkie from one of the firemen and asked the Fire Chief for a situation report.

'The blaze is out and we used the jaws to open the car door. The body is beyond resuscitation,' Owen Ferris said.

Travis suspected the chief was being diplomatic. Based on the flames, he'd have bet on the body being fried to a crisp. 'I'll send the ambulance back to the hospital and call the coroner. I'm declaring the entire area a crime scene.'

'I agree. If you're headed this way, I'd like to point out a few things.'

'Roger and out.' Travis returned the walkie-talkie to the fireman, and then walked over to the ambulance. 'How's it going?' he hollered, hoping it sounded way less stressed than he felt.

One of the paramedics came to the back of the van and squatted in the doorway. 'She's stable. Starting to come around.' He reached out to put his hand on Travis's shoulder.

'She's going to be okay.'

Even though he ducked away from the guy's solicitous gesture, Travis had to fight the urge to jump up into the back of the ambulance and see for himself. At least he remembered his manners enough to say, 'Thanks for the update.'

The paramedic appeared unfazed by Travis's curtness. 'I've been on more than a few calls. It's not a good sign that it's taking this long.' He motioned with his chin to the edge of the cliff. 'What's the scoop?'

'I've sent for the coroner.' Nothing else needed to be said.

'Then we're off to the hospital.'

'I'll check in with you later.'

As the ambulance left the area, Travis called his staff, retrieved his evidence kit and camera from the car, and started back down the trail. He sent Phyllis to the Country Club to tell the relatives, knowing she would manage with sensitivity and tact. He sent Bobby Lee, who was already at the Country Club but too inexperienced and too emotionally involved to handle such a delicate situation, to Barbara's house with instructions to seal it off until he could get there. That left Harlan to help process evidence at the scene.

'I'd rather be there,' Bobby Lee argued.

Travis heard the upset in his deputy's voice

160

even though the young man tried to hide it. He was understandably shaken. The best thing he could do for the boy was to give him some space.

'Understood. And denied.' His small staff was spread too thin.

'My sister — '

'Is on her way to the hospital. The paramedic said she'll be fine. If you wish to disregard your duty in order to hold her hand . . . '

'No, no. I just want to make sure she's all right.'

Travis knew the feeling. 'At this point we have to take the expert's word on that.' He'd slipped and said *we*, but the deputy didn't seem to notice. 'I've assigned you where you'll do the most good. Now, can I depend on you?'

'Yes, sir.'

Travis tucked his cell in his pocket. As he approached the charred remains of the vehicle, he didn't hold much hope of finding any useful evidence. The firemen had thoroughly trampled anything in the area that they hadn't covered with foam. He took pictures anyway.

'Got a minute?' Owen Ferris, the Fire Chief, asked.

'Sure. What's up?' Travis set down his equipment to shake hands. 'Your men did a fine job with the fire.'

'Thanks. How's Caroline?'

'Medic says she'll be okay.'

'Tough when someone you love — '

'Is that all that's bothering you?' From the older man's expression, Travis realized his tone was harsher than he'd intended. He removed his Stetson and ran his hand through his hair before settling it back in place. 'Pardon my hurry. Been a rough day.'

'Yeah, well, my news isn't going to make it any better. Let me start with the fact that I'm not a certified arson investigator. That said, I don't think this fire was caused by the car accident.'

'Show me.'

'When we first heard about the location of the accident and that there was smoke, I was afraid we'd have a range fire because the area's vegetation is so parched due to the dry spell. You'll notice all the brush has been cleared around the car. Not a single tumble-weed for a fifteen-foot radius.'

'Your guys?'

'Nope. We found it this way.' Owen squatted next to the car and pointed beneath the chassis. 'See these marks in the dirt? Apparently, someone shoved all the readily available tinder under here. With the engine running to create additional heat, and possibly a little help from an accelerant, a fire was inevitable. There's what appears to be the remnants of a gas container under there, or it could just be old litter and a fluke that the car landed on top of it.'

'I don't believe in coincidence, and I agree with your assessment. I'm sending the entire car and everything else to the state lab.'

'They're gonna love you,' Owen said with a chuckle. After agreeing to wait for the coroner and send her down the trail, he followed his men up the trail.

While Travis took dozens of photos, his mind raced to recreate what had happened based on the evidence so far. Barbara's car had skidded to a halt in the parking area above. Then the car was either driven or was pushed over the edge. His money was on pushed. He couldn't picture her getting out of the car and moving the parking bumper. Nor could he see her sitting there while someone else made it possible to drive over the cliff. That meant she was probably already dead and brought here to make it look like an accident.

The killer rigged some sort of volatile material to start a fire and burn all the evidence. Unfortunately, he or she had been mostly successful. The rear of the vehicle was a charred, twisted mess suggesting something in the trunk had exploded.

Travis slowly circled around the wreck to the driver's side taking plenty of photos. The door stood open as a result of the firemen's useless rescue effort. Once they'd determined she was beyond saving, they hadn't moved her.

'Poor woman. Horrible, horrible. As if dying on the way to her wedding wasn't bad enough, she had to get burned up, too.'

Travis turned to face Marlene. She was flanked by her assistant and by his deputy, Harlan, on the other.

'I heard they took Caroline to the hospital. She's your witness. Why don't you go interview her,' Marlene said. 'You know you want to,' she whispered as she stepped toward the body. She gave him a sly grin and a bump on his shoulder with hers.

'We can handle everything here,' Harlan said, hooking a thumb in his belt.

Marlene assured Travis she could handle everything, including Harlan. After issuing a lengthy list of instructions, Travis left for the hospital. If he was right and this was another murder, that made it four in as many weeks and he still hadn't made any progress on the other three. At least this time he had a witness.

From the ER nurse he learned Caroline had been treated for smoke inhalation and a bump on her head. According to the report from the paramedics, her first concern was whether they'd gotten her cousin out of the car. The doctor had given her the grim news. Despite recommendations that Caroline stay overnight under observation, she'd insisted on being released and had gone home.

★   ★   ★

Judging by the cars parked beside and in front of the house, the entire Tucker clan had gathered at Mimi's after Phyllis had gone to the Country Club to break the bad news. Travis grabbed his briefcase and took the front steps two at a time. Mimi answered the door.

After greeting the woman and expressing his sympathy, Travis said, 'Unfortunately, I'm here in an official capacity. I'd like to ask Caroline a few questions.'

Several kids chased each other noisily into the hall.

'Isn't that outside behaviour?' Mimi asked the children, a note of censure in her tone. She didn't raise her voice, but gave them the sort of stare that promised no cookies for miscreants.

They stopped in their tracks, nodded wide-eyed, and then raced for the back door.

165

Mimi shook her head. 'Everything's a bit chaotic here. Rose is understandably devastated. That husband of hers won't leave her side, which means his kids are running wild. Poor Dirk alternates between near catatonic depression, and the manic need to *do* something, but Leon Rondale won't even discuss funeral arrangements until the coroner releases the body. Said it might take days. Why would it take days?'

'Marlene has to do her job. We need to find out exactly what happened. Caroline may have some information that will help.'

'What could she possibly know?'

'She was first on the scene. She might have noticed something important without realizing it.'

'She went right upstairs to take a quick shower and change her clothes, but that was over forty-five minutes ago,' Mimi said, checking her watch. 'That's not at all like her.'

'Maybe someone should check on her.'

'Thank you for taking care of that for me.'

'I didn't mean me.'

'She probably fell asleep,' Dirk Vandergelt said as he entered the hallway. 'Poor Caroline has had a physically and emotionally traumatic day. Can't you let her rest?'

Travis raised an eyebrow at Vandergelt's

166

reaction. His spider-sense went on alert, but was it because of his police experience or because another man tried to protect Caroline? From him?

Vandergelt turned to Mimi. 'You're not going to let him go upstairs, are you?'

Mimi took Vandergelt's arm with one hand and patted his shoulder with the other. 'It's sweet of you to be concerned about Caroline when you're suffering too. You are such a gentleman.'

'We should treat each other with kindness every day, but especially so on a day like this,' Vandergelt said. He ducked his head and covered his eyes with his free hand.

'Don't make me gag,' Lou said as she pushed her way forward with the help of her walker. She faced her lifelong friend. 'You know as well as I do Travis would never intentionally hurt Caroline, but he has a job to do.'

Mimi agreed and stepped aside to clear a path to the stairs.

'Go on,' Lou said to Travis. 'And when you're done, don't forget to pay your respects to Rose.'

Travis went upstairs with a sense of relief, and surprisingly, a degree of anticipation.

8

Caroline heard his soft tread and light tap on her bedroom door. Of course Travis would want to question her. She closed her eyes in hope he would go away. The door opened a crack.

'Caroline?'

His voice was a mere whisper but she recognized the underlying determination. She wouldn't be able to avoid his interrogation, but she could delay it. If she pretended to be asleep, maybe he would go away and come back tomorrow, or next week. She maintained the ruse even as she heard him come into the room and move a chair to beside the chaise where she was half sitting, half reclined.

'I know you're not asleep,' he said in that low and smooth tone that sent shivers down to her toes. 'How are you feeling?'

He moved to share the chaise, stretching his long legs out next to hers and taking her gently in his arms. She scooted to the side to give him more room and then gave in to temptation and snuggled her cheek against his chest. How could something so hard be so comforting? His tender embrace smashed through her emotional guard, the strength of his presence her safety net. All the tears she'd held back suddenly gushed forth. Deep sobs wracked any attempt to talk, to explain.

To his credit, he didn't try to hush her or mutter any useless, senseless platitudes. He just held her, rocked her, and let her cry herself out. As the flood of tears became a trickle and then ran dry, she didn't want to move, didn't want to leave the safe circle of his arms. So she closed her eyes and held still, breathing slow and steady.

'Why are you pretending to be asleep?' he asked, his deep voice slightly amused.

She did not respond.

'Come on. If you were really that sound asleep, you'd be snoring.'

Her eyes popped open before she could stop them. 'I do not snore.' Her voice sounded gravelly from the smoke inhalation and was thick from her recent bout of tears. She sat up and pushed him away. 'You, on the other hand . . .'

He slid over to the chair in one smooth motion, as if he'd expected rejection. 'Granted, we're not in the same league. Your snoring is more of a breathy humming noise.'

'What?'

'Best I can describe it.' He'd always thought her little snores endearing, but he'd never told her that. 'A definite giveaway as to your sleep state.'

'Yeah, well, you reek of smoke.'

He raised one eyebrow. 'So do you. Mimi said you came upstairs to shower and change.'

Caroline turned to face the window with a deep sigh. 'I don't have any energy. I can't sleep, but I can't seem to move either.'

She heard him move away and go into her bathroom. 'What are you doing?' she called as she sat up. The noise of running water was an ominous omen. 'Hey, you!' She swung her feet over the edge.

Travis strode back into the room. He'd removed his shirt and shoes. He scooped her up without a word and headed back to the bathroom.

'Put me down this instant or I'll scream.'

'Go ahead.' He stopped for a moment. 'I'm sure pretty-boy Dirk would be more than happy to rescue you,' he snapped without thinking.

Not a possibility she even wanted to consider. 'Fine. I get the hint. Just put me down and I'll take a shower.'

He did put her down, once they were both standing in the tub under the spraying water.

She swiped the wet hair off her face and glared up at him. 'Are you crazy?' she sputtered.

For a long moment time seemed to stand

still as they stared at each other, enclosed by the intimate space, nearness generating heat and electricity.

'I must be,' he said. And he turned, climbed out of the tub, and walked away.

Caroline collapsed against the tiles, leaned her head back and let the warm water cool her body.

Did he mean crazy to get into that situation, or crazy to walk away? Or both?

Travis asked himself the same questions as he grabbed his shirt, shoes, and headed down the narrow back stairs, a feature in older homes that used to be called the servants' staircase. His hopes of getting out the back door unnoticed were dashed when he ran into Mimi and Lou in the kitchen.

'Ladies,' he said. Mentally gripping his last shred of dignity, he managed a nonchalant tilt of his head. Ignoring the wet footprints that marked his path, he headed straight for the door without slowing his pace. 'I will return shortly.'

The two women stared after him for a moment, giving him time to get across the deck and down the hill to the gate. Then they turned to each other with knowing expressions.

★   ★   ★

By the time Travis had taken a cooling shower and donned a fresh uniform, he had four text messages on his phone, three from the coroner. The third message was from Caroline. He read it first.

Her text said, *Mimi says U hve q's? I prmis no brkdwn. BTW U 4gt yr bc.*

What the hell was a *yr bc*? He hated text shorthand. He mentally reran his hasty exit, remembered carrying his shirt and shoes. Nothing else had come off. And nothing else came to mind. He shrugged. He'd find out soon enough.

Marlene wrote, *No smoke in throat/lungs. Dead b4 fire.*

Her second message said, *Post mortem bruising lft upr arm & shldr & knee sggsts dead b4 car over cliff. More. See me.*

Marlene's third message said, *FTR her big-ass diamond engagement ring was NOT on her finger.*

He returned next door to Mimi's house. As he rang the doorbell, it occurred to him he didn't have his briefcase. Ah, now he got it. 'Yr bc' meant your briefcase.

Dee Ann answered the door. 'Thank heavens you're not someone bringing food. One more casserole and the refrigerator door will bust off its hinges.'

As she stepped aside and motioned for him

to enter, Phyllis showed up at her side.

'About time you got here. Dirk Vandergelt has been cooling his heels in the den for a good seven and a half minutes.'

'Because?'

'Sounds like police business to me,' Dee Ann said. 'So I'm going to leave and go sit with my feet up while I have the chance.'

'You took longer to get back than I anticipated,' Phyllis said. 'Oh, and I put your briefcase on the desk in the den.'

'It's kinda spooky when you do that.'

'What?'

'Anticipate what I'm going to do. Is that ESP or — '

'Ha.' Phyllis shook her head. 'You are so like your grandmother it's not funny, and I've worked for her for over thirty years. When you're finished with Dirk, Caroline said she would be available to talk to you about the accident.'

The second prospect held more appeal than the first. 'The sooner started, the sooner done.' With a short nod, he turned on his heel and went into the den.

Vandergelt was seated in the middle of the green brocade sofa, his head in his hands. He looked up when Travis came into the room. 'Why do you want to question me?' He didn't bother to rise or shake hands but instead

173

swiped tears from his red-rimmed eyes with a large handkerchief. 'All I know is what your people have told us, which is precious little.'

'It's standard procedure to interview those close to the deceased to get the full story of what happened.' Travis picked up his briefcase and laid it on the coffee table as he took the leather wingback chair across from the sofa. Even at that distance Vandergelt's cologne was strong, nearly overpowering, spicy with an underlying note of the onions he must have eaten at lunch. A subtle reminder that Travis hadn't eaten since an early breakfast.

'I'd like to record our conversation,' Travis said as he took out a tape recorder and a fresh tape. 'My memory isn't as good as it used to be,' he added in a joking tone. A lie he'd often used to put subjects at ease.

'I'd rather you didn't,' Vandergelt said with an arch expression.

Travis hid his surprise and held his tongue.

'I have an aversion to hearing my taped voice.' He waved his hand in a dismissive manner. 'I know everyone says they sound different on tape but it really freaks me out, like someone else spoke my words.'

'You'll never have to hear it.'

'Doesn't matter. I'll know. And considering all I've been through today, I'm sure my voice

174

will sound even stranger than ever. Can we just get on with it? I really should be getting back to the family.'

Travis took out his notebook and pen. 'When did you last see Barbara?'

'Early yesterday evening. She picked me up at the airport in the afternoon, we went back to hers and I left just after six.'

'That reminds me, do you need someone to pick up your relatives and groomsmen?'

'No. I called my parents. Their private jet had enough fuel to turn around and go back to Miami and the groomsmen only got as far as London before their plane had to land due to bad weather. I spoke to one of them and told him to pass on the message to not worry about coming here.'

'Don't you at least want your family here with you?'

'Of course I do, but my mother's health is delicate. Stress is not good for her. And they're afraid the accident might spawn a paparazzi feeding frenzy.'

'I don't think the Haven press corps, which consists of Harlan's cousin June and the digital camera she got for a graduation present, counts as paparazzi.'

'We decided it would be better for my mother if they stayed in Miami.'

Fine with him. Fewer people for Rose,

Mimi, and Caroline to deal with.

'What time did your plane land yesterday?'

'About two o'clock.'

'And then what did you do?'

Vandergelt looked down at his tightly clasped hands. He sniffed. 'We went to her house and we made love.' His voice was husky and thick. 'She was so sweet and giving. Oh, God, what am I going to do without her?' He threw himself to the side and tried to stifle his sobs in the sofa cushion.

Travis had had plenty of experience with distraught witnesses. He gave the man a few minutes and when his sobs started to slow, he said, 'I know this is rough, but if you can just get through a few more questions . . . '

Vandergelt sat up, wiped his face, and blew his nose. 'I'll do my best.'

'What did you do next?'

'Well, I'd made a reservation for a romantic dinner at La Maison in El Paso, but Barbara decided she didn't want to get all dressed up. She seemed out of sorts. Not sick, but, like, antsy, pacing. And she was testy, biting my head off for being concerned. I wrote it off to nerves and went to my room at the inn about seven.'

'The Arbor Inn?'

'Yes, it's the only hotel in town even marginally acceptable.'

'Did you usually stay there?'

'That is, frankly, none of your business.'

'I'm not judging. I'm simply trying to establish a pattern.'

Vandergelt blew out a breath and looked upward for a few seconds as if deciding whether or not to answer the question. 'No, I did not usually stay at the inn. For this one night, Barbara arranged it ahead of time because of a superstition, something to do with me seeing her before the ceremony or some such silliness. Or rather Caroline arranged it. Poor, dear Caroline. This whole day has been so terrible for her.'

Travis nodded and even managed a sympathetic pursing of his lips. Again with the poor Caroline bit. This guy was beginning to get on the wrong side of his nerves. He blamed his response on his own concern for her and pushed his anxiety aside. Emotions had no place in police work. 'And you keep a car at Barbara's?'

'Really, I don't see any point in — '

'Bear with me.'

'Yes. An older model that I have no other use for. I didn't want to be tied down like some fifties hausfrau. What was I supposed to do while she worked? Clean the house?'

Travis nodded as if he agreed. 'What happened after you arrived at the inn?'

'I checked into my room, watched a little television, and went to sleep. In the morning, I had breakfast . . . '

Travis only had to look up from his notes for Dirk to add the time.

'At quarter to eight. Then I checked out, put my overnight bag in the trunk. When I saw my tux hanging in the car, I realized I'd left a small shopping bag at Barbara's. I'd forgotten to pack black dress socks. You know, one of those things you remember *after* you're seated on the airplane. We'd stopped at a store near the airport and I never put the sales bag with the socks into my garment bag.'

'Yesterday? You went shopping after she picked you up? You didn't mention that a moment ago.' Even though it wasn't necessary, for effect he flipped back through the pages of his notebook.

'I ran into the store and picked up a pair of socks. What in the world is so — '

'Nope, you didn't say that earlier.'

'Why are you making a big deal out of this? My sock problem is insignificant in light of what's happened, don't you think?'

'Actually, this is about Barbara and her whereabouts. Did she go into the store?'

'No, she waited in the car.'

'Did the two of you stop anywhere else?'

178

'No.'

'Okay, let's go back to the point after you left the hotel room.'

'I called Barbara but got her voicemail so I decided to stop by her house. When — '

'Whoa.' Travis held up one hand. 'Why did you decide to go to her house when she didn't answer her phone? That strikes me as illogical.'

'Not if she didn't answer her phone because she was either in the shower or otherwise unavailable. I *logically* decided that if I drove there she would be *available* by the time I got there and I could get my damn socks.'

Travis suppressed a slight smile. So Gentleman Dirk had a short fuse and didn't like to have his word questioned. Sometimes interrogation was as much about what they didn't say as it was about the answers given. And sometimes questions were asked solely to elicit a reaction.

'Did you?'

'What?'

'Did you get your socks?'

Vandergelt sighed. 'I think you should seek qualified help for your fixation.'

Travis smiled ruefully. On the one hand Vandergelt had a point. His fixation on getting to the bottom of an issue and finding

179

the truth was a professional asset and a personal liability. He looked down at his notes. 'So you decided to go to Barbara's house?'

'Yes, only she wasn't home. I presumed she'd already left for the beauty parlor. So then I decided to go there and borrow her key. On the way, I washed my car and topped off the gas tank. Oh, just so you know I'm not leaving anything out, I bought some breath mints.'

Travis kept his face a blank, which seemed to annoy Vandergelt even more. 'Go on.'

'Then I drove to the beauty parlor, but her car wasn't there either.'

'You don't have a key to her house?'

'What's that supposed to mean?'

'Just a question.'

'Well, she did give me a key, but I've never used it because I can't remember the code to her security system. Whenever I was visiting and she knew I would be going in and out, she didn't arm it. That rarely happened because we were almost always together.'

'Except this morning.'

Vandergelt stood. 'Are we done?'

Travis purposefully remained seated, his body relaxed, non-threatening. 'Just a few more minutes of your time. Take me up to your meeting with Caroline at the Country Club.'

He sort of drifted back into his seat almost as if he sat down unwillingly. 'It seemed obvious that Barbara's plans had changed and I was sure Caroline would know where to find her. She's smart as well as beautiful.'

'Hmmm. Why didn't you just call her? Why drive all the way out to the Country Club? How did you know she was there?'

Vandergelt's eyes widened and he pushed backward into the sofa cushion. Travis realized he'd let his tone become slightly heated. 'Sorry. I'm trying to wrap this up since you're eager to be done.' Sure, that was the reason for the bombardment. 'Why didn't you call her?'

'Because I don't have Caroline's cell phone number.'

Travis nodded sagely. Good to know. 'Why not call the club and have her paged?'

'I didn't think of that.' Vandergelt straightened his collar. 'I can only blame any illogical actions on pre-wedding nerves. Surely you understand a case of groom's jitters.'

'Not really.' Of course, his wedding had been more a spur-of-the-moment decision and had consisted of hours of frustrating bureaucratic red tape, about five minutes with a sleepy *Oficina del Registro Civil*, and an idyllic weekend honeymoon at a tiny beach cottage in Los Cabos.

'Anyway, I assumed Caroline, being as efficient as she is lovely, would be at the Country Club on the morning of the wedding and I went there to find her.'

Travis had gathered enough answers to provide a verifiable base of Vandergelt's whereabouts and he was getting fed up with the other man's annoying habit of adding compliments whenever he referred to Caroline.

He closed his notebook and leaned forward to rest his elbows on his knees. 'Even though you usually stay at Barbara's house when you're here, I'm afraid you'll have to extend your residence at the inn.'

'No problem. As soon as I pick up the rest of my — '

'Sorry. If you need anything from her house, one of my deputies will fetch it for you.'

'I don't understand.'

'We still have a few questions about Barbara's death, so her house will be under supervision until we clear up a few matters.'

'You people are unreal.'

'Do you mean — '

'I mean, what passes for law enforcement in this backwater settlement? A woman has a fatal accident and because you can't seem to fathom that fact, we, her friends and family, are put through a second emotional wringer in order to satisfy your sub-rational curiosity.

I find your questioning unnecessary and offensive, and if it doesn't stop immediately, I will call every New Mexico politician I've ever met including the Governor, senators, congressmen — '

'I get the gist of your — '

'And before I'm done, you'll be begging for a job at the local Dairy Queen.'

'I heard they're looking for someone to work nights and weekends.' Travis grinned. 'Good benefits. Free chili dogs and ice cream. Oh, oh, they have that new flavor blizzard. What's it called?'

'Arrrgh!' Vandergelt grabbed a sofa pillow, crushing the fabric in his fist. He jumped up, threw the cushion down, and stormed from the room.

'Don't leave town,' Travis called after him. He was still grinning when Caroline came to the door.

'I don't think Dirk likes you very much,' she said.

'And I think he likes you too much,' Travis said. 'I think that's kinda creepy considering . . . '

Caroline walked to the sofa and sat down. 'At least someone agrees with me. Everyone else thinks of Dirk as Mr Wonderful.'

'Why don't you? Has anything — '

'It's nothing. He just reminds me of

someone back in LA that I didn't care for.'

She was lying but he let it drop. For now.

'Mimi said you had some questions for me? I don't know how I can help.'

'I'd like you to tell me what happened. Everything you can remember. That is, if you're feeling up to it.'

'I'm fine.'

He waited.

She wanted nothing more than for him to take her into the safety of his arms again. Not that she felt unsafe other times. She shook off her silliness and sat up straighter. With her permission he taped the interview and she related everything from the moment Dirk said he was looking for Barbara to when Mimi brought her home from the hospital. 'I couldn't stay downstairs.' She grabbed a tissue from the box on the end table and dabbed at her eyes. 'I keep seeing Barbara and thinking if I'd done something differently maybe I could have saved — '

'You couldn't.' He clicked off the tape recorder.

'But if only I'd — '

'Caroline!' He lowered his voice to continue. 'Nothing you could have done would have made any difference. She was already dead before you got there. I think her car was pushed over the edge.'

'All . . . ' Her eyes widened. 'You mean murder?'

'Preliminary evidence suggests so.'

She bit her bottom lip and he could practically see the thoughts spinning around in her brain. 'That makes sense.'

Travis sat back in the chair and crossed his arms. 'Why would you say that?'

'You might consider this silly, but I kept thinking someone else had dressed Barbara, which is logical if she was either dead or incapacitated when she was put into her car.'

'I'm not following you. What led you to believe someone else dressed her?'

'It's what she was wearing, for one thing.'

'Her wedding dress? On her wedding day? What's so unusual about that?'

Caroline rolled her eyes. 'It's more than the fact that we'd planned for her to dress at the Country Club right before the wedding, or that she had bought a special outfit for the rehearsal. No way would she have put on her wedding dress that early in the day.'

'Maybe she was showing it to someone.'

Caroline shook her head. 'Sitting in a car would have wrinkled the dress terribly. She never would have done that. That's the major reason for dressing at the Country Club. And we know she never made it to her beauty shop appointment. Her hair was down and loose. That particular veil was designed to go with an upswept hairstyle.'

'Circumstantial.'

'She bought special lingerie to wear with her wedding dress, a white, strapless corselet among other things. And I'm sure I saw bra straps. Beige bra straps. Not only was Barbara very particular about matching her underwear to her outfit, Miss Perfection would never allow her bra straps to show. Ever.'

'Maybe she was in a hurry.'

'What is your problem? I'm trying to help you prove your theory, and you're countering every bit of evidence as if it's useless.'

'Opinions are not evidence.'

'Well, I think she was murdered at home, early in the morning, and — '

'This is not a game of Clue.' Although he was glad he'd thought to send a deputy to Barbara's house, even if he couldn't have said why until now.

She ignored his sarcasm. 'Then the murderer dressed her and drove her to Indian Point. Wait. Tommy G said he saw her drive by at about seven-thirty. How could that be?' She paused but not for long. 'He must have seen someone else dressed in white and wearing the veil driving her car.'

'You're making deductions, jumping to conclusions.'

'You said she was murdered, didn't you?'

'I said I think she was murdered. Right now it's still just a theory. And I don't want you to say anything to anyone about it. Not until I've had a chance to collect more evidence, real scientifically provable evidence. Okay?'

She hesitated for a moment before agreeing. She stood up and he did the same.

'Just put it out of your mind,' he said. He reached out and took one of her hands in both of his. 'If you need someone to talk to, I'm available twenty-four seven.' When he realized how that sounded he added, 'Or any member of my staff. We're here to serve and protect.'

'I wish I could forget what I saw.' She removed her hand from his grasp and shook her head. 'I know Barbara and I didn't often see eye to eye, well rarely, actually almost never, but still, no one deserves such a terrible . . . I can't seem to think of much else.' She blew her nose and pasted a forced smile on her face. 'But thanks for coming by, for listening to me.'

'Do you want me to spend the night?'

'In your dreams.' Her refusal seemed to have a combined tone of indignation, surprise, and, maybe just a little, amused interest.

He waggled his eyebrows at her. 'I know a surefire way to take your mind off — '

She slapped at his arm. 'When pigs fly.'

'And here I was offering to subject myself to an all-night session of cards and/or board games for your amusement.' Not something he enjoyed, probably because he'd grown up without brothers and sisters. 'Nope,' he said, holding up his hand, 'Too late. You can't rescind your rejection.' He chuckled as he two-stepped toward the exit and ducked into the hall. The tissue box hit the door just as it shut.

Lou met him in the hall.

'Is your phone off?' she asked. 'Marlene has called me at least ten times looking for you.'

'I always turn my ringer off when I'm in an interrogation session. I got her texts. She thinks she's found something important so I'm on my way there next.'

'Don't be surprised if you get a call from Mayor Keyes. Irene called to warn you. If he can get a quorum, he's going to call an emergency council meeting.'

'What did I do now?'

'It's what you didn't do, as in solve the murder cases. But don't sweat it. You can handle him.'

Travis kissed her forehead. 'Did I tell you today that you're the best?'

Lou pushed him away. 'Yeah. Right after you took the car keys away from me. Again.'

'Right after you promised to heed the doctor's instructions and not drive while you're on this new medication.'

'I haven't suffered a single dizzy spell.'

'You can discuss the side effects, or lack thereof, with him on your next appointment. Until then I'm going to hold you to your word and expect your cooperation.'

'Humpf.' Lou pushed her walker around him and headed toward the kitchen. 'You won't solve this new murder by standing around jawing with me,' she called over her shoulder.

Travis caught up with her in two long strides. 'Who said it was murder?' he asked in a low voice. 'It could have been an accident. Or suicide.'

Lou stopped and faced him. 'Poppycock. I'm physically weak not mentally impaired. Do you really think a reasonably intelligent woman — '

'No.' He lowered his voice even more. 'I don't want anyone to speculate before I get hard evidence back from — '

'Lab reports can take weeks.'

'I asked Marlene to run a few tests right away. She's sent me some texts already to say she's found several indications that Barbara was killed prior to the accident.'

Lou slapped her thigh. 'I knew it. Wait till I tell — '

'Whoa, Nellie. Let's not spread the word until the lab reports — '

'Bah! Police work is more than forensic reports. Good old-fashioned grunt work — '

'I know, I know. You've always said labs provide proof for the lawyers, but investigation solves cases. And to a considerable extent I agree, but in this case the coroner's findings have determined the direction of the inquiry.'

'So go investigate. After you pay your respects to Rose.' She left him and went to the kitchen.

He went into the living room and expressed his sympathies to Rose. She grabbed his hand. 'I want you to find the monster who did this to my sweet Barbara Jean.'

'Yes, ma'am. I intend to.'

He was saved any additional discussion and avoided the necessity of admitting he currently didn't have a clue by the arrival of the minister who immediately usurped Travis's position next to the grieving mother. With a sigh of relief, he returned to the den to pick up his briefcase. Phyllis met him there.

'I'd like you to stay on here to assist the family in any way you can,' he said. 'And for my peace of mind, keep Lou away from the coffee pot.'

'On the first, sure. On the second, no way. I can't start back-talking her at this late date.'

'Just give her the Mom look.'

'The what? Are you insulting me?'

'No, no. I wish I could do it. You know. That fabulous squint-eyed stare moms use that says, *I'm watching you and I don't approve and you're going to hear about this later.*'

'The wait-till-your-father-gets-home-because-there-will-be-punishment look? Very effective, even if there's no father involved.'

Travis shook his head. 'No. That's way too much. I was thinking more along the lines of a glare that says, *if you drink that coffee, I'll tattle to Travis as soon as I get the chance.*'

'Ah. You want the bratty little sister look. Good choice. That I can probably do. According to my older sister, I used to be quite good at it. I may be a few years out of practice, but I presume it's rather like having sex.'

'I beg your pardon?'

'You know. Once you learn, you never forget how to do it.'

'I thought that was riding a bicycle.'

Phyllis patted his arm and gave him a sympathetic smile. 'You can ride a bicycle if you want to, Sonny-boy, I'd rather have sex.'

Lou and Mimi entered the den. 'Who's having sex?' Lou asked. 'Did we miss some juicy gossip?'

Travis threw his hands in the air. 'I'm leaving before the three of you start talking trash that'd make a bronc buster blush.' He left knowing that if there was any information to be gathered, Phyllis and Lou would ferret it out.

9

'What have you got?'

Marlene Rondale jumped as if the corpse in front of her had spoken. 'Don't sneak up on me like that,' she said, putting her hand to her throat. 'What are you doing here?'

Travis shrugged. 'Your brother said this is where I'd find you.'

'No one ever comes down those stairs unless they absolutely have to. Including my brothers. They handle the living and I handle the dead.'

'No problem. What have you — '

'If he'd called, I would have come upstairs. We can use one of the consultation rooms — '

'It's okay. This is not my first autopsy.' Although he would admit he preferred to avoid them whenever possible. Then he realized his discomfort wasn't the issue. He'd invaded her space, and that made her uncomfortable. 'We can go upstairs if you — '

'No, no. This is fine. You're here.' Her manner was quick and businesslike. 'As you can see, the body is quite charred but not a complete cinder. Cremation takes two to three hours at fifteen hundred to two thousand degrees Fahrenheit. Even after all that, the remains must be ground up to make a consistent grain. After removing, of course, any metal like dental fillings, orthopedi — '

'Do you have a time of death?'

'Man, you have a one-track mind.'

'That can be a good thing.' He paused to look at the ID of an incoming call on his phone. 'Excuse me. I have to get this. Hello, Mayor Keyes.'

'Beaumont?'

Who else did he expect? The Mayor's voice boomed so loudly, Travis leaned away and held the phone at arm's length. There was a volume control, but he didn't have time to look for it. 'I'm here.'

'I've called an emergency meeting of the town council. I, um, we would like a report from you regarding the recent crime wave and the status of your investigations.'

'I'll have a report by tomorrow — '

'That's not good enough. I, um, we want to see you in person so we can ask questions. We're waiting for you right now in the council chamber.'

'I'll be there as soon as I finish my meeting with the coroner.' Travis clicked his phone shut, tucked it in his pocket, and turned to Marlene. 'Where were we?'

194

'We can finish later. You should — '

'I can handle that. We were talking about TOD.'

'Too many unknown factors, to call it accurately. Liver temp is usually a good indicator, but allowances must be made for ambient temperature and conditions. I don't have a temp for the inside of the car. How long was she in there? Was the engine running with the air conditioning on? Cause of the fire would give a clue to the temperature reached. How long did it burn?'

'Marlene — '

'Okay, okay. My best estimate for her time of death is between four and seven a.m. but due to extenuating circumstances, I have to hedge that with a margin of error of six hours one way or another.'

'Well, we know it wasn't after nine-thirty, so that gives me a window of almost twelve hours starting at ten o'clock last night.'

'Sorry.' Marlene shrugged. 'Maybe I'll know more later. And you shouldn't keep the Mayor waiting. He's gunning for you and the longer he has to fret the worse it will be. Too bad his wife's not there. I heard she — '

'I hate when you do that. You and Phyllis and Lou and Mimi and — '

'Do what?'

'Know stuff. Be in the loop. The Sheriff

should not be the last person to know . . . whatever.'

'You want to be included in on the gossip?'

'No! That's not — '

'Because I would be real uncomfortable — '

'No. I mean, so would I. What I do want to — '

'Especially when it's about you.'

'Me?' Travis asked.

A moment of awkward silence filled the air between them.

'Forget I said that.' Marlene turned back to the body. 'I'll have more results for you later.'

'Why would anyone gossip about me?'

She turned back to face him with her hands on her hips. 'What? You think you're exempt because you're related to Lou? Family members are prime sources.'

'I've been leading the life of a freaking monk. I work long hours. Take care of my grandmother. What is there about my current life that could possibly be gossip-worthy?'

'Mrs Keyes wants you to stick around and she thinks that if you marry a local girl . . . '

'Tell her I'm not looking for a wife.'

'Oh, not just any woman. She thinks she knows the perfect match for you. Somewhere she read that those in the nurturing careers make the best wives for cops. And she has

196

three nieces, two elementary school teachers and one nurse.'

Travis held his hand out in a halt gesture, which became a wave as he turned toward the exit. 'Later.'

'Never say I didn't warn you.'

'Thanks.' At least he now understood why the Mayor's wife had started giving tours of the courthouse to each of her nieces. Tours that just happened to include a visit to his office, an introduction, and an invitation to lunch. Fortunately, he'd been busy every time.

★　★　★

Travis entered the council chamber and found all six members of the council in their chairs at a large horseshoe-shaped desk, three on each side of the Mayor. The nameplates identified the members Arcelia Rodriguez, Gloria Stanley, Veta Basilio, Dr Karl Dieter, Cesar Ramirez and Werner Whitson. By their solemn expressions it appeared that no one was happy to be there, except maybe Mrs Stanley who loved any opportunity to gather gossip. Travis took a seat in the otherwise empty audience area.

Owen Ferris, the Fire Chief, was standing before the council and just finishing giving his report on the day's proceedings. 'We returned to the firehouse at ten after two o'clock. I've sent samples to the state capital for arson analysis. I'll forward the results as soon as I have them.'

'Thank you, Chief Ferris,' the Mayor said. 'Does any council member have a question? No. Very well. That will be all.'

Owen gave Travis a sympathetic nod on his way out.

'Sheriff Beaumont,' Mayor Keyes said.

'Present.'

'You may step forward.'

Travis refused to be treated like a recalcitrant schoolboy and remained in his front-row seat. 'Thanks, but I prefer to remain here. I'm sure you'll appreciate that it has been a long day.'

'We've all been as busy as a stump-tailed cow in fly time,' Dr Dieter said. He turned to the Mayor. 'I haven't even had my supper yet. Get on with it.'

The Mayor stood up as if he were addressing an assemblage. 'The good people of Haven deserve to sleep peacefully at night without worrying they might be murdered in their beds.'

The council members murmured their agreement. Travis declined to point out that none of the victims were found in their beds.

Poor Annabelle Dawson was technically found in a bed but it wasn't hers and she apparently hadn't been sleeping.

'Four murders without a single arrest is unacceptable.' The Mayor pounded his gavel, now in full hero-of-the-people mode. 'Action must be taken.'

'Hear! Hear!'

'As your mayor I will not stand idly by. We all know who threatened the latest victim on multiple occasions. That same person was at the scene when emergency personnel arrived, although at a safe distance.'

Dr Dieter frowned. 'Now just a minute — '

Gloria raised her hand. 'Mr Stanley cautions — '

With a dramatic gesture, the Mayor whipped out a folded piece of paper from his pocket. 'We must show the people of this town that we mean business.' Holding the paper high, he marched around the desk, most of the council clapping hands to mark time. He came to a halt in front of Travis.

'We have been informed that one suspect arrived at the hospital with dirt on her hands and scratches consistent with handling driftwood and mesquite, just as the arsonist would have received from the actions taken to promote the fire under the car. While there may not be any evidence to link this murder to the others, nothing like this crime spree has ever happened in our law-abiding town until she returned. At least we can take action on one murder.'

With a self-important flourish, the Mayor shoved the folded paper toward Travis. 'This warrant is for the arrest of Frances Caroline Tucker.'

Somehow Travis refrained from jumping up and punching the Mayor. Armchair detectives were a pain in the ass and those with political agendas were the worst. Keeping his voice level, he said, 'There's still a lot of evidence to gather and process. Results from the crime lab take time. Until then, circumstance and hearsay do not make a prosecutable case.' He eyed the warrant with disdain. 'I suggest you reconsider a hasty move that may result in a suit for false arrest.'

But the council's collective conscience had been prodded, and like a team of runaway horses they didn't respond to the reins of reason. They wanted an arrest, any arrest, so that they would be viewed as proactive by their fellow citizens. Never mind that they were wrong.

'I fully understand your reluctance,' Mayor Keyes said, his tone sliding slyly to the oily smoothness of a used-car salesman. He leaned forward on the balls of his feet,

200

towering menacingly over Travis who was still seated. 'We all know you had a . . . shall we say *relationship* with the suspect and this must be difficult for you. Perhaps you should resign your office due to conflict of interest.'

Travis could kick himself. He should have anticipated that move. The Mayor had been the one dissenting vote when Travis had been appointed to fill the balance of his grandmother's term as Sheriff. If he were to resign, the Mayor would most likely push through his nephew's appointment as Sheriff.

For fifty cents Travis would walk away and leave the fools to their own devices. But where would that leave Caroline? In order to prevent them from making her into the sacrificial scapegoat on the altar of public good, he would have to keep his job. And to do that, he would have to arrest her for murder.

Travis stood, forcing the older man to take a couple of steps backward.

'Bad time to bluff,' Travis said in a low voice that only the Mayor could hear. He forced his shoulders to relax and hooked his thumb in a belt loop. 'Only a lousy gambler would go all in with nothing, nine-two off-suit. And since I'm holding pocket aces . . . ' He snatched the warrant out of the Mayor's hand. 'I call.'

Caroline realized she couldn't delay going downstairs any longer. She made it to the kitchen without running into Dirk.

'How's Aunt Rose holding up?' she asked Mimi.

'I'm just fixing her a cup of tea.' She shook her head. 'I wish Rose would call her doctor in El Paso and see if she'll prescribe a mild sedative. Poor Rose has worked herself into quite a state.'

'Isn't that to be expected after such horrible news?'

'Maybe some hysteria, but not for hours. I think she doesn't know what to do to get past this point, and nothing I've suggested has worked.'

'It's like a case of the hiccups you can't get rid of,' Lou said as she entered. 'You just keep trying different folk remedies until something works.'

'You want me to jump out of the closet and scare her?' Caroline asked, getting a couple of chuckles in response.

'No,' Mimi said, shaking her head but still smiling. She picked up the tray. 'Hopefully this tea — '

'Oh, dear.' Phyllis stared down at her phone. 'He can't arrest Caroline.'

'What?'

Phyllis snapped her phone shut.

'Cat's outta the bag,' Lou said. 'You might as well tell us.'

'Especially if it has something to do with Caroline,' Mimi added.

'Yeah.' Caroline didn't like hearing her name and the word 'arrest' used together.

'It's ridiculous,' Phyllis said, 'but Mayor Keyes, in his infinite wisdom, has decided an arrest must be made and he's settled on Caroline as the guilty party because all these murders have happened since she arrived in town. And so far we don't have any evidence that contradicts his theory.'

'That's insane,' Caroline said.

'He can't force Travis to arrest her,' Mimi said. 'Can he?'

'There's a warrant,' Phyllis said. 'It's his job to arrest Caroline for Barbara's — '

'Did I hear laughter?' Aunt Rose said in a loud, strident voice. She shuffled slowly into the kitchen, leaning heavily on her husband's arm. 'I'm sure I heard . . . wait a minute.' She held up a finger and then mentally retraced her steps. 'Barbara's what?'

'Now that you're here, how about a cup of nice hot — '

'Tell me.' Rose pushed past Mimi and glared at Phyllis, her face inches away. 'You said Travis has a warrant — '

'Not Travis. Mayor Keyes.'

'Whatever. A warrant for Barbara's what?'

Phyllis looked to Lou.

'You might as well tell her,' Lou said with a shrug of one shoulder. 'News like this spreads like spilled buck-shot.'

'The Mayor has a warrant to arrest Caroline for Barbara's murder.'

'What?'

Suddenly everyone talked at once. Except Caroline. She was still in shock. Comments zipped around like angry bees and she caught only a word or two here and there.

' . . . how dare — '

' . . . well I never — '

' . . . Travis wouldn't — '

' . . . crazy? — '

How could anyone think her capable of doing such a monstrous, terrible —

A scream jerked her focus back to the present just in time to see Aunt Rose curl her fingers into claws and launch herself at Caroline with a second blood-curdling screech.

'You killed her.'

'No!' Caroline backed away.

Aunt Rose's husband grabbed her round the waist and hauled her to his chest. 'Now, darlin', you know that isn't — '

'She was always jealous of Barbara. Let me go. I'll scratch her eyes out.'

'We'll be in the living room,' Chuck said as he backed out of the kitchen hauling Aunt Rose with him in spite of her grabbing cabinets and doorjambs in an attempt to thwart him. 'She'll see reason as soon as she calms down. Ouch. Stop kicking, darlin'. You're not thinking straight and you might hurt yourself.'

Mimi turned to Caroline. 'She doesn't really believe that. She's just — '

'I understand. She's upset.'

'No one thinks you killed Barbara.'

'It's a common misconception that an arrest is the same as a conviction,' Phyllis said. 'Perhaps a testament to a good record by the force, but unfortunately it means Caroline will be judged guilty by many people when she's taken into custody.'

'Travis would never arrest Caroline,' Mimi said.

Caroline wasn't so sure.

'He may not have a choice,' Phyllis said.

'This isn't about Caroline,' Lou said. 'The Mayor is making a power play, hoping to back Travis into a corner.

An animal howl and a few stifled curses echoed from the living room.

'I'd better go and help Chuck,' Mimi said.

'Maybe it would be wise if you made yourself scarce for a while,' she said to Caroline before bustling away with the tea tray.

Wyoming was nice this time of year, lovely mountains, open spaces. If she left tonight, she could —

'Don't even think about leaving town,' Lou said as if she'd read Caroline's mind.

'Who, me?'

Lou snorted. 'The arrest warrant is already issued. If you leave town, you'll become a bona fide fugitive. Cross state lines and the FBI sticks its big nose into your business. Only frog legs jump out of the frying pan into the fire.'

Rrribbit.

'I'll kill her,' Aunt Rose shrieked from the other room.

'Ignore that,' Lou said. 'It's just her grief talking. Why don't you come over to my house? We'll look at my photo albums. I have tons of pictures taken when you and Travis were kids. I'm sure Mimi will help Rose see reason soon.'

The sounds of scuffling reached the kitchen.

'Maybe an hour or two,' Lou added.

A crash of broken glass sounded like the breakfront being broken by something large smashing into it.

'We're okay,' Mimi called. 'Everything is under control.'

Or not.

'I'd better help clean up that glass,' Phyllis said. She got a broom and dustpan from the closet and headed into the fray.

'You could stay overnight with me,' Lou offered. 'I have a lovely guest room.'

Caroline shook her head. She couldn't believe all this was happening.

'Don't worry, my dear,' Lou said, putting an arm around Caroline's shoulders. 'Travis will stand up to Judge McKay and that meddling Mayor.'

'Judge McKay? What does he have to do with this?'

'Who do you think signed the arrest warrant?'

'Crap.' Caroline had managed to stay out of his courtroom all these years but she wasn't one of his favorite people. She'd inadvertently found out one of his secrets and he wasn't likely to forget or forgive even though she'd never told anyone.

'Travis won't let the city council railroad you,' Lou said.

Except Travis didn't know . . .

'Where is he now?' Caroline asked.

'Travis?' Lou scratched behind her ear. 'I imagine he's at the courthouse. The Mayor called a special council meeting, going to great lengths to get a quorum. An audience for him and a — ' She bit her lip.

'Go on. It's okay for you to tell me. I'm going to find out eventually and forewarned is forearmed.'

'Well, a quorum would be necessary for the town council to vote on the impeachment of the Sheriff.'

'They can't do that.'

'Well, technically they can, if there's justifiable cause. Refusing to serve a warrant might be considered . . . Anyway, the Mayor's cause is to get his nephew appointed Sheriff. Don't you worry. Travis will think of something. He won't arrest you.'

Yeah? And that would get him fired. Being impeached would destroy Travis's career. She realized that innocence alone wasn't enough to save her. As much as she hated to admit it, she needed Travis. And she needed him to be the Sheriff so he could help clear her name.

'I'm going for a drive. To clear my head,' she added as an excuse even though everything was pretty obvious to her. She grabbed her purse and keys from the hall table on her way out.

'Don't leave town,' Lou called after her.

Oh, Caroline was tempted.

But that would only make matters worse.

She passed the turn to the highway and headed straight downtown. She wasn't doing this to save Travis, she was only interested in saving her own skin.

★　★　★

She met Travis coming out as she approached the main doors of the courthouse. He grabbed her arm and pulled her off to the side of the steps and behind a large oleander bush.

'Don't you know the mayor wants to arrest you?' he asked.

'Oh, no. I'm too late.'

'What?'

'Lou said you'd refuse to arrest me and then the council would fire you or else you'd quit and then the mayor would appoint Harlan as Sheriff. Then Harlan would arrest me and it would be up to him to investigate and I wouldn't have a snowball's chance in hell and go straight to jail do not pass go, do not collect — '

He took her by the shoulders. 'I didn't — '

'Two hundred dollars. I didn't kill Barbara and I don't want to go to the big house and wear one of those horrid orange jumpsuits and you know that's my least favorite color except at Halloween but if you're leaving the

209

courthouse that means you've already been to the council and it's too late. I'm doomed to — '

'Caroline!' He gave her a gentle shake. 'I didn't quit and I didn't get fired. Frances Caroline Tucker, you're under arrest for the murder of Barbara Jean Jennings.'

She stared at him for a long second.

'You have the right to remain silent.'

She threw herself at him and wrapped her arms round his neck. 'Oh, thank you, thank you.'

He had no choice but to catch her in an embrace. 'Anything you say can and will be used against you in a court of law.'

She leaned back and took his face in her hands. 'You are my last best hope of getting out of this mess.' She punctuated her words with kisses all over his face.

'You have the right to speak to an attorney, and to have an attorney present — '

She silenced him with a searing kiss. He returned it with hot intensity.

'Get a room,' a stranger said as he walked by.

They jumped apart.

'Um, I guess I got carried away,' she said. 'Don't read anything into that . . . um, kiss of . . . gratitude, because that's all it was, between-friends kind of gratitude.'

Travis cleared his throat. Not his typical arrest. He started over reciting her rights, using the short break provided by the familiar routine to pull himself together. If he wanted to help Caroline he needed to remain detached both emotionally and physically. And he could only do that if she kept her distance.

'Perhaps we should conduct your questioning at the station,' he said, holding aside the oleander branches that had failed to provide privacy.

'Of course.' She raised her chin and stepped past as if she were exiting a fine restaurant. They walked around the corner of the courthouse in silence and entered the station, catching Harlan by surprise.

The deputy's boots fell from his desktop and hit the floor with a jolt.

'Relieve Bobby Lee,' Travis said to him. 'Tell him I need him here.' He didn't want loose-lipped Harlan hanging around while he questioned Caroline.

'But I was just — '

Travis raised one eyebrow.

'Yes, sir. I'm on it.'

'Where is Bobby Lee?' Caroline asked after Harlan left and she'd taken a seat in front of Travis's desk.

'He's guarding Barbara's house until I can

get there to investigate.'

'Go. I'll wait here.'

'Can't do that. You're my prisoner.'

'I'm here voluntarily.'

'You're under arrest.'

'That doesn't mean you have to treat me like a criminal.'

'Yes, in some ways it does.'

'Oh, are you going to handcuff me?'

The corner of Travis's mouth twitched. 'Why? Do you want me to?'

'In your dreams.'

'Only doing my — '

'Fine. Congratulations, you've done your duty. Now what?'

So much for short-lived gratitude. 'Finger-printing, questioning, and then I'll assign you a cell for the night.'

'No need to bother with a cell. I'll just post bail or bond or whatever it's called and go home. True, Aunt Rose sort of freaked when she learned I'd been officially accused of murder, but Mimi will settle her down in a few hours. I can go back and then you can get on with your investigation.'

'A judge sets the amount of bail at a hearing. In your case he's already ruled you're a flight risk and no bail is available.'

From the flat tone of his voice Caroline realized just how serious her situation was.

She was actually going to have to sleep in a jail cell! Make that spend the night in a jail cell because there was no way she was going to get any sleep.

Half angry, half terrified, she was silent during the fingerprinting. His touch was formal as he rolled her inked fingers on to the paper. Then there were the mug shots. His voice was cold and official-sounding as he issued instructions. Toes on the white line. Hold this. Face front. Turn to your left. Even knowing she was innocent, the process was mortifying. And Travis did nothing to make it any easier on her. And that pissed her off.

'What other fun activities designed to humiliate me do you have planned?' Caroline asked. She ripped open a second packaged alcohol wipe and scrubbed her still-stained fingertips. 'You're really enjoying humiliating me, aren't you?'

Bobby Lee entered and leaned silently against the wall.

'This isn't personal,' Travis said.

'Well, it sure as heck *feels* personal.'

'Procedures are established to efficiently handle — '

'Blah, blah, blah. What happened to innocent until proven guilty?'

'That will be decided in a courtroom. Until then — '

'Until then I'm a criminal. I get it. Why don't you — '

'Now, now,' Bobby Lee said. He stepped between his boss and his sister like the referee of a boxing match, using his arms to direct them to seek neutral corners. 'We're all after the same goal.'

'He has a funny way of proving my innocence,' Caroline said.

'My job is to find the guilty party, whomever it may be,' Travis responded, crossing his arms over his chest.

She mimicked his action and stuck out her chin. 'Are you insinuating that might be me?'

'Of course he isn't,' Bobby Lee said. 'Come on, you guys. When he catches the murderer your name will be cleared,' he said to Caroline. Then he turned to Travis. 'And since Caroline spent more time with Barbara lately than anyone else, she's your best resource for clues to finding the murderer. So truce. Okay?'

After a moment of uneasy silence, Travis said, 'Truce.'

'Truce,' Caroline grudgingly agreed.

'Great,' Bobby Lee said. 'Let's get to work.' He rubbed his hands together. 'I've never been in on the questioning of a suspect.'

'Don't call me that,' Caroline said. 'I'm an innocent bystander, a victim, even, but not a suspect.'

'We will refer to your sister as the detainee,' Travis said. 'If that's all right with you,' he asked Caroline in an overly polite tone that irked as much as his earlier rudeness. He held out a chair next to one of the desks in the outer office.

She gave him a gracious if cool nod as she sat down.

As Travis indicated, Bobby Lee took a seat at the neighboring desk, which put him sitting next to his sister. 'You can call a brown dog Spot, but he's still a brown dog,' he muttered.

Travis sent him a quelling look. He set up a tape recorder and then folded his hands on the desk. After identifying the date, time, and those present, he said, 'Ms Tucker has been Mirandized so we will begin the questioning with a reminder that she should consider herself under oath to tell the truth, the whole truth, and nothing but the truth. Do you agree?'

'Of course. Why wouldn't I tell the truth?'

10

Caroline tried to view the questioning session with a positive outlook. This was her opportunity to convince Travis, beyond a doubt, that she was totally innocent. Of course, she would tell the truth. Lying to him would only make matters worse. She held up her hand as if swearing in court. 'The whole truth and nothing but the truth.'

When she looked Travis in the eye, a zing of understanding sparked between them. He wanted to take advantage of the opportunity and ask her about their former relationship, but with her brother hovering close by to referee he wouldn't. She heaved an inward sigh of relief. Some secrets she would take to her grave.

If there were an unspoken agreement to avoid that topic, it was the only subject Travis considered off limits. He questioned her about her reason for returning to Haven, forcing her to reveal the failure of her business.

'Yes, I did say I'd kill Barbara,' Caroline admitted under his intense stare. 'And yes, more than once. But it's just a figure of speech that expresses frustration. It's not a real threat.'

Apparently, the legal system didn't see it her way. Neither did Travis, but he moved on to questions about that morning. He'd had some time to think about what had happened and under his skillful guidance she recalled several helpful details. She hadn't passed any cars on the way to Indian Point which meant whoever had been there with Barbara must have left and made it to the highway before Caroline made the turn on to the access road.

'Dirk Vandergelt told me Barbara was acting differently to usual last night. Antsy, was the word he used. When was the last time you saw her or talked to her before you found her body?'

'She called on her way to the airport to pick him up. Just a quick touch-base kind of call. In her pursuit of wedding perfection, everything had been planned with military precision. Which is why I was so surprised to hear she'd veered from the schedule.'

'Why would she go to Indian Point?'

'I have no idea. What could possibly be so important that she would put her perfect wedding at risk?'

'The obvious answer is that she was meeting someone.'

Caroline shook her head. 'After the last

three weeks of dealing with Barbara's obsession, I would have bet all in that she wouldn't risk anything getting in the way of her goal.'

'Perhaps something, or someone, threatened to stop the wedding coming off as planned. Anyone upset about the wedding? Anyone pissed off enough to sabotage the event?'

'I presume you mean other than me?' Caroline mentally ran though the not-short list. Three stood out. 'The caterer was on the verge of a nervous breakdown due to Barbara's last-minute changes. The florist claimed she was sending him into bankruptcy with her demands. The baker was hospitalized last week for a stress-induced heart attack and his daughter only agreed to complete the job to avoid a lawsuit.'

'At least that gives me somewhere to start,' Travis said. 'Now I want you to close your eyes and visualize the scene as if it's a movie replaying in your mind. I want you to describe it to me as it happens. Start with when you first came up to her car. What do you see?'

'I already told you all that.'

'Just do it,' Bobby Lee said.

Travis turned to the deputy. 'You are here to witness and to learn.'

'Not to speak. I get it.' He made a locking

motion over his lips.

Travis returned his attention to Caroline. 'Sometimes when you describe something a second time you're less concerned with getting facts across and that frees your brain to remember small details.'

'If you say so.' She closed her eyes and described everything much as she had before. But not like a memorized report, which gave her story more credibility in his mind. 'What happens next?' Travis prompted gently.

'I lean over the windshield trying to get her attention. Her eyes are closed like she's sleeping and . . . omigod — '

'What do you see?'

'Freckles. She wasn't wearing any make-up. Barbara hated her spots, as she called them, and hasn't left the house without full cosmetic coverage since the age of fifteen.'

'So the meeting was of the last-minute, urgent type. Any ideas?'

Caroline shook her head. Additional questions didn't reveal any new facts. She had to look away from the frustration furrowing in his brow as he reread his notes. At the next desk, Bobby Lee was using a laptop to page through pictures from the crime scene. Close-ups of footprints, and dents in the car, and what appeared to be skid marks. A photo of Barbara's corpse flashed on to the screen.

Caroline quickly closed her eyes and turned her head away. Too late. She couldn't get the image out of her head.

Travis stood as soon as he heard her little mewl of distress. 'Turn that off,' he said to Bobby Lee, his voice harsher than he'd intended.

'Huh?' The deputy looked up in surprise, but as soon as he figured out what was going on, he shut the laptop. 'Sorry, sis. I thought you were occupied.'

Caroline shook her head. Then something hit her as out of place. Was she imagining things into the picture? 'Wait. Bring back that photo.'

'That's not necessary,' Travis said.

'I think I saw something,' she said. 'No, evidence.'

Travis motioned for Bobby Lee to open the computer. The picture slide show started over.

Caroline leaned closer to the screen. 'That one! No, no. Back up. Stop.' She stood up straight and said to Travis, 'There is absolute proof Barbara did not dress herself,' she said with a presenting motion of her hand. Ta-dah.

Travis looked closely. 'I don't see whatever it is you're talking about.' He glanced at Bobby Lee, who indicated he didn't see anything either.

She pointed at the screen. 'Those shoes were not white.'

'Well, not now.'

'Not then, either. I recognized that little bow on the heel. Those are her pink spectator pumps,' Caroline finished triumphantly.

'So?'

She rolled her eyes and shook her head. 'Anyone, make that any woman, who knew Barbara could tell you her shoes always matched her outfit. She would never have worn pink and white shoes with her wedding dress, not even for a minute. Plus that dress was specifically designed to wear with Christian Louboutin cut-out peep-toe pumps with four-and-seven-eighths-inch heels.' Caroline had practically drooled with envy when she first saw them. 'If Barbara had walked to the car in those sensibly heeled spectators, her wedding dress would have dragged along the ground. She never would have done that.'

'Marlene could check for dirt residue along the hem of the dress,' Bobby Lee suggested.

'If there were enough left to test,' Travis said. 'Whatever material the dress was made of, it — '

'Tulle lace and silk taffeta.'

' — did not do well in the fire.'

'But surely lab tests can prove the shoes were once partially pink,' she said.

'Probably,' Travis admitted. 'But those results would only prove she didn't wear matching shoes on that particular day. That fact alone isn't enough to convince a judge, much less a jury, that whoever dressed her did it after her death.'

Would be if the judge knew her as well as Caroline did.

'Dee Ann wore cowboy boots to her wedding and Mary Lynn wore red Chucks,' Bobby Lee said in a helpful tone.

'Our dear sisters are not exactly what one would call fashionistas like Barbara was.'

'Well, they always look nice,' Bobby Lee said, raising his chin in a defensive attitude.

'I'm not saying they don't it's just — '

'Can we focus on the case?' Travis asked. He rose and walked around the desk. 'Can you look at all the pictures and tell me if anything else strikes you as significant?' He leaned one hip on the other desk that held the laptop.

Caroline blew out a deep breath. 'I'll try.' She followed Travis's advice and broke each photo into small bits approximately one-inch square. She could almost forget what she was looking at and see each piece as a part of the puzzle. Finally, she sat back. 'It's not what's there that's significant, it's what's missing.'

'Like what?'

'Her large diamond engagement ring, for one.'

Travis nodded. 'Marlene already noted it was missing.'

'Could robbery have been the motive?' Bobby Lee asked.

'Maybe,' Travis said. 'But it seems a bit far-fetched to think someone lured her all the way out there on the morning of her wedding just to steal her ring.'

'It would have to have been a powerful lure for her to miss her hair appointment,' Caroline pointed out to the men who might overlook the huge importance of that fact.

'Robbery gone bad could have led to murder, but a more likely scenario is that the murderer took advantage of the opportunity.'

'A trophy?' Bobby Lee asked, more excited than seemed appropriate considering the circumstances. 'I read serial killers often take something from the body as a remembrance.'

'I think that's jumping to a conclusion without evidence at this point,' Travis said.

'And we don't want to do that,' Caroline cautioned, her tone a tad sarcastic because he'd said the same thing to her earlier. 'When do you come to some conclusions? After I'm on death row? In case you've forgotten, this is my life we're talking about.'

'I am completely aware of the significance of this investigation,' Travis said. 'Our being thorough now is your best chance for complete dismissal of all charges.'

'Then by all means take your time.'

'Did you notice anything else?' he asked.

'Her purse is missing.'

'We found a pile of what were probably items from her purse on the floor of the passenger seat.' He flipped through the file pages to find the list of items that had been bagged as evidence.

'That in itself is an issue. Barbara loved her purse collection and never put them on the floor. If she was driving she put her purse on the passenger seat. If someone was sitting in the seat, she put her purse on the back seat.'

'It could have fallen to the floor when the car went over the cliff,' Bobby Lee said.

'Good point,' Travis said and the deputy practically glowed under his praise.

'I didn't think of that.'

Travis handed her the list of the purse's contents.

'Her date book is missing. She not only kept track of her appointments but noted what she wore each day and details of her activities. Also there is no mention of her checkbook. She didn't always carry it but she was supposed to bring several final payment checks to the rehearsal. What is this?' She turned the paper so Travis could see.

He stepped closer, his arm brushing hers.

She ignored the tingling warmth his touch caused and pointed to one of the last items.

'What is a three-by-eight-inch piece of woven material?'

Travis shrugged. 'It was found with the other purse objects. Photo two-fifty-seven,' he said to Bobby Lee.

After examination, Caroline said, 'I think that's the bottom of a straw purse.' She leaned closer. 'And if this color is accurate, it was once navy and red.' She stood and turned to face Travis. 'Even more . . . '

He'd moved to look over her shoulder and suddenly mere inches separated their bodies, nearly touching in all the right places. Her train of thought left the station without any passengers. Neither spoke for a long moment and then both babbled apologies as they sprang apart.

'Even more what?' Bobby Lee asked, still focused on the computer screen.

'Even more evidence that Barbara didn't choose the clothes she wore because the purse doesn't match the shoes,' Travis said.

Caroline smiled. He'd listened to her and had taken her opinion seriously.

Travis grinned back. He loved her smile and hadn't seen the genuine article in way too long.

The door to the station burst open. A tall woman dressed in cowboy boots, jeans, oversized man's work-shirt, and ten-gallon hat held the door for Mimi and followed her inside.

'Mom?' Caroline said.

'Don't act so surprised,' Jean Tucker said. 'You knew I'd planned to attend the wedding. I just had to leave the ranch a little later than I'd expected.'

'We've been so worried about you,' Mimi said as she put an arm around Caroline's shoulders. 'We came as soon as we could. We had to take care of — '

'I can imagine how bad Rose's fit was if what I saw is any gauge,' Jean said. 'I nipped that in the bud. How dare she accuse you.'

'She was upset,' Caroline and Mimi said in unison.

'And rightly so, I'll give her that. But after a while she should pull herself together. Not that anyone expects her to stop grieving but there are things to be done. I called that silly ex-wife of Chuck's and arranged for the ex-mother-in-law to pick up the children. Have you met her? That acorn didn't fall far from the tree, which gives me pause about those stepchildren. Then I called Doc Dieter and had him give Rose a shot of something to take the edge off her hysteria.'

'How's Rose doing?' Travis asked. 'Is Lou with her?'

'She's holding down the fort at the house until we get back,' Mimi said. 'Rose calmed down and Chuck took her home.'

'Which is what we're going to do with you, young lady,' Jean said. 'Gather up whatever — '

'Just a minute,' Travis said. 'She's under arrest.'

Jean swung her large shoulder bag on to the desk and pulled out a folded sheet of paper. 'I've posted bail. She's free to go.'

'How did you do that?' Caroline said, speaking Travis's thoughts.

'We stopped by Judge McKay's house on the way here,' Mimi explained. 'Interrupted his supper, as a matter of fact.'

'I was told he's convinced she's a flight risk and that he wouldn't set bail,' Travis said.

'She probably is,' Jean admitted.

'Stop talking about me as if I weren't here.'

'But I couldn't not bail her out after all the times I've done this for her brother.'

'This is not the same,' Caroline protested. 'I'm innocent.'

'So what changed the judge's mind?' Travis asked.

'Back to that, are we?' Jean said.

'I never give up.'

'He's like a dog with a bone,' Caroline said, shaking her head. 'Believe me, I know.'

'The judge and I go way back,' Jean said. 'Let's just say we came to a mutual agreement.'

'She put up the ranch,' Mimi said.

'Shh. You weren't supp — '

'Mom! You didn't.' Caroline sat down hard. Her mother had actually put her beloved ranch at risk. For her. Now she absolutely couldn't leave town. She hadn't known how much having the possibility meant. Without that, she was truly stuck.

Caroline appeared wilted. 'Why don't you take her home,' Travis suggested. 'We can go over whatever else we need tomorrow.'

Caroline took her car keys out of her pocket and held them listlessly.

Travis took them from her hand and tossed them to Bobby Lee with instructions to bring her car around to the door. As the deputy left, Dirk Vandergelt entered.

Vandergelt sauntered directly up to the Sheriff and brandished a piece of paper under his nose. 'I have the evidence that clears Caroline and, if she takes my advice, she'll sue you for false arrest.'

'I can't read it if you won't stop waving it around,' Travis said. He took it from Vandergelt's hand and spread it out on the desk. A single printed page.

My dearest love,

I can't go through with the wedding but I also can't bear the thought of living without you. That leaves me only one course of

228

action. I'm so sorry for what I must do. Believe I love you above all else.

Barbara

'After everyone left, I asked Bobby Ray if I could borrow his computer to check my email. I found that note dated this morning at seven a.m.' He shook his head. 'I only wish I'd checked it sooner. I might have prevented Barbara's suicide. At the very least I would have saved Caroline from this unnecessary harassment.'

Travis crossed his arms. He wasn't a computer expert but he did know it wasn't difficult to dummy-up an email. None of the other evidence pointed to a suicide, at least not yet. The email was probably a well-meant but futile attempt to rescue Caroline. He kept his suspicions to himself but wondered why Vandergelt was so interested in her welfare.

He was also solicitous of her as he held out a hand to help her rise and offered to drive her home.

'No, thanks, no one drives my car except me and I don't want to leave it downtown.'

'I'll ride with you,' Jean volunteered. 'Mimi can follow us.'

'I have to stop at the minimart and pick up some eggs and bread,' Mimi said. 'I have a feeling we're going to have a bunch for brunch tomorrow.'

'I'll get those for you,' Vandergelt volunteered.

And they all left with him asking if she needed anything else.

Bobby Lee returned after only a moment of silence. 'What's next, boss?'

'Forward the phones to county dispatch. We're going to Barbara's house.'

★ ★ ★

'Take a break,' Travis said to Harlan. 'Be back here in thirty minutes. And bring plenty of coffee. You're going to have a long night.'

While Travis pondered on the best way to break into the house, Bobby Lee found a spare key under a flowerpot.

Travis wasn't sure what to expect inside. He noted the alarm was not set. He hadn't known Barbara all that well, and had only run into her a few times in the months he'd been home. Even back in high school they'd hung out with different crowds. Barbara had been the cheerleader-honor society-teacher's pet type. In fact, he'd been surprised to learn she hadn't left Haven to move on to bigger and better things. He'd never been in her house before but the overblown Victorian femininity seemed characteristic of her.

'I want pictures of everything,' Travis instructed the deputy.

'Yes, sir.'

Everything was neat and clean, and there were no signs of a struggle. With nothing particular to search for, Travis simply remained open to what the scene wanted to tell him, to anything out of the ordinary. A suitcase by the door containing new clothes of the sort worn at high-priced beach resorts indicated Barbara was prepared for her honeymoon. 'Why would she pack for a trip if she planned to commit suicide?'

'Maybe the suicide was a spur-of-the-moment decision? Or maybe she packed a long time ago. I don't understand why, but my girlfriend Stephanie started packing for a weekend trip to Vegas nearly three weeks before we left.'

'Point taken.'

A garment bag lay open on the sofa. He checked the zippered pockets and found white underwear, slip, stockings and shoes with very high heels; everything for a bride's attire except the wedding dress and veil. This all seemed to support Caroline's claim that Barbara had planned to change into her wedding dress later in the day.

Travis moved on to the kitchen. Spotlessly

clean and with an air of being seldom used. Barbara's voicemail password was posted next to the phone on the kitchen wall. Travis listened to angry, desperate, and pleading messages from the caterer, florist and baker and saved them all.

In the bedroom he found a make-up case larger than a professional fisherman's tackle box sitting open on an overcrowded vanity with a large mirror. Few signs indicated that Vandergelt had ever stayed there. A handful of hangers in an otherwise jammed closet, one small, empty drawer in the dresser, and one barren nightstand showed Vandergelt had packed everything before moving to the hotel for his last night as a bachelor.

Other than his things, nothing appeared to be missing. The jewelry box was overflowing, there were no blank spaces to indicate anything missing off the walls, and all the electronics seemed to be new and to be in place.

'What did you think of Barbara and Vandergelt?' Travis asked Bobby Lee.

'As a couple? They both enjoyed and expected the finer things in life, both were shallow and self-absorbed. Seemed perfectly suited to me.'

'Did Barbara talk about her future?'

'I really didn't hang with them. But I do remember this one dinner Mimi gave in their honor about a month ago. The whole family had to show up with bells on. Barbara and Dirk said they planned to return to Haven after their honeymoon on his yacht but they would only stay in town long enough to sell her house. They'd discussed looking for some property nearby, maybe a small ranch where they could keep a few horses, but for the first year they planned to split their time between his luxury penthouse in Miami and his rustic ten-room cabin just outside Vail. Stephanie was so jealous of Barbara. We nearly split up over that dinner.'

Travis moved on to the spare bedroom Barbara used as an office and to store more clothes. He powered up the computer on the desk. When a password was required, he could neither guess it nor find it written down. He decided to leave it and call in a forensic computer specialist to access her data files and email.

Satisfied he'd learned all he could for the moment, Travis replaced the new CRIME SCENE DO NOT CROSS tape after he and Bobby Lee exited.

'Why do I have to stay here all night?' Harlan whined as Travis passed his deputy's car parked in the driveway.

'Your job is to prevent anyone from taking or damaging anything that might later prove to be evidence in a murder trial.'

'Isn't guarding the victim's house overkill, pardon the pun? Just because your ex — '

'Stop right there before your runaway mouth costs you your job.'

'You can't — '

'Are you willing to risk it?' Travis flashed a cocky grin.

After a long hesitation, Harlan said in a low voice, 'No.'

'Fine. I'll send someone to relieve you at seven.' He turned and walked to his squad car.

'You couldn't really fire him for that, could you?' Bobby Lee asked as he buckled his seat belt.

'Nah. But Harlan thinks I can.'

'You sounded so sure of yourself.'

'If you're running a bluff, you gotta act like you believe your own bull. Any sign of weakness and you'll get called holding trey four off-suit, every gambler knows that.'

'You'd never bluff with a hand that weak, would you?'

'If you're bluffing, what do the cards matter?'

11

'You didn't have to do that,' Caroline said to her mother as soon as the car moved out of the parking space.

'Did you want to spend the night in jail because I could — '

'No, of course not. But to put up the ranch . . . '

'Oh, that. Well, don't be getting all misty-eyed. I didn't exactly bet the ranch.'

'But Mimi said — '

'What I told her to say, and that has to remain what everyone believes. But I've never lied to my kids and I'm not about to start now. Judge McKay set bail for you because I called in a favor he's owed me for close to thirty years. The whole bet-the-ranch bit is what we came up with to explain his change of mind. Everyone knows he's coveted my ranch from day one.'

'So you won't lose it, if I take off?'

'Don't be getting any ideas. If you light a shuck the devil will be paid his due. McKay would manage to take something, make no mistake. Maybe Mimi's house. Maybe the lake property. Oh, not straight up but he'd figure a way. He's a powerful man. The shark in a peaceful goldfish bowl.'

'Then I'm truly stuck here.'

'Yep.'

'That must have been one helluva favor you called in,' Caroline said as she pulled into the driveway.

'A real humdinger,' Jean admitted. 'I won't lie to you and say it wasn't.' She picked up her purse and rested her hand on the door handle. 'But I will tell you this . . . '

Caroline turned in her seat and faced her mother. 'Yes?'

'It's absolutely none of your business,' Jean said. She exited and the car door clicked shut before Caroline's jaw hit her chest.

Mimi pulled into the drive and parked her car behind Caroline's. As they walked up to the house together, another car arrived. Then she remembered Mimi had asked Dirk to bring something from the store. He bounded up the walk with a grocery sack in one arm and his suitcase in the other hand.

'What's with the luggage?' Caroline asked in a low voice.

'I couldn't let the dear distraught boy stay at a cold lonely hotel when we have an unused guest room, now could I? You'll learn to like him when you know him better.'

Before Caroline could think of a rational

reason why he could and should stay in a hotel rather than in the room across the hall from her, he entered the house just steps behind her.

'Where should I put these?' he asked, apparently meaning both his burdens.

'I'm going to take something for my head-ache and probably lie down,' she said to Mimi. She was halfway up the stairs before Mimi gave Dirk directions and he started up with his suitcase. Caroline practically ran down the hall, and as soon as she shut her door, she flipped the old-fashioned key in the lock.

Even though the evening was still young she flopped back on her bed. Too emotionally drained to get herself moving and too keyed up to sleep she just stared at the ceiling and thought about taking a long hot shower and changing her clothes.

The slight noise of her door handle moving startled her. She levered herself up on one elbow and watched it turn to the left and then to the right.

'It's locked for a reason,' she said. 'I'm resting.' It was a lie but she didn't want to deal with family just yet.

'Oh, Caroline, is that you? I guess I have the wrong door.'

Really? Caroline had heard Mimi's direc-tions and 'door on your left at the top of the stairs' seemed a copper-riveted cinch. She stood up. 'Your other left,' she called through the door.

'As long as you're awake, I could really use someone to talk to,' he said.

She couldn't think of anything she'd rather do less. 'You should really talk to Mimi or . . . or Bobby Ray! Yes! Bobby Ray took Internet courses on counseling while he was incarcerated. Including grief counseling. He's the perfect person for you to talk to.'

'It's just that you're such a good listener.'

Since when? She was a party of one when it came to shying away from Dirk and she couldn't even give a concrete reason other than her gut said not to trust him. She didn't want to spend any more time around him than necessary and absolutely no time whatsoever alone with him. Was she totally missing the mark and everyone else was right about him? She shook her head. 'Sorry. I'm exhausted and in for the night. Try Bobby Ray's door.'

His footsteps indicated he went into the room across the hall, and she moved the chair from her dressing table and wedged it under the doorknob. After she took her shower she was able to fall into a restless sleep until a dream jolted her awake. Breathless, her heart pounded as if she'd been running, trying to escape. She flipped her pillow over to the cool side and closed her eyes.

Voices from the patio drifted up through her open window. She recognized Mimi, Lou, and Jean's voices dissecting every aspect of the horrendous day.

'Evening, ladies.'

Caroline recognized Travis's voice instantly.

'You riding night hawk?' Jean asked. 'Got a fresh pot of Arbuckle inside.'

He wouldn't have minded sitting a spell in good company but his deputies needed breaks and he still had to get back to Marlene. 'Thank you, ma'am, but I have to decline. I'm just here to walk my best girl home.'

'Helluva day today,' Lou said. 'We've just been catching Jean up on everything that's happened.'

Travis wasn't about to fall for her obvious bid to get him involved in a conversation and thus delay her bedtime.

Mimi shook her head. 'Another murder. Unbelievable.'

'Why did you arrest my daughter?' Jean asked.

'I didn't have a choice,' he explained, not giving away any secrets because the entire story would be all over town before breakfast. 'Right now, jumping to conclusions is the worst thing anyone can do, as our esteemed town council has proved.'

'But you don't believe she's guilty?'

'Of course not. Now I just have to prove it.'

Jean leaned back in her chair and gave him the once over. 'I always said you were no more than a curried wolf, but I think you'll do just fine. My daughter's fate is in good hands.'

High above the patio, Caroline smiled at her mother's words. She turned over and smoothed the pillow under her cheek. Travis believed she was innocent. For the first time in hours she breathed easy.

★   ★   ★

When Caroline went downstairs the next morning her mother was cooking breakfast for Bobby Ray and another man.

'Hungry?' Jean asked. 'I've got hot rocks with sausage gravy, hen fruit to order, and brown gargle.'

'I'll take some coffee but pass on the eggs.' She took her cup and stumbled to the table in the alcove. The stranger made to stand but she waved him back to his seat. She inhaled the aroma from her cup and closed her eyes for a moment, letting the morning sunshine warm her shoulders.

'We've been waiting for you,' Bobby Ray

said. 'When you're awake, I'd like to introduce my friend Joe Strager, Junior.'

Caroline took a long swig from her cup and then held out her free hand. 'Nice to meet you, Mr Strager.'

'You can call me Junior,' the large man with a shaved head and lots of tattoos said. Despite looking as if he belonged to a motorcycle gang he had a nice smile. 'I'm one of Brother Ray's flock of ex-cons.'

'Junior was incarcerated for hacking into the Government's computers to get information on Area fifty-one,' Bobby Ray said.

'You mean the supposed aliens?' Caroline asked.

'Nothing supposed about them.' He looked around as if G-men were hiding behind the fridge or in the broom closet. 'I could tell you things — '

'But we'll do that some other time,' Bobby Ray said. 'Remember we have important information that takes precedence.'

Jean sat down next to her daughter. 'The boys wanted to help you prove your innocence.'

'That's sweet, but — '

'Wait until you hear what we found,' Bobby Ray said.

'Drum roll, please,' Junior said. 'Most computers have an automatic security auditing function that keeps a log of sign-ins within the operating system. By accessing the event log of Barbara's computer, we could tell — '

'You did what?' Caroline turned to Bobby Ray. 'Ohmigod, I can't believe you busted into her house and — '

'Relax, sis. We didn't steal anything.'

'It's still breaking and entering. You're on probation. Hello? Another conviction and you could be sent away for half your life.'

'Actually, a simple B and E would fetch three or four years, certainly no more than fifteen.'

'That is not the point. You're supposed to be reformed.'

'I am. This wasn't a job, I was trying to help you.'

'Yeah, tell that to a judge.'

'Like it would ever get that far. Come on. Harlan Keyes was parked in the driveway guarding the place. If we'd been carrying a party sack of Krystal burgers he might have noticed us.'

Even though her stomach growled at the thought of the small soft burgers that she hadn't tasted since the last time she was in Fort Worth, she was not letting a hankering for grilled onions sidetrack her. 'Again, not the point,' Caroline said. 'Mom, you could jump into this conversation any time.'

'Bobby Ray is old enough to make his own decisions and reap any consequences.'

'I know you're not used to listening to the family screw-up,' Bobby Ray said, 'but I have talents, resources, and information. For instance, did you know her big flashy engagement ring is a fake? And not even one of the best quality imitations.'

'And you can tell that how? By looking at it? Because I can't imagine Barbara handing her diamond ring over to a paroled thief so he can look at it under a jeweler's glass.'

Bobby Ray placed his hand over his heart and pasted a sad expression on his face. 'You wound me.'

'Sorry. I guess I don't know the politically correct terminology for someone who steals other people's jewels.'

'Thief is fine. No, I can't believe you're questioning my ability. There are ways to determine if a diamond is genuine even if the jewel never leaves the hand in question. Besides visual clues there's the breath test. Easy enough to do if you're looking closely at the ring. If you breathe on the surface of the stone, quartz, glass, and cubic zirconium will stay hazy for a moment before the condensation dissipates. Diamonds are good at heat conducting. You shouldn't be able to see any moisture on a real diamond. However, one rock, called moissanite will pass this test, so — '

'I should not have doubted you. My apologies.' Caroline emptied her cup and stood up. 'Now, if you'll excuse me — '

'Sit down,' Jean said. 'I think you should listen to what your brother has to say.'

'It's not that I don't appreciate his offer to help, but it's no longer necessary. Dirk gave Travis the suicide note he received from Barbara via email. So the charges will be dropped.'

Bobby Ray and Junior exchanged looks.

'I'm afraid not,' her brother said.

Junior opened his laptop. 'When the cops verify that email was truly sent from her computer, they're going to find out it's a fake.' He turned the screen so she could see for herself. 'This is a copy of Barbara's event log. Someone logged on to her computer at five fifty-four last night. That person, obviously not Barbara, reset the system clock to six fifty-four a.m. Then approximately fifteen minutes later, plenty of time to type and send an email, the clock is reset back to the correct time. See here at five minutes after seven a.m. and then the time becomes five after six p.m.'

'Why would someone do that?'

'The logical conclusion,' Jean said, 'is that

244

someone who wanted to help you manufactured the note and sent it to Dirk.'

She looked at Bobby Ray.

'Not me. I don't even know enough to bypass a password request.'

Caroline turned to Junior.

'I could have, but I didn't,' he said. 'Passwords are only protection against honest people, computer neophytes or children, and not all of them. If you're interested in protecting your computer, I'll give you the names of several good security programs but, remember, no program is completely tamper proof.'

'We're telling you about the time change because we think you should make Travis aware of the evidence in such a way that he won't feel obligated to arrest either of us and so he can obtain the information legally so that it can be used in court,' Bobby Ray said.

'Knowing Barbara as you did, you never believed she committed suicide, did you?' Jean asked.

Caroline sighed. 'No, but the suicide note is keeping me *out* of jail.'

'Refuting the note may harm your case, but since you were in custody at the time the changes were made, it proves someone else wrote the suicide note,' Junior pointed out.

'Poor Aunt Rose. From murder to suicide

and now back to murder? Who would do such a terrible thing?'

'Obviously someone who knew Dirk's email address,' Jean pointed out.

Caroline shook her head. 'That would be the entire town. He's been passing out business cards to everyone. As if Mr Lopez who has the taco stand on First Street needs an investment banker.'

'I'm ashamed to hear you say something like that. Don't be in such a hurry to judge by appearances. Cesar Ramirez happens to be an astute businessman. It wouldn't surprise me to hear he'd made his first million. And his business isn't likely to fail like someone's we both know.'

'You're right. I don't know the first thing about Mr Ramirez's finances. And I shouldn't make judgments based on appearances.'

'Can we get back to the point? There is still a real murderer out there,' Bobby Ray added. 'Caroline might be in danger. I think the note should be taken as a warning that she should be more careful. Maybe she should be in protective custody.'

'All the note proves is that someone wanted to help me.' And she wasn't convinced that person wasn't her brother.

'Can't they backtrack the email from Dirk's computer?' Jean asked.

'Even if he would volunteer his computer, we already know it came from Barbara's computer,' Bobby Ray said. 'Verifying the time received would prove nothing, even if it shows after six p.m., because the email provider isn't going to open its records to trace the routing.'

'I could hack in,' Junior volunteered.

'No!' Caroline said. 'I don't want you to put yourself at risk for me.'

'Not worth the trouble,' Bobby Ray added. 'Won't tell us anything we don't already surmise.'

'Thanks for your efforts but I want both of you to promise that you won't do anything illegal, not even if you think it might save me. I already have enough to worry about.'

Junior nodded.

After a long moment of hesitation, Bobby Ray also agreed. 'I'll start a prayer chain for you.'

'Thank you.' She had a strange feeling she was going to need all the help she could get.

★ ★ ★

Travis pulled up to Barbara's house at seven-fifty, a good ten minutes before the arranged meeting time with the forensic computer expert he'd requisitioned from the State Police Headquarters in Santa Fe. He dismissed Harlan for

247

the day and unlocked the door of the house. When Dolly DuPree parked in the drive, Travis hid his disappointment behind a welcoming smile.

'I'm pleased you could get here so soon,' Travis said after opening her car door. 'Frankly, I was surprised to get the message that someone could be here this quickly.'

'Oh, honey, you are just the luckiest man alive. I was already scheduled to drive to Las Cruces so I volunteered to stop off here.' She got out and juggled her coffee mug to look at her watch. 'I made good time. Less than three hours.'

He didn't know what to say to that. She must have been doing ninety-five on the highway.

'Guess you haven't had a chance to get back to the capital since we had drinks at the Law Enforcement Conference last spring.'

She made it sound as if they'd had a date when in truth it had been a group of people getting together after the last seminar of the day. The brief contact had been nothing more than the usual networking done at such events, but her resulting emails had intimated much more could happen between them. He hadn't answered any of them. 'I've been busier than a long-tailed cat in a room full of rocking chairs.'

'I understand. I haven't had three days in a

row off in months. That's why I'm thrilled that I don't have to be in Las Cruces until Wednesday.'

Travis let the hint fall like a stone boot. He led Dolly into the victim's bedroom.

'Nice bed,' she said, looking up at him from under her eyebrows with what she obviously thought was a seductive expression.

He was not interested in the least. He didn't even blink in response.

She straightened her shoulders and cleared her throat. 'If you're into the frilly canopied Victorian lace sort of thing,' she said. 'Which I'm not.'

Travis pointed to Barbara's computer. 'While you do your thing, I'm going to continue my investigation. You know the first forty-eight hours are crucial.'

'Indeed, I do. After that, evidence gets corrupted, memories fade. You go ahead. I'll be right here if you need me.'

'Uh, thanks.' He gave her a sort of half-wave, half-smile, and half-nod before he fled the room.

He walked outside and took a deep breath. Another hour and the desert would start heating up but for now the remnants of the night still cooled the air. He spotted a young man wearing a black shirt with white stripes and a black baseball cap exiting the house catty-corner across the street. Travis waved him down and jogged over.

'Morning, Sheriff,' the boy said.

After establishing his name was Eugene Vale and that he lived in the house with his parents, and worked weekends at the Burger Stop, Travis asked, 'Did you leave for work around this time yesterday?'

'Yeah, this is my middle-shift weekend. The schedule rotates. Last weekend was late shift. Next week I start at six a.m. Man, I hate making breakfast.'

'Did you see any activity at Ms Jennings's house recently?' He pointed across the street.

'I heard about the suicide.' He shook his head. 'Course I didn't know her that well, even though I used to mow her lawn when I was a kid. Ma said that shows you just never know what goes on behind closed doors. She seemed to have everything a woman could want and she still wasn't happy.'

'Did you notice anything yesterday morning?'

'I saw the Porsche. Carmona Red 911 Carrera 4S. Have you seen that car?'

'Yes, I — '

'Man, talk about a sweet ride. Zero to sixty in four point five seconds. Three hundred and eighty-five horse power. Top track speed one eighty-five.'

'Who was driving?'

'The old guy, I guess. You know, the blond city dude. He's the only person that ever drives it. Like I would piss in my pants if he offered me a chance to drive it.'

Which might be why an offer was never made.

'Did you see Ms Jennings leave? She drives — '

'That pink abomination. I know. I'd rather drive my POS than that thing. Didn't see it yesterday. You know, if I had a Porsche like that, I could ask Maiya Palmasano to the Homecoming Dance and I bet she'd say yes. Did you notice that the air intakes on the front end have been enlarged? They say it's to increase the cooling power but I think it just makes the grill even more kickass.'

'Well, I don't want to make you late to work.'

After sending the kid on his way, Travis mulled over what he'd learned. The boy's answers made it likely that Vandergelt was in the area around eight-fifteen just as he said he was.

Travis started back across the street.

'Yoo-hoo! Sheriff!'

Travis turned to see an elderly woman shuffling in her worn sandals with rapid baby steps down the sidewalk of the house next

251

to the Vales'. 'Hold up,' he called. 'I'll come to you.'

The woman stopped with a visible sigh. She took his arm and as they walked slowly to her front porch she introduced herself as Mrs Alberta Tacket, widow, retired fifth-grade teacher.

'Would you like a cup of coffee? A glass of sweet tea?'

'No, thank you, ma'am, but please serve yourself.'

She settled on to a red-and-white-striped lawn chair and smoothed the skirt of her hot-pink, caution-yellow, and fire-engine-red housedress over her skinny knees. Even though Lou had several similar dresses she would never have been caught outside in one. To Mrs Tacket's credit she hadn't planned to be entertaining the Sheriff that morning.

'I saw you questioning young Eugene, and I thought you might be interested in what I saw.' She sniffed. 'Not that I owe Ms Jennings anything, but I want to do my civic duty. I did see her pulling out of the driveway yesterday morning wearing her wedding finery.'

'What time was that?'

'I was out getting my newspaper. You'd think they could throw it up on the porch like I've asked them to do a thousand times, but they just drop it at the end of the driveway. I always get the paper as soon as I get up. Every day at seven just like clockwork. Well, right after I take care of my personal business and start the coffee. Maybe after I eat a bite of breakfast because I'm diabetic and I get shaky if I wait too long. But definitely before I turn on the television at nine.'

'So, sometime between seven and nine you saw Ms Jennings leave her house and get in her car.'

'Oh no, I just saw her driving away. I, of course, gave her a neighborly wave, but she turned her face so she didn't have to return the friendly gesture. Ashamed, I suppose, that she didn't invite me to the wedding, even though we've lived across the street from each other for more than six years.'

Travis stood. 'Well, thank you. I appreciate your information.'

'Shame you have to leave so soon. I'd thought you might be interested in the veritable parade of angry people coming and going on Friday evening.'

12

Travis resumed his seat on Ms Tacket's front porch. 'Perhaps I'll have that cup of coffee after all, if it isn't too much trouble.'

She grinned. 'I'll be right back.' She scurried into the house and returned carrying a blue plastic tray. She handed him a steaming mug and offered a plate of small chocolate-covered doughnuts. He took one to be polite and quickly regretted it. She must have been saving the doughnuts for potential guests for quite some time. He choked it down, took a big gulp of coffee and nearly gagged.

'I know cops like strong coffee, so I added an extra spoonful of instant powder.'

Travis could only nod and blink.

'After supper on Friday night, I heard squealing tires and thought it was young Eugene again. But all I saw was the van from Bennett's careening down the street. I remember thinking it was an unusual time for a floral delivery, due to the lateness of the hour. I like to eat my supper while I watch television and reruns of *NCIS* were on.' She stifled a girlish giggle with her hand. 'I just love that Jethro Gibbs.'

'But you're sure it was the florist's van?'

'Hard to mistake a lavender van with flowers painted all over it.'

'I suppose so.'

'Not too long after that, maybe half an hour or so, I happened to glance out the door again and saw a different van pull into the drive. Plain white, the kind that doesn't have any windows. A man in a white coat went into the house but only stayed a short time. As he left, I noticed he dabbed at his eyes with a large bandanna.' She crossed her arms and leaned forward in her chair. 'I don't think he had allergies, if you get my drift.'

'Can you describe the man?'

'Not really. Just normal. Nothing distinctive. Except . . . I remember wondering if he was drunk and then dismissing that. I think he had a limp — not pronounced, but just enough to make the rhythm of his gait uneven.'

Sounded like Lewis Warner. He had just opened a catering business out of his family restaurant. Lewis had been injured in high school football and his knee could well be acting up. Travis made a note to check with Phyllis or Lou, either one would know.

'Then, it must have been quite late, because the news was on, a young girl with blue and orange stripes in her hair arrived. She didn't go into the house, but she did have words with Barbara while standing in the drive. I had opened my door to catch a breeze and couldn't help but notice them. I couldn't hear what the argument was about but the tone was definitely angry.'

'Anything else about the girl?'

'Young. Maybe Eugene's age. Slight build.'

'Did you recognize her?'

'I don't know her name but I think I've seen her working in the bakery downtown.'

'What was the make and model of her car? Color? Did you happen to get the license-plate number?'

'It was quite dark by then and I don't know anything about cars. It might have been black or navy or even dark gray. I didn't get the impression that it was new. And it seemed like she'd borrowed her parents' car to run her errand, but I don't have any facts to back up that feeling.'

Half a dozen more questions failed to reveal any new information. He stood. 'I certainly do thank you for your cooperation.'

'Are you going to have your deputy sleep over again? I couldn't exactly miss the squad car parked in the drive.'

'I'm not sure. I think that depends on what we find today.'

'Is that blonde you brought a CSI?' Her eyes lit up when she asked the question.

'We don't have a crime scene unit like they do on TV.' But Travis didn't want her to carry stories to the proverbial gossip fence. He glanced right and left as if to make sure he wouldn't be overheard. 'You'll have to keep this to yourself until the investigation is over, but she's a forensics computer expert from Santa Fe.'

'Mum's the word.'

He took out a business card and handed it to her. 'Call my office if you think of anything else or if you notice any suspicious activity across the street.'

She gave him an assessing stare. 'I'm thinking this isn't the usual investigation for a suicide.' She scooted forward in her seat. 'Do you think she was murdered for something in her house and the perp will return and break in to get it?'

Another one who watched too many cop shows. He put his finger to his lips. 'You know I can't divulge any information about an ongoing investigation. I'm trusting you to maintain silence until we're through.'

She made a little twist-the-key-in-the-lock motion over her lips. Her eyes sparkled with excitement.

* ★ ★

Travis returned to Barbara's house and decided not to bother posting a deputy there during the day. Mrs Tacket would be an efficient lookout, probably better than Harlan, who had apparently slept through his watch.

At least now he had suspects. Although anxious to find and interview the caterer, florist, and a young girl who was most likely the baker's daughter, he didn't want to rush the computer expert. Travis paced the curving driveway to the back of Barbara's house to see if any neighbors could see the garage entrance. The gravel alley behind the property, used by trash collectors and children on bicycles, was lined with fast-growing cottonwoods. The low-limbed trees effectively blocked the view, and six-foot tall hedges between the yards gave almost complete privacy. Good for users of the hot tub, bad for investigators looking for witnesses.

His cell phone rang with a call from Marlene. 'Whatcha got?'

'Hello, to you, too. I'm fine, thank you very much. Tired, after working most of the night on lab tests for your investigation.'

'And more than a little cranky.'

'Is that the pot calling the kettle black?'

'Sorry. Glad you're fine. Appreciate your

efforts. Whatcha got?'

The coroner sighed. 'I faxed a complete report to your office and a copy to the lab in Santa Fe. Barbara died prior to the fire and prior to the crash. Cause of death was asphyxiation. Time of death was between seven and nine with a margin of error of two hours.'

'Great. That makes it between five o'clock and nine-thirty when the body was found. Four and a half hours is a big window of opportunity.'

'Best I could do with the tools I have. I forgot to bring my crystal ball to work today.'

'Hey, Marlene. I really do appreciate you.'

'I know. I can't help teasing you because you're always so dang serious. You gotta lighten up or this job is gonna kill you. By the way, the family is asking when the body will be released. I don't have any more tests to run. What do you think?'

'Your call, but I don't see reason for further delay.'

'Okay, I'll let the boys upstairs know.'

'Later.'

He flipped his cell shut and spoke before turning around. 'Didn't anyone ever tell you it's not a good idea to sneak up on a cop?'

'I wasn't *sneaking*,' Dolly said in a defensive tone. 'I was being courteous by not interrupting your call.'

'Were you able to figure out the password?'

'Didn't bother trying.' She handed him a stack of papers. 'By using my forensic software I was able to bypass her password. I printed out the last two weeks of system records and emails both sent and received, at least the ones that didn't pertain to online shopping because there were hundreds of those. I put the store-related emails relating to purchases on a CD.'

Travis flipped through the pages and realized he would need to invest several hours in reading them. 'Did anything strike you as unusual?'

She blinked. 'Do you mean other than the massive online shopping?'

'Is that unusual?'

'Depends. What was her career? Did she work in the fashion industry?'

'She was a court stenographer.'

'There's no transcribing equipment in the home.'

'She had an office in the courthouse.'

'That means she was probably salaried. I don't know off the top of my head what salary a court stenographer makes, but there is so much that is out of sync here.'

'Like what?'

'Why don't we discuss this over an early

lunch? It's been hours since I had breakfast on the road.'

That actually made sense and he would have taken her up on it except for the fact that she twisted a lock of hair round her finger while she made the suggestion. And he was definitely not interested in more than a working lunch. 'I think we should stay here so I can see whatever it is you're talking about.'

'Fine.' She stomped toward the door and he sauntered after her.

'The house itself is appropriate for a white-collar, civil-service-type worker,' she said beginning the tour in the living room. 'Three bedrooms, one and a half baths, hardwood floors, updated kitchen and mature landscaping in a quiet, well-kept neighbor-hood. The furnishings are tasteful and of decent quality. But then here and there are the unexpected luxuries, a Tiffany sterling silver tea set on a side table in the living room, restaurant-quality cappuccino machine in the kitchen, and antique ormolu clock in the bedroom. Outside there's the spa that looks new and a Trek bicycle — now that's a real top-of-the-line piece of sports equip-ment.'

'To me that only suggests she received some expensive gifts. Not unusual, consider-ing her fiancé is wealthy.'

'The real question is in the clothes and shoes. That's why I asked if she worked in the fashion industry. Designer labels do not come cheap. And based on the spare room that functioned as a huge closet and her purchases online, she most likely had a monster creditcard bill. I counted fifty-two pairs of shoes, name brands that cost an average of six hundred dollars a pair.'

'Who would pay that much for shoes?' He was astounded.

'Not me, but apparently Barbara did.'

'That's more than thirty thousand dollars all told. For shoes?' He shook his head. Now he understood why the old country song advised keeping your woman barefoot. 'That's . . . that has rendered me speechless.'

'There are more than twenty handbags, all the big names. And they're not knock-offs. I checked.'

'How could you tell?'

'Each designer has something. For instance, a genuine Chanel will have a numbered tag with a hologram that can be registered.' She held up a pink leather bag with back-to-back twin Cs on the side. 'One of this size costs over a thousand.'

'Dollars? For a purse?'

'You really had no idea?'

'If there is one area where I'm completely

lost, fashion is definitely it.'

'I'll let you find out on your own what the clothes cost. I'm sure you'll enjoy reading those store charges. I'd say this was a woman living way beyond her means. What kind of car did she drive?'

'A new Mercedes.' Maybe he should rethink the situation. 'If Barbara was deeply in debt, that might be a motive for suicide.'

'Ah, about that suicide note.' She explained what she'd discovered in the system's event log. 'Someone changed the system clock, wrote the note and then changed the clock back. Someone other than Barbara wrote that note.'

'The question is why?'

'My guess is that whoever it was, killed Barbara before pushing her car — '

'Where did you get that information?'

'I checked in with your deputy before meeting you here. As I was saying, that person must have felt guilty for involving an innocent party and tried to fix things by writing the suicide note so she would go free.'

'That's an interesting interpretation.' But he didn't agree. Whoever it was that went to the trouble to fake a suicide note didn't break in to Barbara's house with altruistic motives.

Dolly packed up her briefcase and they headed out the door. 'I've made copies of the hard drive and I'll send you a copy of my full analysis,' she said. 'Probably in three weeks or so.'

'Thank you. I appreciate your input.' Travis turned and locked the door behind them.

'Are you sure I can't interest you in lunch? I'm buying.'

'Thanks for the offer, but I have to decline.'

'Well, call me if there's anything else I can do for you. In the meantime, you should suggest to the family that they have an appraiser come in before they dispose of her personal belongings.'

He tipped his hat as Dolly drove away.

Barbara had lived pretty high on the hog for a court stenographer, and Travis mentally kicked himself for not noticing earlier. He'd give Barbara's financial papers a closer look after talking to his three suspects. Lewis Warner, the caterer, and Paul Bennett, the florist, both lived in town. Had Barbara used the local bakery? He would have to call Caroline to find out the name of the baker and whether or not he had a young daughter with a punk hairstyle. Maybe he should stop by and see how Caroline was doing.

He checked his watch. If he hurried he could beat the Sunday-morning rush.

He got to Maybelle's Diner and was sixth in line. Not the line to be seated at a table.

That line had one person in it. A separate line for Victory Cinnamon Rolls made by Maybelle herself. Age ninety-four and still baking her specialty, as she'd done every weekend since the end of WWII. Five minutes later, twelve people had lined up behind him. The place was busier than fifty cent beer night at a cowboy bar.

'Morning, Ms Maybelle,' he said as he stepped forward in turn.

She gave him a bright smile. 'Morning, Sheriff. Your usual?' she asked as she broke off one large roll and started to put it in a white bag.

'Actually, I'd like a six-pack this morning.'

'Oh? I seem to remember Lou's birthday isn't until November. What's the occasion?'

'Grandma!' Susan talked while she quickly folded a piece of thin white cardboard into a flat, square box and slid it to within her grandmother's reach. 'We don't pry into a customer's personal business.'

'Maybe you don't, but I do. It's the main reason I'm still doing this,' Maybelle said.

Susan tutted and walked to the other end of the counter to pour fresh coffee for the single remaining breakfast customer.

'She gets a little testy on Sunday mornings,' Maybelle confided. 'Not only does she think I take away all her business, but I leave a terrible mess in the kitchen.'

'I'm glad you do,' Travis said. 'Wouldn't be Sunday without your cinnamon rolls.'

'Or a special day?' Maybelle was obviously fishing for information and not about to stop until she'd landed a decent catch.

'No special day. It's a peace offering.'

'You and Caroline have a lover's quarrel already? She's only been back in town a few weeks. What did you do? Get drunk? Look at another woman? Get drunk *and* look at another woman?'

'You do remember we're not a couple any longer, don't you? We haven't dated since high school.'

'All I know is that you never bought cinnamon rolls for anyone except Lou and Caroline. And these aren't on Lou's diet.'

Travis heard the crowd behind him shuffling their feet with impatience at the delay, but Maybelle stood there with an expectant smile on her face, ready to exchange his captive box of rolls for a juicy tidbit of gossip. Not that he would be revealing a secret or anything. The news was probably in the morning paper. He leaned forward. 'I arrested her last night,' he said in a low voice.

'I heard the Mayor was pushing for an arrest. Can't imagine why he'd think dear

266

Caroline could do such a heinous thing. But that must have put you between a rock and a hard place,' Maybelle said with a worried frown. 'Handcuffs may get a woman's attention but it's not the best way to rekindle a lost love.'

'Caroline and I are just friends. No, not even that. Acquaintances, neighbors. And I was only doing my job.'

'So why the sweet apology?'

'Not an — heck, I suppose it is an apology. And a little grease for the wheels. I need some information from her.'

'Well, here are your rolls. I'll pray for the two of you to find your way back to each other.'

Arguing with her was futile but he had to try a parting shot. 'Thank you, but I'm not looking for romance. I'd prefer you pray that I find the real murderer.'

Before he or she killed again. Even though the MO of the fourth murder wasn't the same as the other three, Travis couldn't dismiss a gut feeling that they were somehow related.

13

Dear Frustrated,

Caroline erased that.

Dear Angry,

She jabbed at the delete key. How could she concentrate on answering letters about wedding problems? She flipped through the letters the editor had forwarded to her. Seating dilemma, jealous best friend, groom's ex bringing his children, they all seemed so inconsequential compared to what had happened to Barbara on her big day.

But *Weddings! Weddings!* paid by the word and her car payment had the annoying habit of coming due every month. She was barely making ends meet with her freelance articles and couldn't afford to lose a steady gig.

With a shake of her head, she tossed the letters on to the table and leaned back in her chair. Morning sunshine dappled through the grape-leaf-covered roof and warmed her face. At least sitting on the patio was more pleasant than being imprisoned in an office. She reached out to shut her laptop but paused. If she was too preoccupied to write about their problems, perhaps she should write about what was on her mind.

Dear Confused,

When a wedding doesn't take place, the gifts should be returned to the givers. The reason for the cancellation is not relevant. The gift was given in celebration of a wedding, not finding your muse, or coming out of the closet, or being abducted by aliens, and the specific occasion didn't happen. Return the gift. Even if you really like it. Even if you really need it.

Please don't ask the giver if they want their gift back because that rudely puts them in an untenable position. What is a person supposed to say to a question like that? Just send the gift back. Include a nice note. You don't have to go into the reason why the event was cancelled, simply thank them and express regret for the short notice.

If you are in the awkward position of already having used the gift (see, your mother was right when she said you should wait until after the ceremony), then you

269

must replace it with a brand-new exact replica so the giver is unaware of your faux pas.

Although sooner is better in the matter, a reasonably generous return window is three or four weeks.

A cancelled wedding is bound to be a topic of gossip for some time. Don't add to your notoriety by mishandling the return of the gifts.

Yours truly,

Mrs Bea Correct

Caroline emailed the letter to the editor and closed her laptop. She still had a deadline for the three-part series on the gold mine legends for *Southwestern History* magazine, and a fifteen-hundred-word article on medicinal desert plants for *Survivalist Gardener* due at the end of next month, but she still had more research to do on those topics.

She was just thinking about going in for fresh coffee when her mother came outside with the pot.

'Looks like a good time for a break,' Jean said.

'Oh, I'm done for the day.'

'Nice hours.' She filled her daughter's cup

and one for herself before taking a seat across the table.

'And the office is fabulous. The pay, not so much.'

'What are your plans now that your business is defunct?'

'Horrible word. I'd rather think of Caroline's Weddings as being on hold.'

'So, you're planning on restarting your business. Back in LA? Or are you thinking of staying in Haven?'

'I'm not sure about LA, but I'm definitely not staying here permanently. I figured on a nice long visit — '

'What exactly does that mean? A week? Two? That would be a really long visit for you, but Mimi seems to think you'll be here longer than that. She mentioned three to four months. Is there something you're not telling me?'

The question itself told her two things. Mimi had less time than she'd said and Jean didn't know anything about her illness. Not only was Caroline unwilling to break a confidence, she didn't want to be the one to tell her. So she just shrugged. 'I needed to get away from it all for a while. I can survive by writing freelance articles, so I guess a couple of months here is a good time frame.'

'I suppose that making your ends meet

includes staying with Mimi and sponging off her good will?'

'She likes having me as her guest.'

'For the first week. The second week a guest becomes a nuisance. The third they're a freeloading pain in the ass.'

'But Bobby Ray and Bobby Lee live here.' Caroline's voice sounded defensive and whiny even though she'd only meant to state a fact.

'At my request. I worried about your grandmother living alone, but she's so stubborn. She finally agreed to take the boys in when she believed they needed a place to stay. They pay her a token rent and do a whole list of chores to help out. Who do you think mows the lawn every week? Who do you suppose painted the house last spring?'

'So what do you want me to do? Re-roof the garage?'

'Don't get smart, and that's already been done.' She paused for a sip of coffee. 'I'm not trying to tell you how to run your life . . . '

Since when? 'Heaven forbid.'

'But being on your own was always important to you. Why, I remember you couldn't wait to move out. Said you hated a crowded house like this.'

'It's not so bad. I'm glad to have the chance to spend some time with Mimi. And you, of course.'

'Right. All I'm asking is for you to think about the situation. I'm sure you'll come up with a solution that will make everyone happy.'

'Maybe I'll move out to the ranch and live with you.'

'Hah! There's an idle promise.'

'Or a threat.'

'You'd hate being so isolated. Wouldn't last a week. Although since they paved the road, the trip into town isn't as bad as it used to be. Only two hours.'

'If you call two cowboy bars, a gas station, and a laundromat a town.'

'Besides, I've redecorated your old room and your sisters' rooms — yours is now a combination home gym and sewing room.'

Her room? Not that she'd expected a shrine to her childhood but at the same time it never occurred to her the room wouldn't be available if she needed it.

'What did Dee Ann and Mary Lynn say?' Her sisters had been much more attached to their rooms than she was. 'I'll bet they were fit to be tied.'

'They didn't mind so much, now they no longer live here, and they thought the idea for yours was wonderful. Helped me clean it out and fix it up last Labor Day weekend. We had a great time.'

'Oh.' That brought up a different issue. 'I, ah, left some stuff . . . '

'Anything that was yours, we boxed up and stored in the attic until you have a chance to sort through it. You'll probably throw most of it away like your sisters did their old stuff, but we didn't want to make that decision for you.'

'Thanks. I'll put that on my list of things to do.'

'Don't dawdle too long. I'm thinking about converting that space into a playroom for my grandchildren.'

'Did you . . . go through . . . ah, anything? Sort stuff out?'

'Are you kidding? We only had three days to get everything done. Don't expect more than a jumbled mess and consider yourself lucky I bothered to do that much. It's not like I haven't asked you a thousand times to go through what you left behind and clean it out.'

As far as she could remember, there was little she wanted to save, but she'd hidden a couple of important documents beneath the lining of an old childhood jewelry box. Her copy of the divorce papers that she hadn't been able to bear reading when the hurt had been fresh. They really should be in a safe deposit box. Maybe she should go out to the ranch earlier than she'd planned.

'Is this a private conversation or can I put my two cents in?' Mimi asked as she sat down and held out her mug.

Jean poured a refill. 'Your input is always valued.'

'Humpf.'

'You were out in the studio early today,' Jean said with a smile. 'Dare I ask if you're starting a new project?'

'Do you mean *finally* starting? You have that tone in your voice.'

'Mother, please.' Jean sighed. 'Let's not start arguing so early. Today is going to be difficult enough as it is.'

Mimi nodded.

'If you heard a tone in my voice it wasn't intentional. That's how I always speak.'

Caroline bit her lip and refrained with effort from rolling her eyes. 'I'm glad to hear you're working,' she said to Mimi.

'Anything special?' Jean asked, her voice overly cheerful.

'Something a little different this time, an existential coffee tree.' She looked at Caroline over the rim of her mug, her eyes sparkling with amusement.

'I swear I don't know where you get your artistic ideas from.'

'Oh, sometimes they come from the most unexpected sources.'

Caroline covered her mouth and faked a cough to hide a giggle.

When her mother's eyes narrowed and a frown pinched her forehead, Caroline whipped her head around to see who stood behind her.

Travis stood on the other side of the patio railing. Not too many men were either brave enough or foolish enough to face her mother's scowl with a grin. As if he read her thoughts, he winked at her.

'In my experience,' Jean said, 'a man who winks is either holding the best hand or he has the worst intentions.'

He held up the white baker's box by the string. 'I do believe six of a kind takes the pot.'

'Would you settle for a cup of coffee?'

'Much obliged, Ms Mimi.' Travis mounted the steps and leaned one hip against the railing. 'To be truthful, I'm not here on a purely social call.'

'Surprise, surprise,' Jean said with an I-could-have-told-you-so expression. She took the box and untied the string.

Mimi had poured him a cup and was handing it to him when she suddenly pulled her hand back. 'You're not going to arrest Caroline again?' she asked, horrified.

'No, ma'am.'

The knot in Caroline's stomach loosened. 'What's in the box?'

'I think it's an apology,' Mimi said.

'Can't a neighbor bring over a treat?'

Caroline lowered her chin and looked at him from under raised eyebrows.

'Okay, it's a bribe. I need some information about Barbara's wedding plans,' he said. 'Seems she made a few enemies. Three vendors in particular were angry enough to show up at her home on Friday evening, the caterer, the florist, and a girl I suspect is the baker's daughter.'

Although Caroline hadn't known about the visits, the fact didn't surprise her. 'You know I'll answer your questions, that goes without saying. That doesn't merit a bribe.'

Travis raised one hand like he was swearing to tell the truth. 'It was a last-minute thought. I remembered you liked cinnamon rolls and figured it's probably been ages since you had any of Maybelle's, that's all. Think of it as a belated welcome-back-to-Haven gift. Don't make a federal case out of it.'

'Well, then, thank you.' But she knew him better than to take his gesture at face value. Some guys would have brought flowers; Travis brought cinnamon rolls. 'And for the record, there's no need to apologize.'

'I'm not apologizing for doing my job.'

'I understand.'

'I had no choice.'

'Absolutely. I agree.'

'For the record, I don't believe you're guilty.'

'I didn't think you did.'

Jean stood up. 'I'm leaving before I gag. I liked it better when you two were fighting.'

'I should leave, too,' Mimi said. 'So you two can talk in private.'

Before Mimi could stand, Caroline pinned her forearm to the table and fixed her mother with a firm stare.

'No need for that,' Travis said in a rush. 'Ah, actually, witnesses to the conversation are preferable. In case . . . ah, if I have to testify in court as to where I got the information. Yeah, that's it.'

'I'd like you both to stay, if you can spare the time,' Caroline said sweetly to her mother and grandmother. But she didn't remove her restraining grip on Mimi's arm so there would be no mistaking her reminder of her promise to abstain from any matchmaking activities.

'In that case, I'll get some plates and forks for the cinnamon rolls,' Mimi said, graciously admitting defeat.

Caroline jumped up. 'I'll get them.' She gave her grandmother a stern look. 'You stay right where you are.' When she returned a short while later, she was carrying a tray loaded with plates, napkins, forks, glasses, and a pitcher of milk. She'd tucked her organizer and the wedding paperwork under her arm.

Travis jumped up, took the tray from her, and carried it to the table. 'Why didn't you call me to help?'

'Oh, it wasn't that heavy.'

Small talk dominated as Mimi served and everyone enjoyed the rolls.

Bobby Ray rushed from the house. 'Aunt Rose is here. I saw her from my window.'

The front door slamming echoed through the house. 'Where is she? I'm going to kill her,' Rose hollered.

Jean turned to Travis. 'Get her out of here,' she said jerking her head toward Caroline. 'We'll take care of Rose.'

'Nonsense,' Caroline said. ' 'I'm going to kill her' is just a figure of speech.'

'She's carrying a shotgun,' Bobby Ray said. 'I didn't see Chuck.'

Travis took Caroline's hand but she shook him off. 'I'm sure Aunt Rose doesn't mean anything by it.'

'Let's not find out. Come on.'

'No. I . . . oomph.'

He picked her up and tossed her over his shoulder before striding down the path to his back yard.

'Put me down this instant.'

'As soon as we're a safe distance away.'

'And who appointed you my bodyguard?'

'Your mother.' He lifted her higher on his shoulder. 'And part of my job is keeping people safe.'

'Ouch. I'm not impressed with your caveman act.'

'Stop wiggling and relax.'

'Oh, sure. Have you ever had a shoulder jammed into your stomach?'

He put her down next to his squad car, opened the passenger door and removed his hat from the seat. 'Get in.'

She crossed her arms. 'I'll have to speak to Aunt Rose eventually.'

'She'll be more receptive after I arrest the real murderer.'

'And when will that be?'

'Hard to say. I currently have three suspects and, unlike the Mayor, I usually investigate before I determine whom to arrest.'

'So, what are you waiting for? Go. Investigate.'

'I'm waiting for you to get in the car because I know if I leave you here you'll march right back in there to confront your aunt.'

'Do you usually take one suspect with you

to investigate the others?'

'No, but my only alternative is to put you in a jail cell for your own protection.'

She stared up at him. Was he bluffing? Would he really lock her up? After several long moments, the only thing she'd learned from his expression was never to play poker with him. Without another word she got into the car and fastened her seat belt.

He put his hat on as he walked around the front of the car. Maybe it was his swagger or the hint of a grin, something told her she'd folded her hand too soon. Drat. Travis could aggravate her more than anyone else, yet still she had to admit the man did look yummy in his John Wayne hat.

He drove in silence for several blocks before saying, 'I'll drop you at your sister's house.'

'Great.' Caroline felt a little lost without her purse or her cell phone. 'Except that Dee Ann is on her way to Las Cruces with Stephen and the kids to spend the day at his parents'.'

'Then I'll drop you at Mary Lynn's house.'

'She's on duty at the hospital until three o'clock.' She didn't like being totally dependent on Travis. 'There's Maybelle's Diner. Just let me off there and I'll find a ride home. Oh, I promise to wait for the all-clear signal from Mimi.'

'I was thinking of someplace less public. You never know if someone will report to your Aunt Rose about seeing you. I envision her tracking you down, rifle in hand.'

'Like Elmer Fudd after Bugs Bunny?'

★ ★ ★

He pulled the car around behind the restaurant. A man dressed in cook's whites sat on the back steps smoking a cigarette. Travis parked the car. 'I need to talk to Lewis. I won't be long,' Travis said as he got out.

Caroline blinked in disbelief. Did he just say that? Did he really expect her to wait in the car for him? Not in this lifetime.

'Actually, Sheriff, I expected you sooner,' Caroline heard Lewis address Travis as she followed him.

'You want to tell me about your relationship with Barbara Jennings?' Travis spared a terse glance at Caroline as she walked up behind him but basically he ignored her presence.

'Hate, loathe, and despise are three words that come to mind,' Lewis said.

'Then why did you agree to work for her?'

He took a long drag on his cigarette. 'I'm starting a business. I can't afford to turn down any client.'

'Plus Barbara reminded you of your

ex-wife,' Caroline said. She turned to Travis. 'His ex took him to the cleaners.'

'She took my house, every dollar I had, flushed my credit rating down the toilet, and she stole my business. Her and that shark lawyer she was f — sleeping with. How do you know about Melinda?'

'Susan only told me so that I'd be patient with you.'

Lewis raised an eyebrow. 'I should kill her for blabbing my secrets. Sorry, it's just a figure of speech.'

Caroline nudged Travis with her elbow. 'See. Everyone knows that's not a real threat.'

'I'm confused,' Travis said. 'Your ex took you to the cleaners. So I have to ask, why would you take a job working for someone who reminded you of your ex, even if it was the last job on earth?'

Lewis dropped his head and shook it slowly back and forth.

Caroline spoke on his behalf. 'Susan said he thought that if he survived — '

'I'd rather speak for myself,' Lewis said, annoyance putting an edge to his voice.

'I'm listening,' Travis said. He picked up an empty bucket from the porch, flipped it over and sat on it.

Caroline slid to a sitting position on the step below Lewis.

'Three years ago I would also have said she took my self respect but I've since realized I did that to myself. I'm not sure if losing my wife or my business hit me the hardest but I got drunk and stayed that way for close to a year. Thanks to a couple of friends who snatched me off a barstool and dropped me at Dr Resnick's treatment center, I finally realized there aren't any answers written inside the bottoms of glasses. I've been sober for one year, eleven months, and fourteen days.'

'Good for you.' Travis's praise was sincere. He waited for the rest of the story. When Caroline opened her mouth to step into the silence, he gave an almost imperceptible shake of his head to stop her.

After a long moment Lewis continued. 'I moved back to Haven to help out with the family business. I have a dream of opening another restaurant, but because of my dismal credit rating I've been forced to start small and pay cash. Catering seemed to be a perfect beginning. Barbara was one of my first clients. Big mistake.'

'In what way?'

'Because Barbara reminded me so much of my ex, I got this crazy idea that if I survived working for her, then I could believe I'd really gotten Melinda out of my system once and for all, that I was free to move on. I know it sounds stupid . . . '

'No, it doesn't,' Caroline said. Even if she couldn't say so at that moment because Travis was standing right there, she totally understood how an ex could continue to affect your life even after she, or he, was long gone.

'Why did you go to see Barbara on Friday night? What did the two of you argue about?'

'The same thing we always argued about. The menu. Or rather her constant changes to the menu. Friday morning, on the day before the event, mind you, she left a message saying she absolutely could not serve mini crab cakes with wasabi lemon mayonnaise appetizers. Apparently, some TV person had served crab cakes at her wedding and Barbara flatly refused to be a copycat. She wanted the appetizer changed to prawns and caviar on toast rounds.'

'I can't really blame her for not wanting to copy a reality-show personality,' Caroline admitted.

'It was the day before the event,' Lewis said again, stabbing at the air with his finger and getting exasperated once more. 'I'd already bought all the ingredients, mostly non-returnable items. And I didn't have the cash to buy prawns and caviar.'

'So you went to her house to . . .'

'Convince her that no one would think her a copycat because everyone knows the menu for a wedding is finalized weeks in advance.'

'And that worked?'

'No. I had to borrow my father's credit card and race to the grocery store in El Paso. It's almost as if Barbara was trying to ruin my business.' Lewis folded his hands and took a deep breath, holding for a few seconds before blowing it out slowly, obviously a calming ritual. 'Adversity teaches valuable lessons that can't be learned in leisure. From this experience, I've learned never to give a quote to a bride without an exact description of each dish and clear prices for changes.'

'Where were you between five and nine-thirty on Saturday morning?' Travis asked.

Lewis jerked his head toward the restaurant kitchen behind him. 'Right in there, all night, working up until the last minute before transporting my food to the Country Club.'

'Can anyone verify that?'

'My helper, Urbano Reyes, was with me.'

'I'd like to speak to him.'

'He's not here right now and he doesn't speak much English.'

'I'd like his address.'

'I'm sure I've got a job application inside, but he didn't show up for work today.'

Caroline and Travis exchanged glances. Sounded like Urbano Reyes was an illegal alien who had vanished at the first sign of trouble. Doubtful he would ever be located.

'Come with me,' Lewis said. He led the way to a walk-in cooler where tray after tray of fancy cuisine lined the shelves. 'Welcome to my business. I know it's not much compared to my former five-star restaurant but it's a start and the free rent is a big plus. What you see represents many man-hours of labor, most of it done overnight before the wedding. My food is my true alibi.'

Despite the abundance of appetizers, Caroline noticed several menu items were missing. 'What did you do with the rest of it?'

'I beg your pardon?'

'Where are the beef tenderloins for the carving stations, the ham and green beans, the assorted fruit for the fruit salad in melon bowls?'

'Oh.' Lewis looked uncomfortable for a moment. 'After I learned the wedding was cancelled, I struck a deal with the chef at the Country Club for a substantial portion of the supplies at a discounted price. Perishable items that he didn't want I donated to the homeless shelter. Unfortunately, they wouldn't take the appetizers but I hate to throw them away. I'm waiting to hear back from the food pantry in El Paso.'

Caroline was almost distracted by the good deed donations but she backtracked to his first answer. 'Let me get this straight. You'll be paid in full in accordance with the contract's cancellation clause, but you won't have to pay cooking or serving staff, so your profit margin just shot way up. On top of that you made even more money by selling the food that you didn't serve.'

'I suppose you could say I was paid for some items twice. That's not against the law, is it?' he asked Travis.

'Of course I'm not a judge, but I suppose the food could be considered abandoned by the first owners.'

'But — '

'We'll let you get back to work,' Travis said, grabbing Caroline's arm and dragging her back to the car before she had a chance to speak. 'I may have more questions later,' he called over his shoulder. 'Don't leave town.'

At the car she shook off his hold. 'What was that all about?'

He held the door open. Seeing the futility of arguing, she got inside.

'Why the bum's rush?' she asked as soon as he opened the driver's door.

'I don't want Lewis to think he's a suspect just yet.'

'Oh.' She mulled that over for a few minutes. 'Oh, I get it. He's a suspect because rather than Barbara destroying his business, he profited from her death.'

'And that's what we call motive,' he said with an exaggerated waggle of his eyebrows.

Caroline stifled her giggle. She realized that, despite the seriousness of their visit, she was having a good time with Travis. And that was downright dangerous.

14

As Travis drove to the next suspect on his list, he called Phyllis, giving her the information so she could verify Lewis's story. He parked in front of the flower shop.

'I appreciate your help talking to Lewis,' he said. 'We make a good team.'

Instead of replying, Caroline jumped out of the car, raced past a large sign that advertised pink roses on sale, and went inside.

What did he say to set her off? He'd given her a compliment, for Pete's sake. Shaking his head, he got out of the car and followed her at a leisurely pace. He'd never expected to understand women in general, but every time he thought he had a handle on one particular woman, she proved him clueless yet again. Not a comfortable feeling for a man who made his living finding answers.

When he entered the shop, Caroline was already seated at a small glass-topped table with the owners. 'Paul.'

'Travis.'

'So much for the pleasantries,' Caroline said, rolling her eyes.

Paul Bennett stood and shook the Sheriff's

hand. 'Caroline told me you're here on official business. I heard about the murder and assumed you'd get around to me eventually.'

'He didn't hurt that woman,' Nina blurted out. 'Paul could never hurt anyone.'

'I'm not accusing Paul. I'm just here to ask a few questions.'

'Please sit,' Paul said. 'Can I get you anything? Coffee?'

'No, thank you. Why did you go to see Barbara the evening before the wedding?'

Paul's eyebrows shot up for a second before he got his expression under control. 'I was verifying — '

'It wasn't him,' Nina said. 'I'm the one who went to see Barbara that evening.'

'Nina, don't,' Paul said.

She turned to her husband. 'It's all right. Let me do this. I don't have as much to risk.'

Paul stood and took his wife gently in his arms, bowing his head into her neck. He whispered something into her ear before turning to face Travis, his arm still draped around her shoulders.

'My wife wants to protect me. I did go to see Barbara on Friday evening and we had an unpleasant conversation. But I didn't kill her, even though — '

'What goes around comes around,' Nina

said. 'I won't lie and say I was completely surprised by the news of her death. Barbara exuded bad karma and it was bound to return to her. Without Paul's help, I assure you.'

'Tell me about that conversation,' Travis said to Paul.

The florist looked to his wife and waited for her to nod permission before speaking. 'Barbara had an uncanny knack for zeroing in on a person's most vulnerable spot.'

'Like a laser targeting system,' Caroline said, her tone revealing she'd worn a bull's eye on her forehead more than once.

'Lately, she'd been giving Nina a hard time about her hair.'

'But her hair is beautiful,' Caroline said.

After a moment's hesitation, Nina reached up and took off her wig. She was completely bald.

Caroline's gasp revealed her surprise.

'I haven't told very many people about my chemo because I didn't want anyone to feel sorry for me,' Nina said. 'I don't want to talk about it all day with every sympathetically curious customer who comes in the door. I want *my* life, not the life of a cancer patient.'

'Somehow Barbara knew or maybe she just sensed a weakness and she wouldn't let it lie,' Paul said.

'I know it sounds vain,' Nina admitted, 'But I'm *über*-sensitive about my hair or lack thereof.'

'You're gorgeous,' Caroline said. 'Without the big hair, your fabulous eyes take center stage. You look awesome.'

'See. I told you so,' Paul said.

'If you weren't married, I'd be in the long line of guys waiting to ask you out,' Travis said.

'Hey!' Paul said.

'Behind Paul, of course.'

'You're all sweet, and I thank you.' She turned her back and repositioned her wig before facing everyone again. 'We won't have to discuss this again.'

'So you went to see Barbara to tell her to stop picking on Nina about her hair,' Travis said to Paul to get the conversation started back on track.

'Yes. I'm not proud to say it ended in a shouting match. I told Barbara that if she didn't leave my wife alone she'd be sorry, that I would make her sorry. But I'm guessing you know that since you're here.'

Travis looked at his notebook. Best not to confirm or deny when a suspect assumes you know more than you do. 'Where were you between five and nine-thirty on Saturday morning?'

'On the road until seven o'clock, maybe seven-fifteen. Then in the workroom putting the pink roses into the bouquets and table arrangements. I delivered the first of the flowers to the Country Club around nine-thirty.'

'I can verify that,' Caroline said. Travis shot her a look. 'For what it's worth,' she added. 'Not much, I assume, coming as it does from another suspect.'

Travis ignored her as best he could. He faced Paul. 'You said you were in the workroom putting the arrangements together. Isn't that sort of waiting until the last minute?'

'Professional hazard. Can't make arrangements with roses too early. I'd done what I could to set everything up, you know — foam in the containers, ribbons made, sticks wired to background flowers and greens, all that sort of stuff.'

'I see. What did you mean when you said you were on the road?'

'I was at the wholesale flower mart in El Paso when it opened at four a.m.'

'Nothing but the freshest flowers for Bridezilla,' Nina said.

Paul pinched the bridge of his nose. 'We have a reputation to uphold.'

'And when did you leave the flower mart?'

'Not until almost six. My main wholesaler didn't have enough pink roses so I had to shop around. That delayed my return trip. I didn't get back here to unload the van until around seven.'

'Can anyone verify your whereabouts?' Travis asked.

'I can,' Nina piped up.

'You went to El Paso with your husband?'

'No, but I looked at the clock when I heard him drive up.'

'Did you see him or talk to him?'

'No, but I . . . ' her voice trailed off. 'I went back to sleep until eight-thirty.'

'The chemo takes a lot out of her,' Paul said. 'I keep telling her she needs to rest more.'

'Can anyone verify your whereabouts early on Saturday morning besides your wife?'

'I was with my wholesale guy until about four-thirty.'

'Anyone else?'

Paul shook his head. 'I made purchases at several stalls but I doubt if any of the vendors can be found. Most of them just rent booths for the day and return to Mexico after selling their product.'

'Receipts?'

'Are you kidding? From those guys?'

'Parking voucher?'

'My wholesaler allows me to park in his reserve area.'

'Anyone see you leave?'

Paul shrugged. 'By then I was running so far behind schedule and in such a hurry to get back that I just loaded up and got the hell out of there.'

Travis folded his notebook. 'One last question. What happened to the flower arrangements you made for the wedding and reception?'

'We salvaged everything we could, especially the pink roses. There's been a run on them for funeral flowers.'

'So you sold them a second time?'

'No. We didn't charge for any of the pink roses that were requested. The rest of them we recycled into new creations. See for yourself.' Paul indicated a display of an assortment of table arrangements, a tray of corsages, and a bucket of long stem pink roses. The sign on a large jar said, *All proceeds go to Susan G. Koman For the Cure.*

'That's a great idea,' Caroline said.

'It's not totally altruistic,' Paul said with a self-effacing grin. 'We do have a vested interest.'

Travis thanked them for their time as a way to close the interview. But he did remind them not to leave town.

On the way out, Caroline stopped at the display. She touched the petals of a single rose and then suddenly turned toward him. 'Lend me five dollars,' she said. 'I left the house in such a hurry, I forgot my purse.'

'No,' he said.

Her eyes opened wide.

'But I will buy you that flower.' He pulled out his wallet, surreptitiously folded a couple of twenties together, and bypassed her outreached hand to drop them in the donation jar. He picked up the flower she'd touched. 'Here you go.'

'Thank you.' She ducked her head and sniffed the fragrance with an expression of sheer delight.

My pleasure, he thought. Truly it was his pleasure to watch her. But he didn't say it. Instead, he spun on his heel and walked out the door.

In the few minutes it took her to say her goodbyes and follow him out, he'd phoned the new data into his office so Phyllis could start the verification process.

'The bakery is at the end of the block. Shall we walk?' he asked when Caroline exited.

'Sure.'

'Tell me about this business. I haven't met the owners yet.'

'Rory and Heidi Struthers. They moved here from Chicago about eighteen months ago. Left their high-stress high-tech jobs and cashed in their retirement savings to start their own business doing what they love. They chose Haven for a number of reasons but near the top of the list was getting their daughter out of her environment. They live in the apartment over the store as do many of these small-business owners.'

'How is the business doing? I can't say I've heard anything about them one way or another.'

'They're struggling because the town still considers them outsiders. And that's unfortunate because they really are quite talented. Rory is an artist with icing. His cake decorating is as good or better than those guys on TV. And Heidi makes extraordinary baked goods from old family recipes she's adapted. Her Poppy Seed Strudel is phenomenal.'

'The daughter?'

'Regan. Her parents insist she's a good kid beneath all the Goth make-up and belligerent attitude. I do know she blames Barbara for her father's recent stress-induced heart attack and the subsequent open-heart surgery. Regan tried to get out of the contract due to the circumstances but Barbara threatened to sue for everything her parents had worked for all their lives.'

'Nice.' His sarcasm was obvious. 'Couldn't you do anything?'

'This all happened before I arrived. By then Heidi told me they really needed the business, what with all the additional expenses and times they had to close the store. I worried that it was too big a project for a seventeen-year-old but everything turned out fine. Regan is as talented as her father. The wedding cake was gorgeous and arrived at the County Club on time. The groom's cake and petit fours were perfect. She did a great job.'

Travis reached for the handle on the door of the bakery and paused for a moment to read the notice.

To all our customers,

Thank you for your concern and consider-ation during this stressful time, but most of all thank you for your prayers. We are pleased to share the news that Rory will be coming home Sunday afternoon.

We will CLOSE at 2.00 p.m. on Sunday. We apologize for any inconvenience and will resume our regular hours on Tuesday.

Heidi and Regan

Travis figured they'd have plenty of time to ask their questions but he checked his watch to make sure. He pulled the door open causing the attached bell to tinkle, but paused before he followed Caroline. When had the investigation become theirs rather than his?

Heidi finished helping a customer and then greeted Caroline with a sympathetic smile. 'We've heard all the gossip.' She chuckled. 'Sometimes I think the customers only come in so they can spread the latest news. How are you holding up?'

'Okay. I'm glad to hear Rory is being released.'

'To hear him talk, it's like getting out of jail. Oh, no offense intended.'

'None taken. I know it isn't easy on the hospitalized person, but the family also has a difficult time. It's been a long haul for you and Regan.'

'Yes, we'll be glad not to make that drive to El Paso to the hospital ever again. He'll still have some recovery and outpatient stuff but he can do most of that at the clinic here in town.'

Caroline introduced Travis.

'Ah, Sheriff Beaumont. Glad to finally meet you. I've seen you around but we stay mighty busy, what with the store and an active teenager.'

Travis used the opening to come to the point. 'Speaking of Regan, Mrs Struthers, I'd like to ask your daughter a few questions.'

'I'm right here, Mom,' Regan said as she stepped around the door to the back room, unwittingly telling Travis she'd been eavesdropping just out of sight. She fit the description Mrs Tacket had given of a slight girl with brightly colored stripes in her hair.

'We can talk in the office,' Heidi said in a low voice as another customer came in. She called for assistance from the back. A slim, pale blond woman, who could have been her twin, came forward wiping her hands on her apron. She introduced her sister Inger who had been staying with them and helping out at the bakery for the last month. After a quick whispered conversation, Inger went to wait on the customer and Heidi led the way through the workroom. She sat behind the desk on one side of a small office crowded with extra equipment, supplies, magazines, cookbooks, and too much furniture. Caroline and Regan sat on the sofa across from the desk and Travis took the chair.

'Now, how can we help you?' Heidi asked him.

'I appreciate your cooperation — '

'This is about that bitch isn't it?'

'Regan!'

301

'I'm not sorry she's dead,' the young girl declared. 'She got what she deserved. The only thing better would have been if I'd been able to shove that wedding cake in her face.'

'Regan! You don't mean that,' her mother said in a horrified voice. 'She's still upset about her father's heart attack,' she explained to Travis. 'It's fear talking. She doesn't really mean it. Tell the Sheriff you don't really mean it.'

The teenager crossed her arms, narrowed her eyes, and pressed her lips into a straight line.

'Why did you go to see Barbara on Friday evening?' Travis asked her.

'She didn't — '

'Yes, I did, Mom. The Sheriff already knows that. I took over the taste test required by the contract, that almighty contract she kept harping on about. We needed her final approval in writing. No way was I going to jump through hoops for her and then have her renege on payment because we forgot something.'

'Where was I for all this?' Heidi asked.

'It was right after we got back from visiting at the hospital. You fell asleep on the couch here. I was just starting the cake and pulled out the contract for the specs when I noticed the final approval was missing. I let you sleep

302

and took the taste test over there myself.'

'Why didn't you wake me?'

Regan shrugged her shoulders in response. 'You were exhausted.'

'Where were you between five and nine-thirty on Saturday morning?' Travis asked the girl. She seemed to have a pretty good head on her shoulders. Not what he'd expected when he'd seen her orange and blue hair, multiple piercings, and tattoos. Profiling, yes, but based on his experience.

'Here,' she answered. 'I worked through the night to finish the cake on time.'

'Can anyone verify that?'

'Not really. I sent Aunt Inger home to get some rest around two a.m. But you try to decorate a huge wedding cake like that in less than twelve hours.'

'I was here, too,' Heidi said. 'I can verify she was here working.'

'You were with her all night?' Travis asked, giving Heidi a calculating stare.

'Except for a few hours when I napped on the couch,' Heidi reluctantly admitted. 'But I'm sure she never left the premises. Please don't hold her appearance against her.'

'Mother!'

'What's wrong with her appearance?' Travis asked with a straight face. The shock on Heidi's and Regan's faces made him smile.

303

The beaming approval on Caroline's face caused a different reaction. A fist-sized ball of warmth appeared in his chest and spread through his veins. He blamed the unfamiliar feeling on the delicious scents wafting through the door, but when the church bells starting ringing as if on cue, he jumped up. 'That will be all for now,' he said, heading for the exit. 'I may have more questions later, so don't leave town,' he called back over his shoulder.

Caroline took her time following him out the door and he waited impatiently. She finally showed up carrying a white bakery box. They strolled back to his car.

'I couldn't leave without buying something,' she said.

'I thought you didn't have any money on you.'

'Mimi has an account. I'll repay her when the bill comes. I thought this strudel would be perfect to take to the wake.'

'Do me a favor and send it with your mother and grandmother. Stay home. Take a pass on the funeral rituals.'

She shot him a questioning glance. 'Aunt Rose should have moved past blaming me by now, shouldn't she?'

'Until we find the real murderer, I'm afraid she'll still blame you. Her logic has probably prevailed and she's gotten over the urge to kill you, but why push her back to the edge of that emotional precipice at a time when she's bound to be distraught?'

Travis flipped open his phone. 'Talk to me. Okay. Hmmm . . . Sure. I'll tell her.' He recited the few facts he'd learned from the Struthers girl and requested Phyllis to do what she could to verify the times they visited the hospital and to see if any of the neighbors noticed the lights in the bakery on all night.

When he shut the phone Caroline asked, 'Was that my all clear?' She'd become way too comfy in his presence, unconsciously matching her steps to his stride, speaking easily yet comfortable with the occasional silences. She needed to get away from the danger he represented as much as she needed to avoid Aunt Rose.

'Yep.' They'd reached the car and Travis waited to explain until they were on the road. 'Mimi called the station when she realized you didn't have your phone. Rose has calmed down and gone home. Guess that means it's time for me to take you back.'

'Thanks for — '

'You don't have to act grateful. I literally dragged you out of the house — '

'For my own protection. No problem. I understand.'

'Then I hauled you around with me while I worked.'

'It wasn't all bad. I had an interesting time, saw some friends, got a rose and something to take . . . or send to the wake.'

'So what was the bad part?'

'You took me away before I could eat my cinnamon roll.'

He responded with a bark of laughter. 'You always could surprise me.'

'So glad you find it amusing. The boys scarf up anything remotely sweet, so I figure there's not an ice cube's chance in hell that my cinnamon roll is still sitting on the table.'

Travis pulled up in front of her house and parked. Caroline was halfway up the walk before she realized that Travis wasn't following. She stopped and turned. He was leaning against the fender of his car, legs crossed at the ankles, arms over his chest, hat shading his face.

'Aren't you coming in?' she asked, taking a few steps toward him in order to see his eyes.

'I'm on duty.'

'Oh.' And she was part of that duty. The bubble of pleasure that had built during their morning together deflated with a pop.

'I still have lots to do today,' he said. 'You do want me to find the murderer as soon as possible, don't you?'

She tossed her head. 'Of course. It's not like I want you hanging around here or anything. I was just being polite.' She spun on her heel and marched up the front steps. When she turned to peek at him from behind the screen door, she could have sworn he was grinning as he pulled away.

15

Caroline carried her bakery box to the kitchen and set it on the counter. Then she got down on her hands and knees to look behind the detergent products under the sink for a bud vase to hold her single pink rose.

'I thought I heard you come in.'

She recognized Dirk's voice despite the fact that she'd almost managed to forget that Mimi had invited him to stay in the guest room. Ignoring his greeting, she pushed her head and shoulders deeper into the cupboard.

With one hand Caroline arranged and rearranged the odd assortment of vases in the vain hope that Dirk would get bored staring at her butt and walk away. No such luck. He just kept prattling on about flowers and cards and who had called to express their sympathy. She grabbed a blue glass bud vase, wiggled out, and then busied herself filling the vase and cutting the stem of her rose.

'You were up and about early,' he said. 'Trouble sleeping?'

'Things to do.' She resisted the urge to elaborate. As much as she needed to talk about her morning, and her confusing reactions to Travis, this was not the right time or place, and definitely not the right person.

'I slept really well, all things considered. Your mother said I must have been emotionally exhausted.'

'And she's usually right about stuff like that.' Caroline poured herself a cup of coffee and turned to leave when she spotted her cinnamon roll on the table in a plastic zip bag. Hmmm. House rules said no food upstairs. If she stayed in the kitchen she'd have to put up with Dirk, but on the other hand, the cinnamon roll that she'd thought lost was there, waiting.

She took a seat at the table in the alcove. Dirk poured himself a cup of coffee and sat next to her. He looked nice in his dark suit, pristine white shirt, and dark blue tie that matched his eyes. He did wear clothes well, she had to admit, but that didn't make him any more appealing to her.

'I would pick the one chair in the direct sunlight,' she said moving to the other side of the table, sliding her roll, coffee, and the rose in the vase with her. She could practically see the wheels turning in his head as he tried to come up with an excuse to change seats. 'Is your family coming for the funeral?' she asked to distract him.

'They're back in Miami now. I told them not to make the arduous journey to come back and I didn't want to mention anything about the suicide note. Not with my mother's delicate health.'

'Ah . . . about that suicide note. I heard, through the grapevine, the note is a fake.'

'What? Are you saying some sicko sent me a fake suicide email? Who would do that? How could someone do that?'

He seemed genuinely shocked, which knocked out her theory that he'd sent the email to himself since he probably had access to the computer. Maybe even that could have been faked. 'I don't know.'

He blew out a deep breath. 'I guess in one way it's a relief. I mean, it hurt to think Barbara would rather kill herself than marry me.'

'So not the case. Okay, she may have had an unhealthy obsession with her wedding being perfect, but I know she was committed to marrying you.'

Dirk nodded, then he stared at his hands clasped on the table.

Caroline stuffed a huge bite of roll into her mouth. Whether it was to keep from saying more or just a race to finish it and leave, she didn't bother to analyze.

'I confess I was the one with doubts,' he

said. 'The night before the wedding, I told Barbara I thought we should postpone the ceremony and she went psycho on me. That's the real reason I spent the night at the inn.'

'Ba bight ba-bore?' Caroline blurted out with her mouth full before she remembered her manners. She hurriedly chewed and swallowed, and then gulped a swig of coffee. 'Are you nuts? You couldn't have figured that out just a little bit sooner than the night before the wedding?'

'I've tried to talk to you about — '

'Have you told Travis about all that?'

'I didn't want to provide any additional evidence against you.'

'Huh? Why would that be evidence against me?'

'My feelings for you are the reason I was unsure about marrying Barbara. Since the moment we met, I've known there's something strong and wonderful between us, and I know you feel it too. Your feelings for me are a motive for you to get rid of Barbara so that you could have me for yourself.'

Horrified shock struck Caroline momentarily dumb. Her mouth opened and closed in vehement denial but not a sound came out, while he babbled on about building a house at the lake, living happily ever after.

She finally said, 'Whoa! I don't have any

idea what you're talking about. I am not attracted to you in any way. There is nothing between us and I never, ever gave you any reason to think so. That is utter nonsense.' She stood. 'I think you should move back to the inn.'

'Frances Caroline Tucker!' Jean said as she entered the kitchen.

Dirk immediately stood up. Such a gentleman. Not.

'I heard that,' Jean continued without pause. 'That was rude and I know you were raised better than to act that way.'

Obviously, she'd only heard the last part of the conversation.

Jean turned to Dirk. 'Mimi invited you to stay and it's her house, so you are not to give going back to that inn another thought.'

'Thank you. Your family has been so kind. On the other hand, Caroline is right. I do have to learn to be by myself now that Barbara is gone.'

'Of course you do,' Jean said. 'And you will, but not today. Not even this week. Eventually, you'll be ready to move on.'

'I truly believe there is another woman for me,' he said, giving Jean a hug and looking over her shoulder directly at Caroline.

She rolled her eyes as her mother patted him on the back.

'I'm sure you're right,' Jean said. She turned to Caroline and sized her up and down with a critical eye. 'You'll make more of an effort with your attire for the wake, won't you?'

'I'm thinking it'll be easier on Aunt Rose if I don't go,' Caroline said.

'But you're family,' Dirk said. 'You should be there.'

Jean gave her daughter a long, calculating stare. 'I think you're right,' she said with a curt nod. 'Rose already has much that she will come to regret. No need to add to it, especially in such a public forum. Thank you for thinking of her.'

Caroline shrugged off the compliment. 'I'll be here during the wake to answer the phone, accept deliveries, that sort of stuff.'

'That'll be helpful,' Jean said.

'Won't you be bored?' Dirk asked. 'I'm sure Rose won't do anything to disrupt the wake. You should come.'

'I'll be fine,' Caroline said. Thankfully, her mother supported her decision, a rare event. She'd rather expected to be told she would have to go, even if it put her life at risk, blood being thicker than water and all that. Apparently, averting a public scene took precedence over blood. Not that she minded staying home. 'Beats being shot at.'

'She didn't actually shoot at you,' Jean clarified. 'And there's no need to ever bring up that incident again.'

Okay. Moment of maternal approval over.

'There'll still be the funeral, of course,' Jean said. 'You could probably attend that, but maybe best to wait and see how the wake goes before making that decision.'

'I'm sure your presence would be missed,' Dirk said with a sad expression. 'I know I'll miss having you near because you've always been so encouraging to Barbara . . . and me. However, since we're both Mimi's guests, I'm sure we'll have a chance to get together later.'

To Caroline's ears, his implied promise sounded more like a threat.

But Jean didn't seem to hear anything wrong. 'We're all here for you whenever you need to talk,' she said, giving him a hug.

Caroline bit her lip. No one had believed her when she'd said earlier that Dirk had made passes at her, why should she expect any different a reaction now? Maybe *she* should move to the hotel. The only problem with that was the cost. If he decided to stick around for a while until the funeral, the hotel bill would make a big dent in her already-strained finances.

'Well, I've got to pop into town to run some errands for Mimi,' Jean said. She turned and headed for the front door.

Caroline refused to stay in the kitchen alone with Dirk. She shot him a glare and quickly headed out the back door and across the patio, seeking refuge in Mimi's studio until he left the house. His amused chuckle spurred her on.

★   ★   ★

Travis looked at the pile of papers Phyllis plopped on his desk. Bank statements, credit-card bills, phone bills and more. Rows and rows of numbers started to blur his vision and give him a headache. He wasn't a numbers guy. 'So what am I looking at?'

'We need to have a forensic accountant look at these papers to make real sense of it. Barbara wasn't terribly organized.'

'There's that catch we always run into. We can't requisition a forensic audit unless we can prove we need it.'

'I did find a few suspicious things.'

He pinched the bridge of his nose. 'Just give me the short version.'

'I've marked several spots on these copies of the originals. The yellow highlighted numbers indicate significant regular deposits made to her bank account.'

'That could explain how she appeared to

live above her means. She had another source of income but the question is from what?'

'They were made in cash, so there wasn't any identifying information listed on the statements. They stopped six months ago. The same time that this deposit from Mimi Tucker was made.'

'Are the two items related?'

'I don't see how. She put the money from her grandmother in a separate account that she appeared to use only for wedding expenses. Her regular account maintained a substantial balance even though she spent generous amounts. Like a six-hundred-dollar cappuccino machine she bought online and a dreadfully expensive bicycle from Kasky's Cycle Shop in El Paso. Here are the receipts. I'm sure I can find more receipts. So far I've only gone back six months on the expenditures.'

'Wasn't that about the time she got the car?'

'There aren't any car payments listed and there's no record of a large cash outlay. But the car is registered in her name.'

Travis looked up the phone number of the only Mercedes car dealer within a hundred miles and managed to connect with the manager. 'Are you the car dealer that sold a pink Mercedes?'

'We most certainly are. A special order, that one, right down to the raspberry stitching on the cream leather seats. Quite lovely.'

Travis identified himself to the manager. 'Unfortunately, the car has been involved in a serious crime. I'm looking for information on the owner.'

'Oh, dear. Is the car all right?'

'We won't know the extent of the damage until the lab is finished with its analysis.'

'Please be kind to that car. She's truly unique.'

'I'll pass that along to the lab. In the meantime, I need the date of purchase, original price, purchaser's name, and any other data about the car that you have.'

'You know I can't tell you that information. You think I'm crazy? Some guy on the phone says he's the law and I'm supposed to spill my guts.'

'It was worth a shot. At least I now know for sure where the car was purchased so I know what name to put on the warrant. We'll be speaking again soon.'

Travis practically threw the receiver back into place with a frustrated frown. 'Any idea where I can get a warrant in a hurry on a Sunday afternoon?'

'Judge McKay,' Phyllis said.

'It's a good two hours out to his fishing

cabin and two back, then an additional drive to El Paso to the dealership. They'll be closed by then. Man, I hate when red tape slows an investigation.'

'Maybe the guy would talk to you if you faxed a copy of the warrant to him.'

Travis gave his head a rueful shake. 'If I had a warrant, I'd sure try.'

'About fifteen minutes ago I saw Judge McKay going upstairs, presumably to his office.'

'He's here?'

'Probably came back to town to be closer to the investigation. Barbara worked for him ever since she got out of school.'

Travis jumped up and looked around frantically. 'Where are those forms?'

Phyllis held up a sheet of paper. 'Do you mean blank warrants like this one that I took the liberty of filling out while you were on the phone?'

He grabbed it and smiled. 'You're the best,' he called back over his shoulder as he headed out the door. He took the stairs two at a time and caught the judge just after he'd exited his office.

'Begging your pardon, sir.'

'Beaumont.'

They shook hands. 'I'd greatly appreciate it if you would sign this warrant before leaving.'

Judge McKay gave him a hard stare for a moment before looking at the paper Travis handed him. In response, he turned to unlock his office door. 'I think you'd better come in and have a seat.'

Travis complied but when the judge sat down heavily at his desk and didn't take out his seal or pick up a pen, he raised a questioning eyebrow.

'There's no need for this warrant.'

'Sir, the dealer — '

'I bought the car for Barbara.'

Not exactly what Travis had been expecting. He schooled his face to hide his surprise.

'It goes without saying that nothing I say leaves this room.'

'If it's evidence . . . '

'This isn't related to Barbara's murder, but I understand why your investigation has led you here. Barbara was more than my court stenographer.'

'I kinda figured that much out. Are you also the one who made the cash deposits into her account?'

'Yes. Barbara liked nice things. We'd meet in New York for shopping and the theatre twice a year. Other times we'd find some place local, always very careful to protect our secret, to protect my wife.'

'I'd heard Mrs McKay was on her

deathbed.' Travis shook his head in confusion. 'But that must have been ten years ago.'

'It's a miracle of modern medicine and a testament to her will to live that she's lasted this long. Barbara understood from the beginning why I couldn't ask for a divorce.'

'So you bought her a car instead?'

'That was an engagement present. And a goodbye gift. When she decided to marry Vandergelt she cut off our relationship. The car was a bit of insurance that she'd keep our little secret.'

'She won't be telling anyone now.'

'If you're saying I'm a suspect, I can assure you I was at my fishing cabin.' The judge pulled over a piece of paper and scribbled several names on it. 'These are just a few of the dozen people who can verify my whereabouts.'

Travis noted the Governor, State's Attorney, and a federal judge's name. He folded the paper and put it in his pocket. 'How long were you having an affair?'

'I don't see how that's relevant.'

'Come on, McKay. I can go back through her bank statements and figure it out for myself. Give me a break.'

After a long moment, McKay mumbled, 'Thirteen years.'

'You had an affair with a teenager?'

'Not so loud. I don't want anyone to overhear us. And it's not as sordid as you make it sound. We were in love.'

'Statutory rape is not love. You of all people should have known better.'

'I wasn't a judge then.'

'You were a lawyer, if the certificates framed on your wall aren't forgeries. She was less than half your age and still in high school, how can that not be sleazy and disgusting? If I ever find any prosecutable evidence, I'll arrest you.'

'Young man, must I remind you that I am a judge and you will have to deal with me in the future for as long as you're still Sheriff. As far as I'm concerned, this conversation never happened.'

Travis stood, laid both hands on the judge's desk, and leaned forward. 'Every time you see me, I want you to remember that I know your dirty little secret. If you even speak to an underage girl, I'll have you hoisted up on charges. If you put up a fight when I arrest you, and I do hope you do, then I'll find a way to cut off your balls and make it look like an accident.'

'Are you threatening me?'

'I thought you said this conversation never took place.' Travis smiled. He turned to leave but paused at the door to turn and say,

'Remember, I'm watching you.'

The sheriff left feeling the need to wash his hands.

Was the judge capable of murdering Barbara to ensure her silence? Had Barbara decided she wanted more from the judge than just a car? Was she blackmailing him?

What about Mrs McKay? Had she found out about the affair and killed Barbara in a jealous rage? Improbable. Mrs McKay, aged sixty plus and of fragile health, wouldn't have been physically able to move the seventy-pound concrete safety blocks at the crime scene. However, everyone knew she'd inherited the Butz family fortune, way more than enough money to purchase revenge. Travis added her to his list of people to interview. That roster was beginning to resemble a town census.

Travis's frustration increased. He wasn't eliminating suspects, he was finding more.

Too many suspects was as bad as none.

The other side of the jealousy coin pointed to Vandergelt who had been an automatic early suspect. As much as Travis disliked and mistrusted the judge, he had no doubt his alibi would check out. And if the affair had previously been discontinued on seemingly amicable terms, what was the motive? At least Judge McKay was looking like one suspect he could eliminate. Travis had already discovered that no new insurance had been purchased on Barbara's life and her previous policies listed her mother as the beneficiary. Did she have a will? Had she changed it recently?

Without consciously making a decision to do so, his feet carried him down the hall to Walter DeShane's office. His theory being that if the judge was in the house, his sycophant nephew wouldn't be far away.

Travis found Walter's office open and Earline present guarding the inner entrance to her boss's private sanctuary.

'I'm surprised to see you here,' he said to the secretary. Her fancy straw hat with a plethora of summer flowers, navy suit, and sensible shoes indicated she hadn't planned to be at the office either.

Earline shrugged. 'Walter wanted to make sure everything was straightened out after the break-in.'

'Of course.' And that warranted a special trip to the office on a Sunday afternoon. Although he could hear distinct words through the closed door to his inner sanctum, Walter was talking to someone, and with no other voice coming from that room he assumed he was on the phone.

'I would have gotten in touch with your office tomorrow, but since you're here . . . '

Earline said, as she pulled a small notebook from her desk drawer. 'We didn't find anything missing after the break-in but there was something strange. I keep a record of all copies made on my copier for billing purposes.' She handed him the notebook opened to a page of her neat handwritten list of names and numbers. 'As you can see, there are twenty-seven pages copied that I can't account for.'

'Does anyone else use your copier?'

'Sometimes Walter does.'

'And he records those copies on your list?'

She laughed. 'No. But he does tell me, and remember, he wasn't in the office.'

'Trashing your office seems a bit excessive to cover up some unauthorized copying. Too bad there isn't a way to find out exactly what has been copied.'

Walter opened his door and invited Travis into his private office. After the usual greetings Walter motioned to the chair in front of his desk. 'What brings you upstairs on a fine day like this?'

Just checking out a theory. 'I was wondering if Barbara had a will, specifically one she'd changed in the last six months.'

'No. At least, not that I know of.'

But he'd hesitated a fraction of a second too long before answering which told Travis the lawyer had thought twice about his answer before speaking.

'As I told you at the time of the break-in, I do very little private practice,' Walter said, leaning back in his chair and tapping the tips of his fingers together. 'If Barbara retained a lawyer, she went elsewhere. Why don't you check with the Department of Records to see if a new will was filed? It's not mandatory, but many attorneys recommend registering copies of important documents.'

Could that be a link to the murder of the elderly Records Clerk? His gut didn't have an answer. Travis made a mental note to check it out first thing in the morning. 'Why do I have the feeling you're holding out on me?'

'I assure you any information I have that is protected by lawyer/client privilege is not related to any of your investigations.'

'Really? Cases can lead to some pretty unexpected places. How can you make a broad statement like that when you don't know exactly which thread of what investigation I'm following at the moment?'

'Then allow me to rephrase. To the best of my knowledge, none of my private clients are currently under investigation.'

Travis realized he wouldn't get any more information and closed the conversation. As he walked back to his office he reviewed what he'd learned. Since checking out the purchase of the car had yielded so much information, Travis called Kasky's Cycle Shop in El Paso and fortunately connected with a chatty clerk.

'Yeah, I remember the couple who bought the Trek,' he said. 'We don't sell expensive bikes like that every day. That one is called the Executive. Super-light titanium body. Folds up with one lever to go up in an elevator like it shows on this brochure. I could mail you one. A brochure.'

'That's not necessary. What do you remember about the buyers?'

'Both tall and blonde. Good-looking for an old broad.'

That made the clerk what? Seventeen? 'Go on.'

'Not much else to say. Neither of them seemed to know anything about the sport of cycling.'

'Did they talk about anything while they shopped?'

'Not really. He talked to other customers about local trails. She was buying a birthday present for him and kept suggesting alternatives but he insisted he wanted a bicycle. So she said she wanted him to have the most expensive one in the store. Like I wish my girlfriend would take lessons from her. My last birthday, I got a wallet.'

'Anything else?'

'No. Not even a card.'

Travis cleared his throat. 'I meant anything else about those particular customers.'

'Yeah, in my opinion the rich are weird.'

Travis wouldn't argue that point.

As he sat down at his desk, he couldn't shake a feeling of general dissatisfaction but he was unsure whether it was caused by his inability to make any real progress in the case, or because his instincts seemed to be failing him when he needed them most. Unless something changed and he caught a break, Caroline would stand trial for murder.

16

Caroline paced the length of the shelves in the studio, naming the items she touched in an attempt to bring order to her mind. Three bald baby dolls. 'Curly, Larry and Moe.' Seven little green plastic army men in various poses. 'Sleepy, Doc, Grumpy, Dopey . . . ah, Blinky, Stinky, and Guido.'

'Park it somewhere,' Mimi said. 'Your wandering around and muttering is making me jumpy.'

Caroline stopped pacing and plopped on to a chair at the table. 'I don't know how you can be creative with everything that's been happening lately.'

'What better reason to escape into my work?'

'And that keeps you from worrying?'

'Focusing on a task or process provides a respite, even if it's only temporary.'

'I should be doing something to prove my innocence, not just sitting around and trusting Travis with my entire future. But I don't know what to do.'

Mimi made that noise that sounded like agreement but really meant she was in the zone with her work and not really listening.

Rather than interrupt her again, Caroline fell back on her tried and tested method of organizing research material that she used when writing a magazine article. After writing down all the facts on three-by-five cards, she arranged and rearranged them to find the thread that tied everything together. She finally threw up her hands in frustration. 'It doesn't make any sense.'

'I've found that when a piece isn't coming together, it's a signal that something is missing. If I back away from the problem, the answer pops into my mind when I least expect it, like when I'm cooking, or doing laundry.'

'I already did my chores for the day, thank you very much.' What she should have done was work on the article on gold prospectors she'd contracted to write for *Southwestern Life* that was due in two weeks and not writing itself. She pulled her laptop over and opened the file that held her research notes.

Five attempts to write a topic sentence failed miserably. She kept looking out the window and up the hill toward the kitchen door but whether she was watching for Dirk to come out or Travis to show up she couldn't have said. 'I can't concentrate.'

'Maybe you need a change of scene.'

New state equaled new state of mind?

Move to improve your mood? 'Travis would freak if I left town.'

'The cabin by the lake would be a perfect place for a writer.'

'It's beyond the town limits and I'd rather not give him any excuse to put me in handcuffs.' Again.

'The lake is within his jurisdiction so I'm sure it would be all right.'

Caroline shook her head. 'I need access to the Internet in case I need to check any facts or clarify any issues.'

Mimi walked across the studio and wiped her hands on a rag. She sat next to her granddaughter. 'You haven't been out to the cabin recently, have you?'

'No. I've been so busy.'

'The cabin used to be one of your favorite places.'

'Bobby Ray told me a lot of work has been done. I guess I didn't want to see the particulars of how Barbara had destroyed its rustic charm.'

'Why would Barbara do anything with the cabin? She hated nature,' Mimi said with a smile.

'I guess I just assumed it was Barbara because eventually she would have inherited the cabin from Aunt Rose who will inherit it from . . . you.' Caroline could kick herself.

She hadn't meant to ever bring up Mimi's illness even in the most oblique way. Although she'd always loved the cabin, family tradition dictated the lake property passed to the oldest daughter, which had meant Aunt Rose and then Barbara. 'I always knew Barbara would get it.' Even though that would change now, it would be years before Aunt Rose would have to make a decision in her will.

'I wasn't going to tell you this until you'd decided to stay in Haven — '

'Which I haven't and won't.'

'Well, I renovated the cabin. For you. The lake property is yours.'

'Mine?' Caroline blinked. 'You cut Rose out of your will in favor of me? No wonder she hates me.'

'No, no. Everything is fine. Rose legally relinquished any right to the property prior to her second marriage. She didn't want the cabin any more than her daughter did, and she agreed it should stay in the family. Barbara gladly gave up her place in the will in favor of a large cash settlement.'

'What about Jean?'

'Daughter-in-law. Doesn't count. And she'll get clear title to the ranch.'

'What about Dee Ann and Mary Lynn? They count.'

'Dee Ann wanted cash for the down payment on a house and Mary Lynn is going back to school this fall to become a veterinarian. She said they would probably have full use of the cabin anyway since you wouldn't be around very often. Don't tell me you want cash, too?'

Caroline opened her mouth to speak but hesitated. Cash to restart her business versus a rustic cabin filled with wonderful childhood memories. She could go back to LA and reopen her office. To again have the excitement and thrill of putting a Hollywood wedding together. And the headaches.

She'd never even considered the possibility that the beloved cabin could be hers, never in a million years. Had she just won the lottery? 'Yes.'

'Huh?'

'No. I mean no, I don't want cash instead. I mean yes, I don't want the cash. Or whatever. I'll be absolutely thrilled to inherit the lake cabin at some time far, far in the future.'

'Maybe you should see the renovations before saying you'd be thrilled. I tried to think of what you'd want but we don't exactly share the same decorating taste. You might hate it.' Mimi went to her desk and fetched a key out of the center drawer. She handed it to Caroline. 'You could go out there tonight.

There's still time before it gets full dark.'

'I don't know.' Daylight savings time meant sunset was at almost nine o'clock. Caroline glanced outside to check the light. Up at the house Dirk peered out the kitchen window. She pulled back even though she was pretty sure he couldn't have seen her. 'I guess I could make a quick trip. Want to come with me?'

'No, no. I'm feeling a bit drained. I just wanted to work for an hour or so before calling it a night, and it's about that time.'

Caroline peeked out the window again. Dirk had gone, she noted with a relieved sigh.

'I guess I'll wait on the field trip. Come on. I'll walk you up to the house.'

'Not necessary. I think I can find my way after all these years.'

Caroline turned out the lights and shut the door behind her grandmother. She flipped the strap of her computer carrying case over her shoulder and took Mimi's elbow with her free hand. 'Oh, let me be nice. Just say thank you and take it easy.'

'Thank you.'

They were both smiling when they entered the kitchen. Caroline's grin quickly faded. Dirk, who had been seated at the table on the side away from the window, jumped up and rushed to her side.

'I'm so glad you're back,' he said. 'I've been waiting for you. We need to talk.' He wrapped his fingers round her arm.

She jerked away and stepped out of his reach. 'I have nothing to say to you.'

'Now, now, don't be rude,' Mimi said.

Caroline almost told her grandmother that he had put the make on her earlier but she changed her mind. No one would believe her if she did say something. 'Sorry,' she said to Dirk. 'I don't have time to talk to you tonight. I'm leaving right now on a little field trip.'

Mimi looked at her with a confused expression.

Caroline kissed her on the forehead. 'Sweet dreams,' she said. 'I'll see you in the morning.' Hopefully, her raised eyebrows and emphatic nodding got across the message that she would be staying at the cabin overnight.

'Oh? Oh! Yes. Thank you. And sweet dreams to you, too.'

She picked up her laptop and left the kitchen thinking she should pack an overnight bag. She felt Dirk's gaze on her back and when she glanced back over her shoulder he squinted at her like he was trying to read her mind and figure out her plans. The need to escape shivered up her spine. She snagged her purse as she passed the table in the hallway and ran out the front door.

The drive up into the mountains only took twenty-five minutes. Caroline arrived at the lakeside just as the setting sun smeared the sky with glorious mango, papaya, and passion fruit smoothies. She drove up the winding gravel driveway and parked in front of the double garage that was used to store the boat, sports equipment, and lawn furniture off-season or when the cabin was not in use.

The silhouette of the cabin seemed the same with the steeply pitched cedar shake roof and the porch around three sides of the two-story structure. When she had been a child the porch had been perfect for sleeping on hot summer nights. Mattresses had been dragged out to cover the plank floor and the mosquito screens rolled down. Boys on the left. Girls on the right.

The boy cousins had wrestled and fought and made fun of the girls, laughing hysterically at the squeals that erupted when they tossed various items to the other side of the porch. The never-fail favorite? A stick thrown while screaming, 'Snake! Snake!'

Caroline smiled as she walked up the path. So many memories.

The girls had played games, giggled, told stories, and dressed and undressed their dolls until falling asleep wherever they happened to be when they stopped going full speed. Except Barbara. She always staked out her claim in the corner, outlining her territory with tiny Barbie doll clothes, miniature shoes, and purses. All of which Caroline had delighted in touching, moving, and rearranging for no other reason than to aggravate Barbara.

The cabin seemed bigger than before. The porch wider, floor smoother. Had the workmen found Barbie's red pumps that Caroline had stolen in retaliation for some childish hurt and had hidden in the space created by the porch wall and a knothole in the two-by-four vertical support?

The flimsy second-hand door had been replaced by one of solid oak. Caroline used the key Mimi had given her. Not sure what she'd expected, except maybe the previous oddball collection of hand-me-down furniture and once stylish lamps, she was astonished to find everything looked new. There were a few items that she might not have chosen, like the plaid couch in the living room in front of the big stone fireplace, or the olive-green towels in the bathroom. She also didn't care for the guest bedrooms done in the themes of what she could only call Boat and Tree, but she would probably convert one into an office anyway.

The kitchen was perfect with large black and white tiles on the floor and stainless-steel appliances. Caroline walked around, touching, naming, making it her own. A red vinyl dinette set transported straight from the fifties was kitschy chic. The pantry had been stocked with non-perishables and canned goods and there were two bottles in the wine cooler.

Best of all, the third bedroom had been expanded into a luxurious master suite. Additions included a fireplace, scenic view, floor-to-ceiling windows, a breakfast nook, walk-in closet, and a bathroom to die for. Beach blue and white accessories and seashells set the design tone. The claw-foot tub seemed made for the bathing alcove. A walk-in shower connected via glass doors to an outdoor shower with flagstone floor. Thick towels and a terry robe waited nearby ready to pop into the warming drawer. Caroline picked up a shell-shaped soap and closed her eyes in pleasure as she inhaled the clean scent.

She walked back into the bedroom and turned in a slow circle. 'I am never leaving this room.' Stretching her arms wide, she flopped back on to the bed. She closed her eyes and sank boneless into the plush coverlet, realizing she hadn't really relaxed for days, weeks. First the wedding, then the murder.

Thirty seconds later her eyes popped open. She wouldn't be free to totally unwind until the question of who murdered Barbara was answered. 'Arrrgh,' she said, rolling to a sitting position and rising.

She settled at a small game table in the living room and opened her laptop. The purpose of coming to the cabin was to write her article, but even in the peaceful setting she couldn't concentrate. Instead of working on her article, she decided to use her research skills to find out everything about Barbara and the murder.

Starting with the Internet site of the town paper, she progressed to the Miami papers to see if the engagement announcements there offered anything of interest. What did Barbara's prospective in-laws think of their son marrying outside their elevated social circle? Strangely, there wasn't any announcement in the social pages. What did that mean?

She continued her research. Dirk was described as a multi-millionaire with wide real estate investment interests. In actuality he was a bit older than he looked, and she credited expensive spa treatments, possibly even plastic surgery, for his appearance. His name was mentioned often, but there were no clear photos. A few side-shots, pictures of a man holding a menu, hat, and jacket lapel in front of his face. The news articles referred to him several times as camera-shy and reclusive. So that's why Dirk had insisted on his friend taking the wedding photos, the friend who hadn't shown up, the friend who most likely didn't exist.

Digging deeper into the archives she discovered Dirk had been married before, three years ago. His wife, sole heir to the Wheatly Pot Pie fortune, had died tragically in a private plane accident. Caroline was on a roll. She kept going, skimming articles on polo matches, opera openings, and charity balls. To her surprise, she found another wife, another heiress. That one succumbed to some mysterious illness while on an African safari honeymoon.

Anxious to share the information, Caroline called Travis, but he'd already left the office. Harlan wouldn't give out his cell number, but he promised to pass on the message to call her. Then she found a nine-year-old article in a Miami social column that insinuated a certain handsome camera-shy fellow had a sudden rise in prospects thanks to the generosity of a certain father. Underage daughter of said father had left quite suddenly for an exclusive school in Switzerland. Not hard to put two and two together.

She heard a car engine, tires on the gravel drive, and then a car door shutting. Thank goodness Travis had decided to respond to her call in person. Wondering what he'd make of the new information she'd found, she opened the door wide. And immediately tried to slam it shut.

Dirk pushed his way inside and walked around. 'So this is the inside of the cabin. Not bad. Hate the couch.'

'Really? I love plaid.' Caroline crossed her arms. 'Sorry you can't stay. I'm working.'

He stood next to the table and rudely turned her laptop so he could read her screen.

Fortunately, she'd gotten into the habit of minimizing her work if she left her desk for any reason. 'Goodbye, Dirk.' She held the door open with one hand and motioned him out with the other.

He crossed the room to stand close, putting his hand over hers on the doorknob.

She pulled away and stepped back, not bothering to hide her shocked disgust. He used her movement to slide in next to the door, closing it as he knelt on one knee.

'I know I should have brought flowers or maybe even waited until we could have a romantic dinner, but I just couldn't keep it to myself any longer. I love you and want to be with you. I know your family might object to an immediate wedding so let's drive to Vegas tonight. We can be married by tomorrow.'

'Don't be ridiculous.' Was he crazy?

He reached for her, following her, walking on his knees. 'I love you so. You are the light of my life.'

'Oh, stop it.' He didn't take subtle hints. He ignored outright rejection. What was it with this guy? 'I will not marry you, not now, not ever. I think you should go.'

Dirk laughed as he stood up. 'At least we can stop the stupid love charade.' He pulled a small pistol out of his pocket and pointed it at Caroline, demanding she sit.

She eased down on a straight-back chair, easier to jump up and run if she got the opportunity. Her best chance for escape was to remain calm, and to calm him if possible.

'This will work out just fine,' he said. 'You won't be expected to attend the funeral. Right after that we'll leave for Vegas.'

'Why do you want to marry me? I'm not an heiress. Neither was Barbara. Isn't that your usual choice?'

'Come, come, you can't be as stupid as Barbara. Are you telling me you didn't know the Silverside Resort Corporation wants this

341

land for the development of a conference center and racetrack?'

'This property? There must be some mistake.'

'No, I double checked the official plat surveys. That old bitch didn't want to let me see them, but I took care of her.'

'You killed Mrs Crocket?'

Dirk shrugged. 'She got in my way. Just like your senile grandmother did.'

'She's not — '

'She most certainly is. How else can you explain her turning down my company's reasonable offer of ten million dollars? *I want to keep it in the family,*' he mimicked in a high voice. 'I could have flipped that deal in two weeks and made a sweet three mil, but no. I thought about using Rose to swing the deal but she'd recently married and that complicated the situation. My best choice was Barbara. Once we were married, and dear Granny and Mama had been helped to their final rewards, I'd be back in business.'

'Wouldn't another wife suddenly kicking the bucket so soon after the wedding alert the authorities that something was wrong?'

'That's the beauty of my plan. I wouldn't have had any problem talking Barbara into selling the land. Since New Mexico is a community property state, a simple divorce would net me fifty percent. I'd have made at least five million, which would have done me just fine. Would have made the extra six months worthwhile. But no, it can never be easy. Barbara had to screw that up.'

Keeping her voice calm, Caroline asked, 'Is that why you killed her?'

Dirk gave her a calculating glare, then suddenly his face cleared and he smiled. 'Since you'll soon be my wife and therefore unable to testify against me, I see no reason you shouldn't know.' He paced the room as he spoke, gesticulating wildly. 'Everything was going so well, sweet set-up and smooth execution of my brilliant plan. Then Mimi announced you were returning to Haven, hopefully to stay. Barbara wasn't happy about that, never having been fond of you.'

'No surprise.'

'I tuned out her ranting until she mentioned the lakeside property. Imagine my shock when Barbara said Mimi had changed her will and the land would go to you.'

'Her idea. She told Mimi she preferred a cash settlement.'

'Yeah, right. Fifty thousand instead of a ten-million-dollar property at the very least on the open market. Great deal. Even Barbara couldn't be that stupid. At least, I thought so until I checked out the will myself.

Unfortunately, it had been registered with the county so simply destroying it would do no good. My only choice was to come up with a plan B, but I was running out of time. Once the Silverside Resort Corporation announces their plans to develop at the lake the real estate sharks will have a feeding frenzy. My only choice is to marry you.'

'But Barbara didn't agree?'

'She went ballistic when I told her the wedding was off. She just wouldn't shut up. Why won't they ever shut up?' He brought his fists to his forehead as he paced, and the pistol shook with the tension. He spun around to face Caroline, snapping his hands to his side. 'She actually threatened me. Me!'

Caroline couldn't think of anything to say. She tried not to move a muscle.

Dirk started pacing again. 'I showed her. Nobody threatens a Vandergelt. No sirree. I am the man with the plan.'

He continued muttering to himself, but the walking and talking seemed to calm him down. After several transits back and forth he paused and slid a sideways glance at her. 'I know what you're thinking. You're wondering why you should marry me. Especially after this.'

'The thought had occurred to me.'

He raised a mocking eyebrow. 'By marrying

me you get to be a heroine and save the rest of your family. For instance, if you don't, an anonymous tip will direct the police to the exact place in your brother Ray's room where they'll find Barbara's missing diamond engagement ring. As a third-time offender, he'll spend a long, long time behind bars.'

Caroline hid a smile. Not for possession of that ring he wouldn't. 'I believe the justice system will prevail.' She stuck out her chin. 'I'll never, ever marry you.'

He sneered at her bravado. 'I'm prepared for your resistance. I made it my business to find out all about you. The town doctor's files were most illuminating.'

'You killed poor Annabelle just so you could read my medical file?'

'So I could figure how to swing a ten-million-dollar deal. Oh yes, I know you were pregnant when you graduated from high school. Won't that rock the gossips of your stupid provincial little town? Miss Goody-two-shoes Tucker, unwed mother. Your deep dark secret.'

The heartache of her miscarriage resurfaced, a pain she'd thought long forgotten. Although she had tears in her eyes, Caroline forced herself to laugh at his threat. 'That won't matter to my family, considering we have more skeletons than closets. And for your information, I was married to Travis Beaumont at the time. I didn't get divorced until the end of that summer.'

'No.' He shook his head. His eyes widened and the pupils dilated, the growing panic visible. 'No. My grand scheme can't be unraveling, not again. First that bitch Barbara and now you.' He pulled pieces of rope from his pocket and, after a struggle that seemed to last for ever but couldn't have been more than a few minutes, finally managed to bind her to the chair.

As soon as he walked out the door she wrestled to get free, only succeeding in chaffing the skin of her wrists and ankles raw. She heard a car door slam but instead of the hoped-for engine sound, Dirk returned carrying a briefcase.

He dumped the contents on the table, and after pawing through the papers confronted Caroline. 'I have copies of every single official record filed at the Court-house that contains your name, and there's no record of any marriage.'

'I wasn't married in Haven, we eloped, so there wouldn't be a local record, but my divorce papers were filed here.'

He dug through the papers. 'I was in a hurry when I copied these, but I don't remember a . . . Damn.' He shook the paper under her nose. 'It's an application for divorce. An application that isn't completed,' he shouted. 'You're still married.'

Vandergelt howled in frustration.

Caroline nearly fainted in shock.

17

Travis stopped at the Tucker house to walk his grandmother home. The older women were arranging three-by-five cards in patterns on the dining-room table.

'Is this some weird new card game?'

'Caroline started it,' Mimi said. 'She wrote down everything she knew about Barbara and the murder on three-by-five cards. She thought that by moving them around she might find a connecting thread or pattern.'

'We added a few cards,' Lou said.

'But we're still not seeing any connection,' Jean added.

Travis leaned over and whispered in his grandmother's ear, 'It's time to leave.'

'Just a couple of minutes more. I feel it in my gut. We're close to something, so close.'

Travis shrugged and took a seat. What difference would a few minutes make? He grabbed a few blank cards and added Lewis, Paul and Regan and as suspects. Mentally, he factored in Barbara's affair with Judge McKay.

The women had arranged the cards in a starburst shape around the wedding events.

Even though Barbara was supposed to be the common denominator, Travis kept seeing Caroline's name pop up. Was that just because he was more interested in her than in Barbara on a personal level? He shoved that thought aside and concentrated on mentally rearranging the cards by different criteria. Grouping them by location didn't give him anything, but when he re-shuffled them in date and time order, he saw that Caroline's return home was the catalyst for the crime wave.

'Give me some more cards,' he said, scooting his chair closer.

'Please,' Lou reminded him.

'Shush,' Mimi said. 'I think he's on to something.'

He shook his head. 'Close but no banana.' He stood up and pushed the chair back under the table. 'The puzzle pieces don't make sense. And it's time for us to go,' he said, looking meaningfully at Lou.

'Okay. We'll all sleep on it and try again in the morning.'

As they turned to leave, Travis couldn't shake a feeling. 'I don't know what all that means.' He waved to encompass the table. 'But my gut says Caroline is in danger. When she comes downstairs, tell her to stick close to home.'

Mimi and Jean looked at each other with wide eyes.

'What?'

'Caroline went to the lake house to have some peace and quiet in order to work,' Mimi said.

Travis was out of the house and on his way to the cabin almost before the words were out of her mouth.

*   *   *

'I've invested months of planning and preparation for what? You and that bitch Barbara have cost me five million dollars,' Dirk said, back to pacing the room. 'There must be some way to salvage my brilliant plan.'

'I could get a divorce,' Caroline volunteered. After all she would be doing *that* anyway.

'Shut up.' He pounded his fist on his forehead. 'Think! Think!'

Caroline tried to loosen the ropes on her hands again, but not only had Dirk tied them together but he'd also tied her arms to the sides of the chair back. If she could just make it into the woods, she could find a trail to the main road. She knew the area and he didn't.

'I have to go to the bathroom. If you'll untie

me, I promise — '

'Shut up.' Dirk fired a shot over her head, breaking out the window.

Her ears rang from the explosive shot in such a small area. Her eyes watered and her nose itched from the gunpowder smoke. She couldn't reach for a tissue, so she tipped her head back and blinked, turning her head from side to side. She fought the urge to cry for real. Miles from the nearest neighbor, she couldn't hope that someone would have heard the shot and would investigate. Keeping her spirits up was difficult, but if she were going to escape this madman, she had only herself to depend on.

★　★　★

Travis heard the shot as he ran toward the cabin. His gut clenched but he couldn't allow himself to think of Caroline wounded, or worse. His best chance to save her was to be smart, cautious. The driveway seemed miles long as he traveled on foot from where he'd left his car. He paused next to the second car in the driveway. Vandergelt! He should have known. And now the bastard was with Caroline.

Moving in slow motion while his brain screamed *hurry, hurry*, he crossed the acre of porch and peeked through the window, assessing the situation in a fraction of a moment. Travis paused with his back to the wall long enough to take a deep breath. Then he kicked the door open. But Vandergelt must have heard the porch floor creak because when Travis entered, the felon was standing behind Caroline with a gun to her head.

'If it isn't the nosey neighbor. Come on in, Sheriff. Oh, that's right. You are already in. Well, then, drop your gun and move over to the fireplace with your hands up. That's it.'

Travis allowed himself one quick glance at Caroline to reassure himself that she was unharmed. No blood or visible signs of injury, but he couldn't look into her eyes or he wouldn't be able to pull his gaze away, and he needed to concentrate on the crazy man with the gun.

Vandergelt laughed. 'It's so perfect, one would think I'd invited the Sheriff to join us. Don't you see, my dear? Now instead of killing you, I'll make you a widow and then we can still be married as I'd planned.'

Travis didn't understand what the man was talking about, but he needed to distract him until reinforcements could arrive. 'Perhaps you'll answer a few questions first,' Travis said to Vandergelt. 'You know, clear up a few details.'

'I suppose,' Vandergelt said in a hesitant voice as if the Sheriff's casual attitude confused him. 'What questions?'

'Why did you kill Monique? I saw the Trek bicycle in the back seat of your car and figured out that was how you got back to the inn and your car from the crime scene after killing Barbara, but Monique was killed before that. She couldn't have seen you while out on one of her rides.'

'She's the one who showed me that particular trail. We rode it together several times while I was still solidifying my plans. Then she knew too much and became a liability.'

Vandergelt, distracted by talking to Travis, dropped his arm. Caroline had been waiting for a break, and she pushed off with her feet, threw her head back, and tipped her chair over backwards, knocking him down. Travis lunged forward and wrestled the gun away from him. With his shin pressing one side of Vandergelt's face into the floorboards and his knee planted between the downed man's shoulder blades, he cuffed the villain's hands behind his back. Then Travis freed Caroline.

'Are you all right?'

She nodded.

'When I heard that shot . . . ' No more words would come out of his throat. He folded her into his embrace, rocking her slightly from side to side, wishing he didn't have to let her go. 'You're sure you're all right? He didn't hurt you, did he?'

'I'm shaken up, and my wrists and ankles are sore, but other than that I'm fine.' She straightened her spine and pushed away from him. 'We have to talk.'

Vandergelt moved, as if he were trying to stand and make a break for it. Travis knelt, placing his knee in the small of the other man's back, pushing him back down on the floor, not roughly, but firmly. He leaned over and said to his prisoner, 'If you even twitch in the direction of the door, I'll see it as an attempt to escape.' His voice was low and level, almost soothing. 'You know I'd welcome any excuse to shoot you where it hurts most, don't you, you sick son of a bitch?'

As Travis stood and led Caroline to a seat on the sofa and wrapped his jacket around her shoulders, he heard one of the loveliest sounds in the world: glorious sirens. 'Reinforcements will be here any minute.'

Caroline blurted out everything that had happened, and everything Dirk had told her about killing poor Mrs Crocket and Annabelle, ending with the shocking fact that their divorce papers were never finalized.

Travis wasn't sure what to say to that. The

entrance of two deputies gave him a reprieve. He raised an eyebrow. 'Who's minding the store?'

Harlan and Bobby Lee looked at each other and then turned to Travis with deer-in-the-headlight stares.

'I transferred the phones to county nine-one-one,' Phyllis explained as she sidestepped the boys. 'State troopers are on patrol in town to cover for us.'

'Good job. I want you to process Vandergelt's car.'

'Am I looking for anything in particular?'

'Hopefully evidence linking him to all our unsolved crimes.'

Phyllis left with jaunty steps to get her evidence kit.

Travis turned to Bobby Lee. 'I want you to take your sister home.'

'But I wanted — '

'This is not the time to ask for a transfer.'

'No, that's not what — '

'But that's what you're going to get if you don't leave this instant to pull your car up to the door.'

Bobby Lee saluted and scooted out the door. Travis turned to Harlan. 'First, wipe that grin off your face. You will bring my car close to the door behind Bobby Lee's, and then put the prisoner in the back seat. If he escapes, you might as well go with him because I'll shoot you both.'

The deputy turned and ran. Travis wondered if he had laid it on a little too thick, but shrugged off the thought. He sat on the sofa next to Caroline and took her ice-cold hands in his. 'I've got to take the prisoner to the station,' he said. 'Bobby Lee will take you home.'

'I've got my car.'

'Let your brother drive. You've had a traumatic experience and even if you're all right, he needs to be reassured of that by taking care of you.' Was he talking about her brother or himself?

'Okay,' Caroline said.

'I'll see you soon.' She had some major explaining to do.

★   ★   ★

'Why weren't my divorce papers filed?' Caroline asked as soon as she got to talk to her grandmother alone. She'd had to explain everything three times and to reassure her mother, brothers, and grandmother that she was fine innumerable times. As soon as everyone had calmed down and gone upstairs Caroline had headed straight to her grandmother's room.

Propped up in her old-fashioned poster

bed, Mimi laid her book in her lap, and took off her reading glasses. 'I can't sleep either. I swear, I've never been so afraid as when Travis lit outta here like his skivvies were on fire.' She blinked away tears. 'I'm glad, as I didn't want to lose another granddaughter to that monster.'

Caroline waved away her concern as if being tied up and having a gun held to her head was nothing compared to the fact that she was still married to Travis. 'I'm fine. Don't try to change the subject.'

Only then did Caroline notice that Mimi was wearing the oversized flannel robe that had once belonged to her grandfather. Mimi only wore that particular robe snuggled around her when she needed to feel comforted, safe. Caroline rushed to Mimi's bedside where she knelt and took Mimi's hand. 'I'm sorry.' She laid her cheek on the back of her grand-mother's hand.

Mimi stroked Caroline's hair. 'You have always been a great joy to me, a big pain in the ass at times, but a joy nonetheless.'

'I can't believe I'm not divorced.' She sat up to look her grandmother in the eye. 'I can't believe you kept that fact a secret from me. What if I had fallen in love and wanted to get married?'

'That would have been wonderful. It's what

357

I've always wanted for you.'

'Bigamy is not wonderful.'

'But it wouldn't have been a second marriage. Your divorce couldn't be completed because you were never legally married to begin with.'

'What?' Good thing Caroline was near the floor and didn't have far to fall because she was afraid she might faint.

Mimi sat up and swung her legs over the side, 'Let's talk about this over a nice cup of soothing herbal tea.'

'We're not going anywhere until you explain.' Caroline stood, or technically sat, her ground and blocked Mimi from rising. She held her grandmother's steady stare for several long seconds, finally realizing she couldn't literally make the other woman talk and she desperately needed some answers. She stood. 'You wait here. I'll fix a tray.'

'Oh, that's not necessary. I need to get up and stretch my legs anyway.'

Apparently, they were going to do this Mimi's way or not at all. Caroline let out a sigh and used her foot to scoot Mimi's slippers closer to the bed. 'I'll put the kettle on,' she said, turning on her heel and heading for the kitchen.

'Use the electric one,' Mimi called after her. 'It's faster.'

Caroline wound up making a tray anyway. She settled Mimi in one of the comfy chairs in the den, brought her a footstool, covered her legs with an Afghan, and served her a steaming mug of tea before curling up in the big leather armchair opposite her. 'Okay? Now spill it.'

Mimi cleared her throat. 'When you eloped with the intent of getting married at one minute after midnight on your eighteenth birthday, you forgot to take into account the time difference. You were technically still underage and unable to marry without parental permission. The sleepy justice of the peace assumed you were the age you said you were and recorded the wrong birth year. No one noticed until the divorce papers didn't match. According to the lawyer, you and Travis were never legally married.'

'Why would the lawyer tell you and not contact me?'

'You gave me power of attorney to handle your divorce. Walter Senior did everything he was supposed to do.'

'And you never bothered to tell me about all this because?'

'Well, it's not the sort of news one shares over the phone and every time you were home for your short, very short, visits, the time just never seemed right. And truthfully, after a while it didn't really seem to matter. You and Travis both thought you were divorced, which is the same as not being married.'

'It's not the same.'

'Essentially the same.'

'No. Never having been married is not the same as having been married, failing at that, and then getting a divorce. Being a divorcee influenced many of my decisions over the last ten years. I feel as if I've been cheated somehow.'

'Why? Even if it's different, it's not important. The actual events of your non-marriage haven't changed. No one else would overreact like you're doing.'

Caroline shook her head. 'Of course not. Why should I expect to be told about something so important? This is just another indication of the reasons I left home in the first place. This family is crazy. How can I ever expect to lead a normal life, have a normal husband, when any sane person would run screaming in the opposite direction as soon as he met my family?'

She jerked back in shock when Mimi stood and threw the Afghan on to the seat behind her. 'Frances Caroline Tucker! For the first time in your life I am ashamed of you.'

Caroline hadn't realized she had been

ranting aloud. 'Sorry, I didn't mean — '

'I'm not sure if you even knew what you wanted when you left, but I did. You're still searching for some advertiser-invented chimera named normality, while meanwhile, real life is passing you by.'

'Why is wanting a normal family so impossible?'

'Because there's no such thing. Every family is dysfunctional in a unique and irreplaceable way. If you no longer want to be part of this family, you can have your wish. But remember when the town council thought you guilty of murder, your crazy family stood by you, believed in you, and did everything possible to help prove your innocence including putting themselves at risk.'

Caroline folded her arms. 'I didn't ask anyone for help.'

'Isn't that the point of family?' Mimi walked to the door, paused, and turned back long enough to say, 'Striving to be the best you can be is good, but requiring perfection in others only leads to heartache.'

Caroline stared into her mug as if the murky liquid could provide some answers. Mimi had made it sound as if she was as bad as Barbara and that certainly couldn't be true.

Okay, when she ran her own business maybe she was too demanding, but wedding planning was a stressful industry. Maybe if she'd gotten to know her employees personally her assistant might have felt a responsibility to give her a heads up so she could have done something in advance to mitigate the damage. What, she didn't know.

Or maybe mysterious forces were at work and she was *supposed* to be back in Haven for some reason. Like to be around for Mimi.

Caroline realized her herbal tea had cooled. She gathered up the tea things and carried them to the kitchen. But she wasn't ready to go to bed so she warmed up her cup and carried it outside and across the yard to the rose garden. As a child she had loved stretching out on the bench and looking up at the stars. The constellations had made her problems seem insignificant while at the same time making her feel like she was a part of something glorious and grand, albeit a very small part.

Her near-to-death experience at the cabin gave her a new perspective, made her examine her priorities. What did she really want out of life? Going back to LA wasn't appealing anymore. Whatever it was, she knew she wanted to include her eccentric relatives.

She heard faint music, followed the sound to the back end of the yard next door, and found Travis in his open garage, working on his motorcycle. Dressed in a white undershirt and jeans, he wiped a metal part with a rag that smelled of gasoline.

'Good evening.'

He looked up. 'Hey. Come in and sit a spell. Can I get you a drink? Beer? Diet Coke?'

'No thanks.' She held up her cup. 'Herbal tea.'

He made a strangled sound in his throat.

'Don't laugh.'

'I didn't.'

She shook her head and rolled her eyes.

'How are you doing?' he asked.

'Fine. I'm fine.'

'I'm glad to hear you say that. But you did have a traumatic experience. Probably wouldn't hurt you to talk to a counselor.'

'I'll think about it.'

The uncomfortable silence stretched to several long, torturous minutes. She knew what she wanted to talk about, but she didn't want to blurt it out like she had the news that they were still married. 'This mess reminds me of old times,' she finally said.

He'd spent many hours in his garage and she'd spent many hours watching him, either from her bedroom window or sitting on the chest freezer as she now was.

'Yeah. When I decided to get this ancient bike back on the road I didn't know the extent of damage sitting idle could do. I expected the tires to be shot but this sludge in the carburetor was an unpleasant surprise.'

'And I know how much you like surprises,' she said with a shake of her head to indicate the opposite.

'In my line of work, surprises are at the very least unpleasant and at the very worst can get you dead.'

'You hated surprises before you became a cop.'

He chuckled. 'You might be right about that.'

'You know I am. Well, I probably won't get any better opening so I guess I'll jump in with both feet here. Don't you hate that expression? I mean it's not as if a person could jump in with any less than both feet. Unless they only had one leg, but I've never heard a one-legged person use that expression.'

'You're babbling.'

She had a tendency to run on when she was nervous and they both knew it. 'The good news is that we're not still married.'

He didn't cheer as she expected.

What he did do was put down the carburetor and wipe his hands as he came over to sit next to her. She told him what Mimi had told her about them never being legally married in the first place.

He reacted with a long, low whistle. 'Ain't that a kick in the butt.'

'That's what I said to Mimi, different words, but same meaning and she totally didn't understand. I have to confess marriage to you, and even our divorce, was an emotional anchor of sorts. For better or worse the connection defined me. Now that it's gone, I feel rather like a boat that has slipped its moorings and is drifting rudderless with storm warnings on the horizon.'

'I understand. I've been feeling that way all evening and didn't know how to describe it. Tell you what, let's get married again, then we can get divorced again. Put us both back on an even keel.'

'No, thanks. Not that I don't appreciate the generous offer but I've got my family and right now I think that's anchor enough.'

He ducked his head. 'Whatever happened to us? I know we were young but I would have bet anything we would have beat the odds.'

Her recent reliving of her tragic miscarriage resurfaced. She blinked away tears. Mimi had kept her secret, but he deserved to know the truth. 'I blamed you for going off with your fool friends to that motorcycle race, for being gone when I needed you most.'

'You're the one who left me while I was away. Mimi said you'd changed your mind about being married and had decided to pursue college and a career.'

'That's true but not the whole story. I made that decision when I was in the hospital recovering from a miscarriage.'

'What? I never knew — '

'I called you dozens of times. You never answered and I couldn't leave that news on voicemail.'

'We were so far out in the country there wasn't any cell reception. I saw all the missed calls when I got back into town but by then you weren't answering your phone.'

'That sounds logical now but at the time all I knew was that I needed you and you weren't there. I was afraid it would always be like that, me waiting for you to return and I couldn't face that.'

'I didn't know about the miscarriage — hell, I didn't know about the pregnancy. How can you blame me for something I knew nothing about?'

'Would it have made a difference? Would you have stayed home from that race if you'd known I was pregnant? I don't think so.'

'We'll never know that for sure.'

'Well, back then I didn't think it would make a difference and that's why I decided I should learn to take care of myself.'

'Well, that's two knockdowns today.'

'What do you mean?'

'Being emotionally kicked in the back of the knees. Like when I was running toward the cabin. I heard the gunshot and was afraid I'd lost you for good. I realized then that I want you in my life. I want us to be together. Can you give us a second chance?'

'When pigs fly.'

'You came into my arms easily enough.'

True. And wasn't that what she'd always wanted in her heart of hearts, a second chance with Travis? But she was older now and presumably smarter. 'We can't base a relationship on one adrenaline-filled evening. The reasons we got divorced haven't changed. But we can be friends.'

Travis stood. 'I'm not interested in your friendship.' He walked away, and did not look back.

18

Dear Hopeful,

There are many traditions and super-stitions concerning wedding dresses. As for wearing a dress for a second time, often the dress is the something old or the something borrowed of the time-honored rhyme. It's considered good luck to wear a dress worn by a happily married woman. If I understand your convoluted explanation, the twelve-thousand-dollar wedding dress you want to wear is the one you wore previously when the groom did a no-show. (Hopefully, that was a different man to your current fiancé.) Your reasons are logical: cost of the gown, the fact that you only wore it for a short time, and the new groom had never seen it. Add to that the expense of a replacement gown when you can no longer afford it.

I think it boils down to one question: who did you buy the dress for? Brides choose gowns to please mothers, fathers, friends, the groom, the wedding planner, or their children. If you bought the wedding dress to please yourself, and not any of the others, especially the old groom, and if this is the dress that makes you feel wonderful, then start a new tradition of your own and wear it.

If you're worried that the dress might hold some residual bad luck for you, sell it and use the proceeds to purchase a different gown. There are many wonderful gowns at a much lower price point. If you plan ahead, many bridal shops have clearance days when the prices are slashed on off-the-rack gowns. Have an idea of what you want and enlist your friend's help. I've even heard of women who've gone to the sale with a friend and wound up buying for themselves because the price of the perfect dress was too good to let pass, even though they weren't engaged. Now there's a bride who is dressing to please herself.

Another plan you might consider is to have a seamstress (one with lots of wedding-dress experience) make some minor changes so the dress looks very similar but not exactly the same. You can always point out those differences if anyone is rude enough to say something.

In closing, need I remind you, the wedding should be about your commitment to *each other. Everything else, including what you're wearing, is of lesser importance.*

Yours truly,

Mrs Bea Correct

Caroline sent off her response to *Weddings! Weddings!* and checked her watch. 'Yikes.' Her date would be there to pick her up in less than half an hour and she wasn't ready. She quickly straightened the waiting room and her display of samples. The business had been moderately successful during the four months since she'd opened. She still had to write articles for a second income stream, but that gave her something to do on the days when no one, absolutely no one, came into the store.

Satisfied everything was set for the following day and her nine o'clock appointment, she rushed to the back room to run a comb through her hair, change her earrings from simple gold hoops to rhinestone chandeliers, and apply a darker shade of lipstick. The bell over the door signaled her date's entrance.

'I'll be right there,' she called. She grabbed her satin clutch and lace shawl, re-entered the main room, and skidded to a halt.

Travis Beaumont was the last person she expected to see standing in the middle of her bridal salon, clipboard in hand.

'Hello,' she said. 'I'm just on my way out.'

'I only need a minute. I'm running for Sheriff in the next election and need five hundred signatures on this petition to be included on the ballot.' He handed her the clipboard.

She looked at the top page. The lines were numbered from four hundred and seventy-five to five hundred. Only one more signature was needed to reach the required amount. Her signature would allow him to run for Sheriff and stay in Haven.

'I didn't know you'd decided to stay. Won't you miss the excitement of Chicago?'

'So far things have been less than peaceful, especially since you came back. I think I'll stick around and see what happens.'

She scribbled her name on the petition. 'Well, good luck in the election.'

'Harlan's running against me,' he said with a grin.

'Well . . . ' She waved toward the door. 'I closed at five.'

'Can I use your phone? My cell is low on battery and I need to save it for emergencies.'

'Okay. Sure.' She pointed to the desk against the back wall.

'Actually, that's just an excuse. I wanted to give you this.' Travis handed her a small box that was obviously from a jewelry store.

'What's this?'

'That depends on how you feel about me,' he replied.

She untied the ribbon and opened the box. Inside was a fine silver chain necklace with an inch-tall silver pig pendant with ruby eyes and golden wings. A flying pig.

Before she could think of a response, Walter arrived exactly on time for their date.

The two men greeted each other, wary as two stallions in one corral.

'Going to the tractor pull out at the fairgrounds?' Travis asked.

The lawyer snorted. 'Dinner and the Desabo Art Gallery in El Paso. A friend of mine has an exhibit opening tonight.'

If she didn't do something quickly, they would start pawing the ground and butting heads. 'We need to leave now if we're going to be on time,' she said, taking Walter's arm and leading him out of the store. She paused at the door to flip the lock and hang the closed sign before turning back to say to Travis, 'Feel free to use the phone. Just turn off the light and pull the door closed behind you.'

Walter had parked right in front of the store and he opened the car door for her and closed it after she'd settled inside. While he ran around the back of the car to the driver's side, she opened her purse and dropped in the small jeweler's box. The promise it symbolized gave her a secret thrill.

She named the tiny flying pig Lucky.

Five interesting things about Laurie Brown:

1. I am a true shoe-a-holic and have over a hundred pairs of shoes to prove it. (This addiction probably stems from having to wear ugly brown orthopaedic oxfords as a child.) Now I've reached a point where if I buy another pair, one of the others has to go. Either that or my office/overflow closet will become just a closet and then where will I write?

2. Cotton balls make me shiver like when fingernails scratch across a chalkboard. I can't bear to touch them. I swear they make noise when they're squeezed, but no one else in my family seems to hear it.

3. Cooking shows on television fascinate me but they haven't made me any better at coping with kitchen duty. Thankfully my husband is marvellous. Don't you just love a man who cooks?

4. I love crossword puzzles but must restrict myself to the one in the Sunday newspaper.

If I buy those little books of puzzles all I wind up doing is copying the answers found in the back.

5. I can drink coffee anytime, anywhere, any flavour. Love it.

We do hope that you have enjoyed reading this large print book.

Did you know that all of our titles are available for purchase?

We publish a wide range of high quality large print books including:
Romances, Mysteries, Classics
General Fiction
Non Fiction and Westerns

Special interest titles available in large print are:
The Little Oxford Dictionary
Music Book
Song Book
Hymn Book
Service Book

Also available from us courtesy of Oxford University Press:
Young Readers' Dictionary
(large print edition)
Young Readers' Thesaurus
(large print edition)

For further information or a free brochure, please contact us at:
Ulverscroft Large Print Books Ltd.,
The Green, Bradgate Road, Anstey,
Leicester, LE7 7FU, England.
Tel: (00 44) 0116 236 4325
Fax: (00 44) 0116 234 0205

Other titles published by
The House of Ulverscroft:

A CHANGE FOR THE BETTER

Pamela Fudge

Jo Farrell has spent her whole life caring for others, but with the timely departure of both her alcoholic husband and her demanding mother, Jo finally has the peaceful existence she's always craved. Finally, she has a chance to look at herself . . . but when she does, she doesn't much like what she sees. Jo has no idea where to start so she makes a list of all the things she once planned to do before life got the better of her . . . and as she starts to make changes, her life comes together in ways she never expected . . .

HARD TO GET

Jessica Fox

'Love will come through hope alone', or so a fortune-teller tells Charlotte at her future sister-in-law Zoe's hen night. But Charlotte's love life is utterly hopeless. She's decidedly single and unhappy about her ex-husband Richard working with her at the Arts Council, especially as he's dating her boss. When Charlotte and Richard's work trip to Yorkshire includes a visit to the Hope Foundation, Charlotte has to laugh — although she wonders if the spark between them really has been snuffed out. And what about devoted single dad Paul? And the dark, brooding Heath? Perhaps Charlotte has reason to hope after all . . .

LEOPARD ROCK

Tarras Wilding

Journalist Roo Beckett longs to go on safari, so when she wins a fabulous prize — an all-expenses-paid, month-long trip making a documentary at Leopard Rock, South Africa, at the home of the famous wildlife film-maker Wyk Kruger — she's ecstatic. Unexpectedly accompanied by her freeloading magazine colleagues (tagging along uninvited for some exotic-sounding fun), Roo is concerned that the stern, sexy Wyk won't take her seriously. But Wyk's too busy hiding his family secrets to notice anything — except that Roo is far too attractive for her own good.

TALK OF THE TOWN

Suzanne Macpherson

Sometimes Mr Right is actually Mr Very Wrong, as Kelly Atwood discovers on her wedding day. Her vows said nothing about sticking by a drug-smuggling husband. So, after delivering a neat left hook, which knocks Raymond out cold, she heads to the tiny Washington town of Paradise. When the runaway bride bumps into attorney Sam Grayson, it's clear she makes him hot under his super-starched collar. But Kelly, unaware that her suitcase is stuffed with dirty money, is being followed by some dodgy characters. Meanwhile, passion must take a back seat — right now she's just running for her life . . .

TRUE LOVE AND OTHER DISASTERS

Rachel Gibson

When money-bags Virgil Duffy leaves his widow a stash of cash and his beloved ice-hockey team in his will, team captain Ty 'Saint' Savage is furious. The Chinooks are set to win the biggest prize of the season, and a beautiful young ex-stripper taking over the reins is the last thing he needs. Even if Faith, former Playmate of the Year, is the sexiest woman he's ever laid eyes on. Soon tensions are mounting between the Saint and the Sinner from Vegas — but maybe Ty's forgotten the first rule of play: never underestimate your opponent . . .

ACROSS THE SANDS OF TIME

Pamela Kavanagh

Newly engaged to Geoff, schoolteacher Thea Partington is happy with her career, her show ponies and family life at their farm on the Wirral. But everything changes when Irish vet Dominic joins the local practice and Thea is attracted to him. The engaged pair begin to renovate an idyllic, but empty and ramshackle, property on Partington land. Thea experiences a series of waking dreams of the history of the house, revealing uncanny parallels, stormy relationships and fearful consequences. Meanwhile, Dominic, a man with a past, loves Thea, but believes he is fated. But are the fates on their side?